GÂCHE AN

To Mum
Happy Birthday 2017
All our love
Owen, Shona, Mia, Elsie
& Hamish xxx

GÂCHE AND GOSSIP

A year in the life of a small Channel Island

JILL WATSON

© Jill Watson, 2016

Published by Huitrier Pie Publishing

All rights reserved. No part of this book may be reproduced, adapted, stored in a retrieval system or transmitted by any means, electronic, mechanical, photocopying, or otherwise without the prior written permission of the author.

The rights of Jill Watson to be identified as the author of this work have been asserted in accordance with the Copyright, Designs and Patents Act 1988.

All the characters in this publication are fictitious and any resemblance to real persons, living or dead, is coincidental.

A CIP catalogue record for this book is available from the British Library.

ISBN 978-0-9955512-0-6

Book layout and cover design by Clare Brayshaw
Cover image © Laifa | Dreamstime.com

Prepared and printed by:

York Publishing Services Ltd
64 Hallfield Road
Layerthorpe
York YO31 7ZQ

Tel: 01904 431213

Website: www.yps-publishing.co.uk

Introduction

The Channel Islands lie just off the north west coast of France. Although British, the Channel Islands, which are Crown Dependencies, still retain much of their French heritage. They are self-governing with their own laws, justice systems and taxation. They are not part of the United Kingdom or the European Union. The islands of Jersey, Guernsey, Alderney, Sark and Herm are familiar to many people, but the island of Ormerey and all its inhabitants are fictitious and exist only in the imagination of the author.

Gâche (pronounced 'gosh') is a traditional Guernsey fruit loaf. It is usually served spread with butter, and eaten at tea time or with morning coffee.

Chapter 1

Lizzie clambered into the small aircraft, fastened her seat belt and wondered for the umpteenth time if she had made the right decision. She could feel tears smarting at the back of her eyelids and rummaged in her bag for a clean tissue. She kept her head bent as a tall thin man climbed into the seat next to her and tried to manoeuvre his long legs into a comfortable position.

'I'm sorry, I'm afraid I take up far too much room,' he apologised. 'I think these planes were designed for midgets. I say, are you all right?'

'I'm fine, thank you.' Lizzie made an effort to pull herself together.

'Not afraid of flying, are you?'

'No, it's not that. I've flown to Ormerey before. I'm just being silly. Take no notice.' She smiled at him.

'What takes you to Ormerey?' He noted her smart navy and white suit. 'Business?'

'No,' said Lizzie. 'I'm moving over there to live with my partner. He's an islander.'

The man tried to turn in his seat so he could get a good look at her. She was fortyish, he reckoned, attractive with short wavy brown hair and grey eyes. 'You're not Raoul St Arnaud's girlfriend, are you?'

'Yes, how did you know?'

'A lucky guess. News travels fast on a small island. I'm Geoff Prosser.' He smiled and held out his hand, his soft brown hair flopping over his face. He had hazel eyes, Lizzie noticed, and was quite good looking. She shook hands.

'Lizzie Bayley.'

'Very glad to meet you, Lizzie.' His words were drowned by the roar of the engines as the plane prepared for take-off.

The noise from the Trislander's three engines made further conversation impossible. Geoff Prosser settled down to read and Lizzie looked out of the window, watching Southampton airport receding below. They flew over Southampton Water with its docks and cranes, crossed the Solent and she had a clear view of Alum Bay and the Needles as England was left behind. A cold sliver of misgiving pierced her suddenly like a shard of ice. What on earth was she doing? She had only met Raoul four times before agreeing to move in with him. It had not been an easy decision to make, leaving her whole life behind and throwing herself into the unknown but then she had never expected to fall in love after being single for so long. She shook herself briskly and her common sense took over. After all, she wasn't marrying Raoul; she could always come back if things didn't work out.

The plane broke through the cloud layer into brilliant sunshine. Lizzie immediately felt better and her sense of adventure returned. She settled back into her seat and relaxed. She loved flying. She watched the ever-changing clouds below, stretching as far as the horizon, reminding her of an alien frozen landscape. She thought of Raoul waiting for her at Ormerey's tiny airport. Fog in the islands had delayed the flights and they were over an hour late. She was looking forward to the romantic dinner Raoul had promised her to celebrate her arrival.

Forty minutes later the plane was descending over Ormerey. Lizzie could see the island below, green fields, roads and houses spread out like a map. She suddenly became aware of how small it was. She knew it was only three miles from the cliffs at the western end to the rocky bays and the lighthouse in the east. Would she ever get used to living in such a quiet, remote place? The sea was a deep aquamarine with white frills at the edges where it met the shore. They flew in at an angle, the plane tilting alarmingly before finally touching down on the tarmac and bumping over the grass before coming to a halt outside the airport building.

Raoul was waiting impatiently in the arrivals hall when Lizzie finally made her way through customs. She could see him behind a group of excited people, tall and handsome. In his middle fifties, Raoul St Arnaud was in his prime, suntanned with blue eyes and not a trace of grey in his blonde hair. He caught sight of Lizzie and waved at her.

'Come on,' he said giving her a quick hug and grabbing her bags. 'We'll be late. The meeting starts at seven. I thought you weren't going to make it, there was thick fog earlier.'

He tossed her luggage into the back of his pick-up. Lizzie scrambled up into the passenger seat with difficulty, hampered by her straight skirt and high heels. Raoul glanced at her. 'You're looking very smart.'

'I thought we were going out for dinner.'

'We are, later. I must attend this meeting.'

'What's it about?'

Raoul was driving at speed past farmland and derelict greenhouses. They reached the outskirts of the town and the pick-up careered down a cobbled street, past shops and houses, until it came to an abrupt halt in Main Square outside the Island Hall.

'It's the People's Meeting. There's a controversial planning issue on the Billet. It should be interesting.'

'The Billet?' echoed Lizzie.

'The Billet d'Etat,' explained Raoul. 'It's the agenda for the next States meeting. At the People's Meeting the electorate have an opportunity to comment on what's on the Billet, it's supposed to be democracy in action but the States members rarely take any notice of the public. Hop out and wait here while I go and park.'

Feeling more bemused than ever, Lizzie hitched up her skirt and scrambled down on to the cobbles, nearly turning her ankle. Moments later Raoul was back.

'I'm so sorry, love. I know I said we'd go out for dinner and we will. I've booked the table. I just need to do this first.'

He took her arm and ushered her into the imposing, granite building known as the Island Hall. It was packed with people and it seemed to Lizzie that every head turned to look at them as she and Raoul squeezed into two vacant seats at the side of the room. She felt herself blushing.

'It's all right,' whispered Raoul, 'They all want to get a good look at you. You're the object of everyone's curiosity tonight.'

'Why?'

'Everyone knows you were arriving today. Don't worry, you'll be old news by tomorrow, there'll be someone else to gossip about.'

Lizzie shrank down into her seat. She felt conspicuous and overdressed among all the anoraks and Guernsey sweaters. The overcrowded room smelled of smoke, stale beer and sweat. She was tired and hungry after travelling and could feel a headache coming on.

Two men in suits were sitting at a table on the stage at the front of the room. One of them stood up and raised his hand. The room fell silent.

'Good evening, ladies and gentlemen, and welcome to the People's Meeting.'

'That's Theo Rachelle, the President,' Raoul whispered in Lizzie's ear.

'Of the island?'

'No, of the States of Ormerey, the island's government. He's just the chairman really. The other man is Bertie Soames, the Clerk of the States, our top civil servant.' He took Lizzie's hand in his and squeezed it.

The Clerk, a small fussy-looking man with a thin face and sandy hair, shuffled the papers in front of him and coughed. 'A-hem, as you all know there is only one item on tonight's Billet. It is whether or not the States should give its permission for the house known as Yaffingales to be removed from the green belt so that it can be demolished and rebuilt as a hotel.'

'No, no, no,' shouted someone from the back of the room.

Lizzie looked round. To her surprise she saw her companion from the plane, Geoff Prosser, standing up and shaking his fist angrily.

'It's a bloody disgrace. The green belt should be left alone. Who needs another hotel anyway? And who will be lining their pockets? Not the locals, you can be sure of that.'

'Sit down, Mr Prosser, and be quiet or I shall have you removed from the meeting.' The President banged on the table and glared round the room. A short heavily built man with dark hair greying at the temples he had an air of dignity and authority. 'I would ask you all to stick to the rules and raise your hand if you wish to speak. The Clerk will then indicate who is to speak next. Anyone who interrupts or speaks out of turn will be removed. Is that understood?'

'It's going to be a lively evening,' said Raoul, 'You'll find it very entertaining.'

* * *

It was 8.45pm when Raoul and Lizzie finally made it to the Imperial Hotel for their celebration dinner. The meeting had ended in chaos. After several speeches, some of which were lengthy and all of which were against the proposed hotel, someone spoke out in favour, stating that it would be good for tourism which was, after all, the island's main industry. Geoff Prosser, unable to contain himself, was escorted from the hall by the local police constable. By this time the room was in uproar and the President, after consulting with the Clerk, had closed the meeting. This proved unpopular as many of the electorate were still waiting for their chance to speak, and the President and the Clerk had to push their way through an angry crowd to exit the building. Raoul and Lizzie had left unnoticed.

The Imperial Hotel stood on the main coast road overlooking the island's largest beach. It was the only hotel on the island, boasting twenty five bedrooms and a dining room which was open to non-residents. Built in the 1930s in the Art Deco style, it had been badly damaged during the Second World War when the island was occupied by German forces. The renovations and repairs had been sensitively done and the hotel, painted pale grey and white, retained its period charm. Now, in late August, it was almost full.

The evening had turned chilly as Raoul and Lizzie pushed their way through the heavy glass doors into the warm and welcoming reception area. An attractive woman in her middle-thirties stood behind the desk. She was elegantly dressed in a crimson velvet trouser suit and her long dark hair hung in glossy curls around her shoulders. Her eyes were green with thick lashes, her lips full, and her make-up immaculate. She smiled.

'Good evening Raoul, how nice to see you both.'

'Hello Natasha, we've a table booked for 8.30. I'm sorry we're late.'

'That's OK. How was the meeting?'

'Lively,' said Raoul. 'Geoff had to be thrown out as usual, and then Theo had to close the proceedings. There was so much noise you couldn't think straight.'

'What a pity I missed it. Come this way, I'll show you to your table.' She led them into the large elegant dining room.

'I'm afraid you're too late. We've stopped serving now.' A tall angular woman with grey hair cut in a severe crop approached them.

'I've reserved a table,' said Raoul.

'For 8.30,' Daphne Warrington surveyed him coldly. 'As I've just said, you're too late.'

'But Mother, they've been at the People's Meeting, they couldn't get here any earlier,' protested Natasha.

'Perhaps we could re-book for tomorrow night?' suggested Lizzie.

'I don't think so.' Daphne turned to her. 'It's Saturday, we're fully booked.'

'Are you sure?' Natasha looked puzzled. 'I'm sure we could fit two more in.'

Daphne glared at her daughter, her grey eyes glinting like polished granite. 'We're full. I took a group booking this evening. I haven't had time to write it down yet.'

'It's all right,' Raoul spoke to Natasha. 'We'll go to The Lord Nelson, I'm sure Val will find something for us to eat.'

He took Lizzie's arm and strode out, watched by several diners who had witnessed the exchange with interest.

'Was that really necessary, Mother?' Natasha was cross and embarrassed. 'I'm sure Chef wouldn't have minded, after all the dining room is still half full.'

'I am not having that man flaunting his girlfriend under my nose,' said Daphne. 'They can go somewhere else.'

'Oh, for God's sake, Mother!' Natasha turned on Daphne furiously. 'Will you never let it go? You know full well that I never wanted to marry Raoul St Arnaud and he never wanted to marry me. Just get over it.'

'Maybe I could,' said Daphne bitterly, 'if you hadn't made such an abysmal mess of your life.'

* * *

The drive back to town only took a few minutes. Raoul parked the pick-up in his own yard and they walked the short distance down Main Street to the island's busiest public house. The Lord Nelson was a dark dingy establishment. The windows overlooking the street were grimy and mud splattered and the sign hanging over the door, a portrait of the famous admiral, creaked eerily in the wind. It did not look promising Lizzie thought as she and Raoul entered and found themselves in a room full of noise and smoke. It was badly in need of redecorating, the once cream walls were stained brown with nicotine. The furniture was battered and scarred and the peeling paint on the window sills curled up like miniature scrolls. Had it been empty the whole place would have had a dismal neglected ambience but the buzz of chatter and raucous laughter lifted it into cheerfulness. It was a popular rendezvous for the locals who propped up the bar every evening and an eye-opening experience for holiday makers who raved about its "authentic character". Lizzie's heart sank as she and Raoul pushed their way through the crowd towards the bar. Nobody appeared to be eating.

Raoul managed to catch the landlady's eye. 'Hi Val, you couldn't possibly give us something to eat, could you? We couldn't get dinner at the Imperial and I've nothing in at home. We're starving!'

Val took one look at Lizzie's exhausted face. 'Come along into the back, love, where it's quiet. I've got some lasagnes in the freezer. I can easily microwave them for you. Will that do?'

'It would be wonderful,' said Lizzie gratefully. She noticed an exquisite model of HMS Victory in a glass case on the bar. 'Who made that?' she asked. 'It's beautiful.'

'My old man', said Val. She beamed at Lizzie.

'I'll go and get us a drink,' said Raoul.

'On the house,' said Val, 'to welcome your young lady.' She turned to Lizzie. 'Welcome to Ormerey, my dear, I hope you will be very happy here.'

Lizzie was touched. 'Thank you,' she said. 'It's so good of you to feed us at this late hour.'

'No problem.' Val disappeared into the kitchen. The lasagnes duly arrived, together with crusty bread.

'I'm sorry but we seem to be right out of salad.'

'That's OK. This is perfect.' Raoul grinned at her.

Val perched her ample behind on the edge of the table and watched them eat. She was an amiable north-country woman with greying hair pulled back into an untidy bun.

Generous, out-spoken and popular with her customers, she and her husband, Bill, had arrived on Ormerey in the 1970s and had run The Lord Nelson ever since.

'So, Mrs Warrington's not forgiven you then?'

Raoul laughed, 'Doesn't look like it.'

'Forgiven you for what?' Lizzie relaxed. Warmed by the food, the cosy ambience of the small room and the landlady's welcome, she was beginning to feel better.

'Mrs W had got Raoul marked out for her Natasha. She's never forgiven him for not marrying her.'

'Really?' Lizzie was intrigued. 'Why was that?'

'Oh, it was embarrassing at the time,' said Raoul. 'The Warringtons wanted to attach themselves to a genuine island family and I was the eligible bachelor they selected for their only daughter. It didn't seem to matter that I'm old enough to be Natasha's father. They spent years trying to push us together. Finally Natasha ran off and married a fisherman from Jersey. Her parents were furious. Unfortunately it didn't work out. She's divorced now and lives at the hotel with her little girl.'

'Is that why her mother was so sniffy with us tonight?' said Lizzie. 'I'm surprised the owner of a big hotel like that turns away customers because of a personal dislike. It's hardly good for business.'

Raoul put his arm round her. 'Oh my darling Lizzie,' he said with a laugh. 'This is Ormerey. What a lot you have to learn about us all.'

Chapter 2

Lizzie woke at sunrise with a feeling of happy anticipation. She got out of bed quietly, leaving Raoul asleep, and went downstairs to put the kettle on. She opened the front door and looked up and down the street. It was empty. The crisp, fresh smell of early morning mingled with the salty tang of the sea and a faint whiff of diesel. A few herring gulls circled lazily overhead uttering piercing cries. The sky was clear; it was going to be a beautiful day.

Lizzie made herself a mug of coffee and wandered slowly through the house. The Sycamores had belonged to the St Arnaud family since 1900 when Raoul's grandfather, Jean-Luc St Arnaud, had brought his English bride home to Ormerey. It was a sturdy granite town house on Main Street, a few doors up from The Lord Nelson. There was no front garden, the door opened straight on to the narrow pavement but a side entrance led to a yard at the back and behind that was a small area of lawn, flower beds and two large sycamore trees. The house was not large. There were three bedrooms and a bathroom upstairs, and two spacious reception rooms on the ground floor which were separated by a corridor leading straight from the front entrance to what had once been the back door but now opened into the kitchen.

The room which Raoul called the kitchen was a ramshackle lean-to built against the back wall of the house. Once this area had been part of the yard, it had a sloping flagstone floor and a flimsy corrugated plastic roof covered in moss. It smelled of damp and drains and Lizzie, who was now seated on a fabric covered box under the window, surveyed it with dismay and wondered how she would ever prepare a meal in it.

There was a knock on the back door. It was Raoul's cousin, Francesca, whom Lizzie had met on a previous visit to the island. She was a small, plump woman with a round face and a wide smile. She had been extremely pretty in her youth. Now sixty, her short curly hair was still black and her face had very few lines. A small sandy coloured dog was straining at his lead trying to get in.

'Hello, Lizzie. I know it's still horribly early but I was walking Zapp and I noticed the curtains were drawn back so I thought I'd drop by and see how you're settling in.'

'How nice,' said Lizzie. 'Do come in and have a coffee. Raoul's still asleep.'

'Thanks. Is it all right to bring the dog in?'

'Of course. Hello Zapp, do you remember me?'

The basenji, released from his lead, rushed in excited circles round Lizzie and then made straight for the door into the hall. Francesca closed it quickly.

'No you don't! Raoul will not appreciate being jumped on this early in the morning.' She sat down on the window seat. 'Do you like the house? Raoul's redecorated the sitting room and the dining room in your honour.'

'The house is lovely. The only part I'm not sure about is this kitchen. It's so primitive, no units or work surfaces, just these old cupboards and a very wobbly table.'

'Oh, I know. Raoul's mum, Aunt Juliet, used to moan about it, especially as she got older, but nothing ever got done. It's difficult to fit units because the floor slopes, but the cooker's quite new. I expect you'll get used to it.'

'I'll have to,' said Lizzie, 'but it's not what I'm used to. I hope I can manage.'

'You'll manage all right,' said Francesca with an encouraging smile.

The two women sat on the window seat together sipping their coffee.

'When I came over here at Easter,' Lizzie said, 'I thought Raoul was pulling my leg when he showed me this kitchen.'

'Why?'

'Well, he brought me in through the yard and showed me that awful outside bathroom where the washing machine is, and told me that was the bathroom. I nearly had a fit. He roared with laughter and said not to worry, there was a proper one upstairs. When we came in here and he said "This is the kitchen," I thought he must be teasing me again and there was a better one somewhere else in the house.'

Francesca laughed. 'He always did have a wicked sense of humour.'

Raoul appeared in the doorway. 'Hi Frankie, I thought I heard voices. Get down, Zapp, you little pest.' He gave Lizzie a quick kiss. 'How long have you been up? I thought you'd run off and left me already.'

'She's overwhelmed by your dreadful kitchen,' said Francesca. 'It's a lovely day, Raoul. Why don't we all walk out to Yaffingales this afternoon and Lizzie can see what all the fuss is about?'

'Good idea.' Raoul extracted the remnants of a sliced loaf from the chipped enamel breadbin and looked in the fridge. 'There's not much to eat, I'm afraid.'

'I'll go shopping this morning,' said Lizzie, 'and I'd love to see Yaffingales.'

'That's settled then, I'll call by at two if that's all right.' Francesca retrieved Zapp from under the table where he was looking for crumbs. 'See you both later.'

* * *

By the time Lizzie had got herself organised and was ready to shop, the sun was high in the sky and Main Street was buzzing with activity. St Mark, always referred to as "the town", was the size of a large village, built on the side of a hill that sloped gently down towards the harbour. Main Street ran in an easterly direction from the airport road down towards Main Square. There the street name changed to Valmont Road until it reached the harbour, where it took on another identity as "the coast road" and wound its way round Briac Bay.

Main Square, a large open space graced with sycamore trees and a few seats, was bordered on its northern side by the Island Hall. St Mark's church stood on its eastern side and Rachelle House, home of the President, was on the southern boundary. Most of the island's shops were on Main Street where they were interspersed with offices and private houses, giving the whole area a colourful and informal ambience.

Ormerey's population of around fifteen hundred souls was well provided for when it came to shopping. There was a bakery, with fresh bread baked on the island, a butcher, a wet fish shop, a post-office, a chemist, a newsagent cum bookshop, a DIY and hardware store, two clothes shops, two gift shops and the Ormerey Supermart. There were also three banks and a hairdresser's salon.

Lizzie joined the queue of holidaymakers outside the bread shop and bought a French loaf. She then made her way to the Ormerey Supermart for groceries. It was inappropriately named, she thought, as she entered the dingy poorly-lit cavern of a shop with very narrow spaces between the shelves. Fortunately it was not crowded. She had only found a few things she needed when a woman in a pink nylon overall marched over and took hold of her trolley.

'I suppose you think you've been very clever, coming over here and grabbing yourself one of the island's richest men.'

'Pardon?' said Lizzie.

'You heard,' said the woman who was now joined by a colleague, similarly attired and equally aggressive.

'We don't like strangers coming over here and worming their way in where they're not wanted.' The second woman's voice was as hostile as the first's.

Lizzie's mouth was dry. She felt her heart pounding. 'Excuse me,' she said, 'I want to finish my shopping.' The sound of her own voice gave her confidence. 'For your information I have come over here at the invitation of Mr St Arnaud. I have no intention of grabbing anybody. Now please let me pass.'

To Lizzie's amazement they stepped aside. She was too shaken to concentrate properly and decided to come back later when she had calmed down. She felt sick. There was no queue at the check-out. Still shaking, she unloaded her trolley and put her shopping on the counter. As she did so an elderly well-dressed woman with a mauve rinse elbowed her out of the way and plonked her basket down in front of Lizzie's shopping.

'Excuse me, I was here first.' Lizzie was outraged.

The woman on the check-out, who had earlier grabbed hold of her trolley, ignored Lizzie and began to empty the basket. 'Good morning, Mrs Cleghorn. How are you today?'

'Very well thank you, Prunella, and yourself?'

Lizzie waited, fuming with anger. This was just too much, she thought.

Prunella, who had wispy, straw coloured hair and protruding eyes like pale pebbles, eventually finished her small talk and checked Mrs Cleghorn's shopping through. She did not look at Lizzie or speak to her until she had priced Lizzie's few articles. She barked out the price. Lizzie held her tongue with difficulty. She could not wait to get back to Raoul and tell him what had happened.

Raoul was sympathetic. 'The women in that shop constitute one branch of the Ormerey mafia. They've all worked there for years and think they run the island as well as the shop. A more spiteful bunch you're never likely to meet and Prunella's the most poisonous of the lot. Take no notice of them; they're jealous that's all.'

'Easier said than done,' said Lizzie, 'there's nowhere else to buy groceries.' She paused. 'Are you really one of the island's richest men?'

'I suppose I am. Some of the old island families such as mine and the Rachelles own land and property which has passed down through the generations. That arouses envy.'

'The Rachelles, you mean Theo Rachelle, the President?'

'Yes. Theo's father was President before him and his grandfather before that. The Rachelles go back centuries, like us.'

Lizzie thought for a moment. 'But what about Mrs Cleghorn, she's not an islander is she?'

'No, she's descended from the English aristocracy, or so she says. She's got pots of money and expects everyone to bow and scrape to her. You can either ignore these people or stand up to them, Lizzie, but don't let them upset you.' Raoul laughed and gave Lizzie a hug. 'Never mind all of them, I'm glad you're here and so is Frankie. She's really taken to you.'

'I've taken to her too, and Zapp.'

'Of course, we mustn't forget Zapp.' Raoul kissed her.

* * *

Yaffingales stood in a small valley between high cliffs on the south side of the island. A granite cottage, built in the early nineteenth century, it nestled cosily among the trees. The garden, which was landscaped into terraces, extended down the valley to a shingle beach which covered over at high tide.

An English naturalist, Edwin Draycott, and his wife Muriel had purchased the cottage and the field adjoining its northern boundary from the Rachelle family in 1950 and turned it into their own private nature reserve. After Edwin's death in 1980, Muriel stayed at Yaffingales for the remainder of her life and, since the couple had no children, the house and land were left to a nephew who eventually sold it to the present owner, property developer Simon Brockenshaw.

There were only two ways to reach Yaffingales. One was by a grassy track which meandered its way across pastureland from the western edge of town to the head of the valley. There was no road. The only other access was by boat at low tide. It was along the path across the fields that Raoul, Lizzie and Francesca now walked. Zapp pranced elegantly at the end of his extending lead, pausing every so often to watch the cows, tethered by ropes to stakes in the ground in the open pasture. The cows stared back.

'I'm surprised he doesn't bark,' said Lizzie.

'Basenjis don't bark, they yodel,' Francesca reined the lead in. 'It's more of a howl, like a wolf. He can be really noisy when he wants to be.'

'I never realised,' said Lizzie, 'I'd just assumed he was a quiet dog. He's very unusual.'

'He's a hunting dog from Africa, there's still a lot of wildness in him, that's why I keep him on the lead near animals or traffic, or anything else he can chase.'

The day had continued fine and sunny, the August heat tempered by a fresh breeze from the sea. Skylarks soared overhead, their trilling songs mingling with the cries of gulls and the harsh, guttural bark of a pheasant.

Lizzie breathed deeply and put the morning's events to the back of her mind. 'I've never known such wonderfully bracing air; it's got such a fresh tang to it.'

'Wait till the winter,' said Raoul, 'You'll find out what bracing really means. Look, there's a new fence round the Draycott's field.'

'Mr Brockenshaw's field, you mean.' Francesca surveyed the barbed wire with distaste. 'I suppose this is where he wants to build his hotel.'

'It would have marvellous views,' said Raoul thoughtfully. 'It would be ideal for birdwatchers and people who are interested in wildlife.'

Francesca threw him a furious look and strode off down the path which skirted the field then disappeared into a tunnel of hawthorn trees before coming to a rickety wooden gate. She pushed it open and descended the stone steps to the front door of the cottage. The others followed. They peered in through the windows, the insides of which were festooned with cobwebs and dust.

'There's still some furniture here,' said Lizzie. 'How sad it all looks. How long has it been empty?'

'It must be getting on for two years,' said Raoul.

They walked round the side of the house, through another wooden gate, and found themselves on a verandah overlooking the neglected garden. They could see the sea, a bright shimmering blue, over the tops of the trees. The sun glinted on the white plumage of gannets diving for fish offshore.

'Can you get down to the beach?' Lizzie asked.

'Not any more,' Francesca sighed. 'The path has completely disappeared under the gorse and brambles. It hasn't been used for years.'

They sat down on some stone steps. Zapp was let off the lead and rushed off to explore.

'Won't he run off?' said Lizzie.

'No, he won't venture into the undergrowth; he's a wimp when it comes to prickles.'

'Look!' said Raoul, 'A Jersey tiger, the first I've seen this year.'

The black and cream moth with striking markings landed on the warm stone nearby, then fluttered off showing its scarlet hind wings.

'It's so peaceful here,' said Lizzie. 'What a shame it's so run down, it would make a lovely home for someone. Imagine having your own bit of beach. Why is it called Yaffingales?'

'That's the old country name for green woodpeckers. There used to be a pair here in the valley when the Draycotts first came. We came here a lot, didn't we Raoul? Our family was friendly with the Draycotts, we often came for tea. Old Edwin would take us into the German bunker he used as a bird hide. We could watch the nesting kittiwakes and fulmars up on the cliffs, and the yaffingales feeding on the lawn.'

'Where's the bunker?'

'Down there in the trees.' Raoul got up. 'Let's see if we can still get to it.'

They walked across the rough turf of the terraced lawns which had been kept short by grazing rabbits. Lizzie was entranced.

'Smell the wild thyme when we tread on it,' she said. 'What are these spikes of tiny white flowers?'

'Autumn lady's tresses,' said Francesca. 'They're wild orchids. Edwin taught us the names of all the flowers. He kept journals, over thirty years of records and observations. They are in the Ormerey museum now.'

The old lawns were carpeted with wild flowers; daisies, clover, eyebright and bird's foot trefoil. The humming and buzzing of insects was everywhere. Graceful branches of purple buddleia, festooned with butterflies, reached almost to the ground. Orange montbretia and pale pink Jersey lilies straggled among the leggy, overgrown bushes of rosemary and lavender in what had once been flower borders, now invaded by gorse and brambles from the sloping sides of the valley.

'The bunker's down there,' said Raoul. 'We can't get to it, it's too overgrown.'

'We need sccateurs,' said Francesca.

'You forget we're trespassing, we shouldn't be here at all.' Raoul led the way back up the garden to the verandah where they all sat and relaxed in the late afternoon sun. Zapp was asleep on the warm flagstones.

'A pity we didn't think to bring a picnic with us,' Lizzie laid back, her hands behind her head.

'I wonder what Simon Brockenshaw would have to say if he suddenly appeared and found us here,' Raoul murmured lazily, lying back beside Lizzie.

'Damn Simon Brockenshaw!' Francesca suddenly burst into tears. 'Damn and blast him to hell!'

Chapter 3

'Why is Frankie so upset about Yaffingales?'

Lizzie was washing up the supper things. They had eaten late, having accompanied Frankie and Zapp back to Puffin Cottage after their walk. Lizzie had made a pot of tea while Raoul had tried to comfort his cousin, with little success. Dusk was falling by the time they had arrived home. Raoul had been silent and thoughtful throughout the meal and Lizzie had contained her curiosity until after they had eaten.

'I'll tell you when we're settled in the other room. It's a long story. Would you like some coffee?'

'Yes please.'

'Go on through, I'll bring it.'

Lizzie escaped from the lean-to kitchen with relief and entered the large living room. She loved this room; being part of the main house it had an atmosphere of cosiness and security which the kitchen lacked. The rich colours of the old-fashioned Axminster carpet lent warmth to the freshly painted magnolia walls on which were hung pictures and photographs of island scenes. Above the fireplace was an oil painting of Jean-Luc St Arnaud and his wife Felicity. Settees and armchairs were arranged around the walls and a large TV stood in one corner. Lizzie sat down on a brown velvet sofa. Her eyes closed; it had been a long day.

Raoul appeared with the coffee and settled himself beside her. 'Don't nod off,' he said. 'I'm going to fill you in with some of our family history; it's riveting stuff.'

Lizzie forced her eyes open and took the mug of coffee from Raoul.

'Thanks.'

'When Frankie was little she and her parents lived at Yaffingales. They rented it from the Rachelles.'

Lizzie was suddenly wide awake. 'I thought she lived with you.'

'That was later on. I'd better start at the beginning.'

Raoul took a slurp of coffee and continued. 'Back in the 1920s Ormerey was as popular with tourists as it is now. Every week in the summer my father James and his friends would go down to the harbour and watch the passengers coming off the Weymouth steamer. One day the beautiful Craddock sisters, Juliet and Rosamund, arrived for a holiday with their parents. You can imagine the excitement, two lovely girls from the mainland. They caused quite a stir, all the island lads wanted to date them. To cut a long story short, my father and Juliet fell in love and were eventually married in the spring of 1929.'

'Did they live in this house?' Lizzie snuggled up to Raoul. He was a good story teller she thought.

'No, this was my grandparents' home. My parents lived in Valmont Road, that white cottage near the Catholic church. The first summer they were there my mother's younger sister Rosamund came for a long visit. She had a passionate love affair with an Italian farm worker who had come over for the season to help on the land and by the October she realised she was pregnant. You can imagine the scandal; a seventeen year old upper-middle class English girl pregnant by an Italian labourer. Her parents went mad and promptly disowned her, they couldn't stand the disgrace. My mother stood by her sister and was disowned too. The Craddocks never made contact with their daughters again and so I never met my maternal grandparents.'

'What happened to Rosamund?'

'She and Antonio got married and decided to stay on the island. It was a very quiet wedding, a civil one of course; the churches didn't want to know. The couple were shunned by most people because she was pregnant before she got married, and they were subsequently excluded from much of Ormerey's social life. Frankie was born the following May at Yaffingales, it's her birthplace. Now her mother's dead it's her last link with her father.'

'No wonder she's so upset at the prospect of it being pulled down. Was it a successful marriage?'

'Yes, they were very happy. Our two families were close. My parents always said what a charming man Antonio Saviano was, a devoted husband and father. I never knew him; he died the year I was born. He was only twenty six years old.'

'How awful, did he have an accident?'

'No, he was murdered. He was found floating in the harbour with a bullet in his back. No one ever knew who killed him. The local policeman couldn't be bothered to look into it; Antonio was only a foreigner after all, not a local man. My grandfather wanted President Pierre Rachelle, he was Theo's grandfather, to use his position and insist the matter was looked into properly but Rachelle refused. He said it was nothing to do with him. My father and grandfather went over to Guernsey and asked the Guernsey Police to come to Ormerey and carry out a full investigation which they did. They interviewed a lot of people and got nowhere so the case was eventually dropped. Father and Grandpa both said it was a cover up by someone in the local community. They made themselves very unpopular because they wouldn't let it rest, so the Rachelles evicted Rosamund and Frankie from Yaffingales, threw them out with no prior notice. Grandpa had a huge row with Pierre Rachelle, the reverberations of which are felt to this day. These island feuds pass down the generations, you know. It's the Norman French blood apparently.'

Raoul paused. 'As you can imagine Rosamund was distraught, she'd lost her husband and her home. Her prospects were bleak; there was no social security in those days. People were very nasty, said she should go back to England where she came from. My parents took her and Frankie in and gave them a home. They lived with us until after the war so Frankie and I grew up together; we were more like brother and sister than cousins.'

Lizzie was curious. 'So no one knows who killed Frankie's father?'

'No, it could have been any one of a number of people. It was a dreadful thing to do, shoot a man in the back and it was most likely racially motivated. There were people who thought Ormerey should be exclusively for islanders, there are still a few who think like that today.'

Lizzie thought back to the morning's encounter in the Ormerey Supermart. 'Wouldn't that lead to inbreeding?'

'It has done in the past. The St Arnauds have been criticised in some quarters for marrying English women.

Grandpa and Father both did, and so did I. The island needs new blood but some people can't see that.'

Raoul rarely mentioned his wife but Lizzie knew that the marriage had only lasted a few months. She wondered if it had anything to do with Clare being made unwelcome on the island but she did not like to ask. She changed the subject. 'How do you get on with Theo Rachelle? You say the feuds last through generations.'

'I don't know him. He's always ignored me but that's probably more to do with Frankie than an old feud from our grandparents' time.'

'Frankie?'

'Yes, she and Theo had a teenage romance. It was the summer they were both seventeen and they met in secret because Theo's parents would have gone mad if they'd known. They found out eventually and put a stop to it. Frankie was heartbroken; she's never fallen in love with anyone else.'

Lizzie thought for a moment. 'So that's why she never married. I think Frankie's an amazing person. She's had tragedy in her life but she's not bitter, is she? She's one of the kindest people I've ever met.'

'You're right,' said Raoul. 'She's a happy soul, she doesn't bear grudges; she just gets on with life. It really threw me to see her so upset today but she'll be better tomorrow hopefully, she's very resilient, always been a fighter.'

'It must have been hard for her growing up here, all the animosity towards her and her mother.'

Raoul laughed. 'She soon learned to stick up for herself. Frankie was born here on the island; that means she's local and she's made sure everyone knows that. She's very confident and sure of her place here. No one messes with Frankie.'

* * *

It was another glorious sunny day with only a gentle breeze to rustle the leaves on the sycamore trees in Main Square. Francesca was getting organised for work after the long summer break. Term started next week and she looked forward to meeting the new intake of infants at St Mark's Primary School. She came out of the post office and bumped straight into Theo.

'Oops! Sorry!' she said. 'How are you, Theo?'

'Fine, fine,' muttered Theo. He still felt awkward with Francesca, even after all these years. He watched her walk down the street and sighed. She was still an attractive woman in spite of her dumpy middle-aged figure. He wished he had married her.

He thought back to that fateful summer of 1947 when he and Francesca had fallen in love. It seemed so long ago now. He remembered the night they had first made love, a magical night on a quiet beach with the full moon casting a shimmering light on the calm sea as the waves lapped lazily against the sand. They had fallen asleep in each other's arms, only waking as dawn tinged the sky.

Francesca had tiptoed indoors unnoticed but Theo had received a shock as he carefully opened the heavy back door of Rachelle House.

'At last! Where have you been all night?'

Theo had jumped. His mother was sitting at the kitchen table fully dressed; she had obviously been waiting up for him since the previous evening.

'Who have you been with?' She had almost spat the words out. 'Not that little Italian baggage I hope.'

Theo knew better than to lie to his mother. 'Yes, I've been out with Francesca.' He had spoken defensively, wondering how his mother had found out. 'I love her and she loves me. We want to get married.'

'Don't be so ridiculous.' Claudine Rachelle's voice had risen to a shriek. 'Remember who you are; the President's son. You're a Rachelle and she's the daughter of an Italian labourer and that English woman. They had to get married, you know, she was expecting.'

'That's not Francesca's fault.' Witnessing his mother's fury Theo had felt sick.

'Don't answer me back. I absolutely forbid you to see her again. Is that understood? Find yourself a girl from a good island family and then tell me you want to get married.'

Theo had gone miserably up to his room and from that day on had avoided Francesca. He had spent several anxious weeks wondering if he had made her pregnant, and when he realised he hadn't he had heaved a sigh of relief and taken up his university place in England.

Francesca, hurt and bewildered by Theo's coldness had cried into her pillow every night and finally confided in her mother. Rosamund Saviano, sympathetic and supportive, had realised immediately that it must have been Claudine who had put a stop to the romance, explained the situation to her heart-broken daughter and comforted her as best she could. Francesca had not been the first girl who had been sent packing by the Rachelles and she would not be the last.

When Theo had returned to the island four years later to set up his accountancy business he expected to find

Francesca married with a family but she was still living with her mother at Puffin Cottage. He had tried to keep out of her way but that was impossible on a small island and when they did meet their conversation was stilted and awkward, neither of them knowing what to say.

Now Theo watched as Francesca stopped to talk to Raoul and his new girlfriend. The three of them disappeared into the Rock Café. He was overcome by feelings of loneliness and exclusion. Francesca had always been close to Raoul, like a big sister to him and with her warmth and generosity had welcomed Lizzie into the family. He could have been part of that happy group if only he'd had the courage to stand up against his parents and marry Francesca.

Standing there in the street Theo finally acknowledged how unhappy he was; sixty years old, with no wife or children and not a single living relative. He hated himself for being such a coward all those years ago. He had a sudden crazy impulse to act completely out of character, to join the trio in the café, to walk through the door and say "Hi, may I join you?" but he had always been a shy man who found it difficult to mix unless he was in a work environment. He hesitated outside the door, they were all sitting at a window table chattering and laughing. Raoul looked up, caught sight of Theo standing there looking miserable and waved to him. Theo took a deep breath and walked in.

'Hello, Mr President', Raoul stood up, smiled and gave a mocking little bow. 'Come and meet my partner, Lizzie Bayley.'

Francesca kicked Raoul hard. He ignored her and pulled out a chair. Theo shook hands with Lizzie and sat down. He had not been in the Rock Café for years. It had changed hands recently and had been redecorated and brought up to date. Now with its gingham table cloths and potted plants it had a warm, cheerful atmosphere. 'I saw you at the People's Meeting,' he said to Lizzie. 'What did you think of it?'

'Very interesting,' said Lizzie, 'we don't have anything so democratic at home. It's good that people can have a say on important issues.'

Raoul signalled the waitress and ordered another coffee.

'What's your opinion, Theo, Yaffingales or the new hotel?'

Theo relaxed. He felt safe talking shop. 'I'm supposed to stay neutral. I only hope I don't have to use my casting vote. The hotel plans will probably go through, the new owner's been passing a lot of money around and promising work to people if his scheme goes ahead.'

'That's down to the Planning Committee I suppose,' said Raoul.

'No, it has to go before the full States. Removing land from the green belt is a States' decision; it's not down to just one committee.' He paused. 'What do you think, Francesca? You know Yaffingales better than anyone.'

Francesca met Theo's steady gaze and flushed. Those deep brown eyes still had an effect on her. 'Leaving my own personal feelings aside, I think the valley should be left alone. It's a beautiful part of the island. We don't need another hotel. The Imperial is never full except in July and August and there are plenty of guest houses.'

'But another hotel would be good for tourism,' said Raoul, 'and would provide dozens of jobs. Ormerey needs a larger population, it would help us all, but we shouldn't encroach on the green belt.'

'Simon Brockenshaw has set his heart on Yaffingales as the site for his hotel because of its location,' said Theo. 'He'd never recoup his costs if he had to sell it and start all over again somewhere in the building zone where prices are so high.'

'Everything always comes down to money in the end,' said Francesca bitterly.

'I'm afraid you're right,' Theo looked at her sympathetically. His heart ached, he wanted to put his arms round her and give her a hug.

'I still don't think the island needs another hotel.' Francesca was fighting back tears.

Raoul hastily changed the subject. 'I see you've got a new car, Theo, are you pleased with it?'

'Yes, I am.'

Theo found he was enjoying himself. The conversation flowed easily. Raoul St Arnaud's a nice chap, he thought, strange how they had never got to know each other before. Finally he got up to leave.

'Paperwork calls, I'm afraid. Thanks for the coffee. I do hope we can all do this again.' He gave Francesca a meaningful look. 'Cheers for now.'

'Well,' said Raoul after Theo had gone. 'That's the first proper conversation I've ever had with our esteemed President. Guess who still carries a torch for our Frankie?'

'You do talk a load of rubbish, Raoul.' Francesca blushed and threw him a furious look.

Raoul smirked and winked at Lizzie.

Chapter 4

The late August heat wave ended abruptly in thick fog. For three days Ormerey was cut off from the rest of the world, isolated in a soft grey blanket that swirled around the airport, sent wispy tentacles through the town and hung heavily over the beaches. The small planes were grounded. There was no mail, newspapers or any of the freight which usually came by air. Frustrated passengers paced the small airport lounge, hospital appointments in Guernsey were missed and holidaymakers were stranded. The small airport café ran out of sandwiches and had to phone through to the bakery for more supplies.

Raoul and Lizzie sat at one of the small tables outside the terminal building away from the crush inside, drinking coffee and chatting to a Jersey couple waiting to fly home after a week's holiday.

'Ormerey really needs a passenger ferry,' said the plump middle-aged woman who had introduced herself as Jennifer Pallot. 'We say that every year, don't we, John?'

'We do indeed,' said her husband. 'I should have been back at work yesterday but I'm not complaining; an extra day or two here is always a bonus.'

'Doesn't your boss mind?' asked Lizzie.

John laughed. 'Oh no, we all know how unpredictable the island weather can be. We locals make allowances, it's the

English who fret and fuss. They like to get away from their hectic lifestyles on the mainland and then complain when they can't get back to them.'

A steady stream of cars loomed out of the fog, deposited their passengers and disappeared again.

'It's clear in Jersey,' said Jennifer, 'and I think it's beginning to brighten up here. I can almost see the sun.' She looked up to where a halo of brightness shone through the fog.

'I can hear a plane,' said Raoul. 'There's one trying to get in.'

They could hear a deep drone somewhere above them. John turned to Lizzie. 'You know why these planes are called Trislanders, don't you? It's because they are always trying to land.'

Lizzie laughed politely. She had heard the joke before.

'You're English, aren't you?' said Jennifer. 'How do you like living here?'

'I've only been here a week, it's very different from England. I feel as though I've stepped back forty years into the past. The other day I saw a man kneeling down in the middle of the road painting the white line with a brush. He let me take a photo of him.'

'I'm taking Lizzie to see something else she won't see on the mainland,' said Raoul, 'my German bunker. It's time I checked up on it.' He handed a card to the visitors. 'Here's my phone number. Call me next time you're over here and we'll meet up for a drink or something. I hope you get off all right. Have a good flight back.'

They said their goodbyes and Raoul and Lizzie drove slowly back towards the town. Before they reached the top of

Main Street they turned off to the right and drove down the steep hill towards Briac Bay, the island's most popular beach. They had almost reached the point where the road flattened out and curved around the bay when Raoul stopped the pick-up and jumped out.

'Here we are,' he said, 'my German bunker.'

'Where? I can't see it.' Lizzie peered into the fog.

'Here in the bank.' Raoul pushed his way through the undergrowth at the side of the road and held the bramble stems back so Lizzie could squeeze past. They came to a grey wooden door, so well hidden that it could not be seen from the road. 'This is where I keep my secret stash.'

'What of?'

'Oh, this and that, stuff that might come in useful.'

Raoul produced a large key and unlocked the door. It was jammed tight and he had to use all his weight against it before it would open. He almost fell inside. Lizzie peered past him into the gloom. In the light of Raoul's torch she could see china washbasins, lavatory bowls, cisterns, rusty metal window frames, heaps of wood and numerous unidentifiable objects.

'Why have you got all these loos?'

'You never know when someone might need one. These came from the Imperial Hotel when they refurbished it. All the stuff they took out was taken down to the tip so I went down with a few others and we salvaged what we could. Joe the plumber got most of it including the bath tubs. He's made good money installing them in people's houses. I didn't have the room to store baths.' There was a note of regret in Raoul's voice.

'It's very wet in here.' Lizzie surveyed the water on the floor which gleamed in the light of the torch.

'It must have been all the rain we had last winter.' Raoul was fiddling about at the back of the bunker. Lizzie waited in the doorway; she did not want to get her feet wet. 'What are you looking for?'

'I had some old taps here somewhere; we could do with a new mixer tap in the kitchen.'

Lizzie groaned. 'Couldn't we go to the shop and buy a new one?'

Raoul stared at her in amazement. 'Good Lord no, I'm not wasting money. Here we are, this will probably do.' He extracted a rusty looking object from a heap of stuff on the floor and held it up triumphantly. 'Just the job. It'll polish up nicely.' He looked around. 'I really must give this place a good sort out.'

'Not now, please. Can't we go home?' The damp fetid smell emanating from the bunker made Lizzie feel ill, she could not wait to get away.

'OK!' Raoul locked the door. The fog was still thick, obscuring the view of the bay.

'Do you own that bunker?' Lizzie asked climbing back into the pick-up.

'No, I rent it from the States; it costs me a tenner a year. Most of the bunkers are rented out, some are much larger than mine – and drier,' he added.

'I don't know how you can bear to go in there,' said Lizzie. She shivered, remembering the accounts she had read about the German occupation and the slave workers who had been brought to the island to build the huge concrete fortifications.

All the Channel Islands had been occupied by German forces from 1940 until 1945 and were heavily fortified as part of Hitler's Atlantic Wall. There were reminders of war all over Ormerey; huge concrete gun emplacements on the cliffs and headlands, half-buried bunkers around the coast and inland, metal tank traps on the beaches and coils of rusty barbed wire lying in the undergrowth. The reminders were not only physical but lived on in the minds of the islanders who had been evacuated shortly before the invasion and had returned to find Ormerey in ruins. It was a tragic period in the island's history and Ormerey still bore the scars.

* * *

The Pierre Rachelle room, named in honour of Theo's grandfather, was a small comfortable room at the back of the Island Hall with a pleasant view of the garden. It was used for the States committee meetings and could be hired out to local organisations for social occasions.

On the first Friday of each month it played host to the Ormerey Ladies' Guild regular coffee mornings. These were presided over by Jean Yorke, an English settler in her early sixties who had moved to island with her husband in 1980. She had thrown herself enthusiastically into island life and was on several committees. With her slim build, neatly permed grey hair, smart clothes and acid tongue she was a formidable figure who liked to control every situation she found herself in and ruled the Ladies' Guild with a rod of iron.

On this particular morning she was not feeling at her best. Thank goodness that awful fog has gone at last she thought as she bustled around arranging coffee cups in neat rows. She checked the urn, and then placed some biscuits on a large plate which she pushed to the back of the table well out of reach. She hoped that Francesca would leave her dog at home. She had asked her several times not to bring it but Francesca had ignored her requests. The locals never take any notice of anyone and just do as they like she thought crossly. She buttered some slices of Guernsey gâche which she arranged on another plate and slammed the fridge door. Her new dentures were uncomfortable, making her irritable. She could do without any upsets this morning. She had debated whether or not to wear the dentures in public before she had got used to them but vanity had prevailed. She could not possibly be seen at the Guild coffee morning with no top teeth.

The ladies started arriving in ones and twos. Greetings were exchanged as they settled themselves down. The majority of them were elderly English settlers. The only regular locals were Alison Soames, the Clerk's wife, and Francesca who pointedly ignored each other.

Francesca had been dragged into the room by Zapp who was looking forward to being petted and spoilt by various ladies who slipped him the odd treat.

'I do wish you wouldn't bring that wretched dog,' Jean snapped. 'Last time he gobbled all the left over biscuits.'

'Well, you shouldn't have left them so near to the edge of the table; you know what a little thief he is.' Francesca spoke mildly. 'Don't worry, I'll tie him up.'

She looped the dog's lead over a coat hook on the wall. 'There! Sit down, Zapp, and be good.' Zapp whined a few times then lay down on the floor, giving Francesca a reproachful look.

'I think we're all here now. Let's get started.' Jean took up her position in front of the trestle table facing her audience. 'What has happened since our last little get-together?'

Alison Soames was the first to speak. 'Raoul St Arnaud's so-called girlfriend has turned up. My sister-in-law Prunella doesn't think much of her, stuck-up she says.'

'There's a surprise,' said Jean tartly. She did not care for Alison Soames. 'Your sister-in-law Prunella doesn't like anybody.' She addressed the room. 'What do we know about this Elizabeth Bayley, apart from her name? Perhaps you could fill us in Francesca; you appear to spend a lot of time with her. I'm surprised you haven't brought her with you.'

'She's busy unpacking,' said Francesca. 'Her stuff arrived on this week's boat.'

'Oh, she's intending to stay then?' Alison snorted loudly. Francesca glared at her.

'What does this woman look like? I haven't seen her yet.' Josie Cleghorn spoke up from where she was sitting at the back of the room, the sun glinting on her mauve curls.

'Yes you have,' Francesca spoke curtly. 'She's the woman you shoved out of the way in the Ormerey Supermart the other day.'

Josie looked hurt. 'Who, moi?'

'Yes you. Really Josie it's dreadful the way you treat people sometimes. I don't know who you think you are. You've made a very bad impression on Lizzie and Raoul.'

Josie went a deep red and pursed her lips. She was not used to being criticized.

'Never mind that now,' said Jean hastily. Once Francesca decided to speak her mind things could get very unpleasant. She spoke soothingly. 'Francesca, perhaps you could tell us a bit about Elizabeth. Where is she from? How did she meet Raoul? We'd all like to know.'

Francesca was getting annoyed. 'If you really want to know then I suggest you ask her yourself. I'm not here to gossip and certainly not about my own family. Haven't you got anything else on your list this month? It's not like you to be stuck for a topic.'

Jean rummaged in her handbag and produced the notebook in which she wrote down a list of subjects to be discussed by the Guild. 'Well, there's Yaffingales of course. Does anyone know the latest on that?'

She looked at Francesca who sat back in her seat, folded her arms and set her mouth in a thin line. Emily Platt who was sitting next to her recognised the danger signals. She got up quickly and whispered to Jean. 'Why don't we have our coffee and biscuits now, dear?'

'Good idea.' Jean was relieved. She and Emily busied themselves pouring coffee and handing it round. Jean looked longingly at the biscuits. Her dentures were killing her. She sat down near one of the low tables, checked to see no one was watching her then discreetly removed her top teeth. She wrapped them in a tissue and hid them under the edge of her saucer. That's better, she thought, everyone is too busy chatting to notice.

Susan Cottingham, Francesca's next door neighbour, handed round the plate of Guernsey gâche. Jean took a slice gratefully; it was easier to eat than a biscuit. The atmosphere eased a little as everyone tucked into the refreshments.

Alison sidled up to Francesca, her small eyes gleaming spitefully. 'That woman is only after your precious cousin's money. I'm surprised you can't see that. Why else is she over here? Prunella says…'

Francesca rounded on her furiously. 'I'm not interested in what you or Prunella has to say. It's ridiculous to say Lizzie is after Raoul's money. She's a very nice person, they love each other. That's what you can't stand, isn't it? You're such a misery guts you hate to see anybody happy.'

'Ladies, ladies,' Jean mumbled with difficulty through a mouthful of gâche. 'No one wants to upset you, Francesca, but you can't blame us for being curious. After all, she could be anybody. Don't you think you're being a little naïve, dear?'

Francesca's fiery temper finally got the better of her. 'No, I don't. You're such a snob, Jean, a thoroughly unpleasant snob who can't mind her own business. You can keep your Ladies' Guild. It's not a proper club; it's just an excuse for gossip and tittle-tattle. I don't know why I bother to come. I'm having nothing more to do with it.'

Jean went white. She was stunned. She had founded the Ormerey Ladies' Guild and run it for years without any complaints. She stared in amazement at Francesca who unhooked Zapp's lead and moved towards the door but Zapp had other ideas. Not a morsel had passed his lips all morning and he was usually given a few titbits. He spied Jean's half eaten gâche on the low table and made a dash for it, jerking the lead out of Francesca's hand. He loved gâche; there was no time to lick the butter off like he did at home so he gobbled it down in one mouthful and snuffled around amongst the crockery looking for crumbs.

Jean suddenly let out an anguished shriek. 'Francesca! That dog's got my teeth.'

Francesca stared in horror. Zapp was now under the table delicately picking bits of tissue off Jean's dentures. The room was silent apart from a few supressed giggles. Francesca, her face scarlet, grabbed Zapp's collar and retrieved the teeth. She handed them to Jean. 'I'm so sorry, Jean, I really am. He must have thought they were something edible.'

'You stupid woman! Look at them, they're ruined.' Jean waved the dentures in Francesca's face. She was incandescent with rage, spraying crumbs and spittle as she screamed at her. 'How many times have I told you not to bring that bloody dog in here and now look what it's done.' She dissolved into tears. People crowded round her murmuring sympathetically.

Zapp hated shouting. He flattened his ears and bolted for the door. Francesca only just managed to grab his lead before the two of them fled from the room.

Chapter 5

'Well, that's that then,' said Raoul as he, Lizzie and Francesca left the Island Hall after the States meeting. There had been standing room only in the public gallery of the Court Room where the States meetings were held, now everyone was spilling out into Main Square where the golden evening light filtered through the sycamore leaves. Simon Brockenshaw, surrounded by several States members, had a broad grin on his face as people congratulated him and slapped him on the back.

'Just look at that!' said Francesca furiously. 'How could our island States vote to destroy the green belt, they must have been bribed.' She was fighting back tears.

There were twelve elected members of the States of Ormerey. Seven had voted for the proposal to remove Yaffingales from the green belt and five against. The proposal had been carried; had there been a tie the President would have had to use his casting vote.

'Bribery would be impossible to prove,' said Raoul. 'Come on; let's go to the pub for chicken and chips to cheer ourselves up. I bet Geoff Prosser will be there holding forth, he'll be organising some sort of protest I expect.'

Raoul was right. Geoff Prosser was standing on a chair in the public bar of The Lord Nelson. 'Citizens of Ormerey,' he shouted above the hubbub. 'Are we going to allow our island to be raped by developers? Are we going to sit back and do nothing? Where's the spirit that brought the island back to life after the occupation?'

'He's a good orator,' said Lizzie. 'He should be on the States himself. Is he local?'

'No, but he's been here for donkey's years. He sailed over in his boat one summer and never left. He has tried to get elected but never succeeded. He's too controversial, a loose cannon.' Raoul tried to manoeuvre his way through the crowd towards the bar.

'But he's honest,' said Francesca. 'Geoff would never take a bribe. He'd make a nuisance of himself in the States, that's why he's not been elected. There's a cabal amongst some of the English settlers that makes sure things go their way. The locals don't stand a chance when it comes to the elections; there aren't enough of us, we're always out voted.'

A group of people got up to leave. 'Grab that table, Frankie, while Lizzie and I get the drinks and order our food.' They finally made it to the bar. 'You're busy tonight, Bill.'

'We always are after these meetings; folk like to chew the fat. I see old Geoff's in fine form.' He leaned across the bar and beamed at Lizzie. 'How are you settling in, my dear? Life here's never dull, is it?'

'I'm settling in fine, thanks, but it all takes a bit of getting used to. It's so different to England.'

'You'll soon put down roots. Give it a year. If you can make it through your first Ormerey winter you'll be fine. That's the big test.' He winked at Raoul. 'Val and I have never looked back. The island's our home now; Blighty's just a distant memory.'

Lizzie sipped her drink and smiled politely. She was not sure she would ever fit in. Ormerey was so quiet. She missed the hustle and bustle of the mainland; she missed the shops and all the conveniences she was used to. Most of all she missed her job, her work colleagues and her friends. She was not finding it easy to get to know people on the island in spite of Francesca's efforts to introduce her to people who attended the various clubs and charity events. The response had been cool to the point of rudeness and the few who had been polite and had seemed friendly at the time had shown no indication of wanting to get to know her. She hated the hostility she encountered daily in the Ormerey Supermart, and what was so bad about the Ormerey winter, she wondered, not the weather surely?

Francesca had managed to secure the empty table and Val brought their food over. Geoff Prosser, who had finished speaking and climbed down off his chair, approached them. 'I'm organising a protest march. I wonder if you'd give me a hand, Francesca. I know how strongly you feel about the issue.'

'Of course I will,' Francesca brightened. She liked Geoff; he was so open and direct. 'I'd be delighted, when are you thinking of having it?'

'Soon, while this good weather holds and before the Building and Development Control Committee meet to discuss Brockenshaw's plans. He's already submitted them, you know, they're available for perusal at the States office. All objections have to be in by the 20th.' He lowered his lanky frame into a vacant seat next to Raoul. 'You will write and object, won't you?'

'I certainly will, in the strongest possible terms,' said Raoul.

'Good man.' Geoff helped himself to one of Francesca's chips.

'Here, have them, I'm not hungry,' Francesca pushed her plate towards him.

'Thanks. Can you come round to my place a bit later on to discuss tactics? Natasha's coming; the last thing the Warringtons want to see is another hotel on the island.'

* * *

Francesca was relieved to be back at school. She always enjoyed September. There was her new reception class to settle in and this year the start of term kept her mind from brooding on the fate of Yaffingales and the unfortunate destruction of Jean Yorke's dentures. She was sure she had not heard the last of that episode.

St Mark's School had one hundred and thirty two pupils ranging in age from five to sixteen years. A drab single-storey building, it had been constructed in the 1970s when the old Victorian schoolhouse in the town became too small for the increasing numbers of children. The present school stood alongside the Coast Road opposite Briac Bay. It overlooked Briac Common, a wide grassy area which extended for a quarter of a mile around the bay between the road and the sand dunes.

It was an ideal spot for a school Francesca thought as she watched the children stream out of the playground to their parents and grandparents who were waiting, with picnics and swimming gear, ready to take them on to the beach.

The weather was idyllic; dewy mornings, with the long grass and foliage draped in fine cobwebs, were followed by warm sunny days. The air was clear and bright; the sea still warm, but there was a distinct autumnal tang in the air that heralded the demise of summer.

Francesca queued up with the children and bought an ice cream from the van parked on the common. She sat on the top of a concrete bunker which was half buried in the sand dunes and waited for Lizzie and Zapp to come and meet her for a walk.

Lizzie found that she had time on her hands now that Francesca was back at work. She missed her company. Raoul was often out. Where he went to and what he did Lizzie still had to discover as his replies to her questions were always along the lines of "this and that" or "just pottering about with Henri".

Lizzie knew that Raoul and Henri spent a lot of time together. Friends since childhood they shared many interests including shore fishing, tinkering about with motor vehicles and sifting through rubbish at the tip looking for treasures. Separated from his wife, who had returned to Guernsey with their two sons several years previously, Henri viewed Lizzie with suspicion, concerned that she would monopolise all Raoul's time but he need not have worried. Raoul and Lizzie respected one another's space, one of the reasons we get on so well Lizzie thought to herself as she collected Zapp from Puffin Cottage and walked down the hill to meet Francesca.

'I need a part-time job, something clerical,' Lizzie said as they walked along the common, watching the children down on the beach laughing and splashing at the water's edge.

'Why on earth do you want a job?' Francesca stared at her in surprise.

'I've always worked. I'm not used to being at home all day.' The truth was Lizzie was lonely. It would be a good way of meeting new people and it would be nice to have work colleagues again, she thought.

'Hmm! I don't think Raoul will be too keen on the idea. Ormerey men like their wives to be at home. You'll find it hard to believe but some island women never go out except to shop or collect their children from school. They might go out for a drink with their husbands occasionally but they don't meet up for coffee like the English women do. They're expected to stay at home and do the housework and have dinner on the table at 12 o'clock sharp.'

'Really, how old-fashioned! Like England was back in the 1950s. I don't think Raoul will mind me working, and anyway I'm not his wife.'

Francesca glanced sideways at her friend's set face. Of course, that was it! Why hadn't it occurred to her before? No wonder Lizzie was finding it hard to settle down. As Raoul's wife she would have been accepted; as his live-in girlfriend she was being cold-shouldered by the upper echelons of Ormerey society in the same way that she, Francesca, and her mother had been ostracised. The influence of the church was strong in the islands and living in sin, as it was still called, was disapproved of.

She kept her thoughts to herself. There was no point in upsetting Lizzie further and she knew that any mention of marriage to Raoul would be like red rag to a bull. He never spoke about his brief unhappy marriage to Clare and no one else was allowed to mention it either.

Francesca tucked her arm through Lizzie's. They walked to the far end of the common where there was an old broken slipway leading down to the shore. Francesca let Zapp off the lead and he raced on to the beach startling a couple of whimbrel feeding among the rocks. A flock of oystercatchers flew up, piping shrilly, the sun glinting on their black and white plumage as they skimmed over the sparkling water.

The two women sat on the edge of the slipway soaking up the warm afternoon sun. This end of the beach was covered with large stones and ended a few yards away in a rocky promontory. It was deserted except for Zapp who snuffled about in the seaweed pulling at fronds with his teeth. He found a dry kelp stalk and sat holding it upright between his front paws like a cigar while he nibbled the end of it.

'He's so funny,' said Lizzie. 'I've never known a dog with so much character. What made you choose a basenji?'

'I didn't. He used to belong to an old lady and when she died I took him. He'd have been put down otherwise; not everyone likes basenjis, they're such a handful.'

'Did he settle down all right?'

'No problem at all, I think it helped him moving from one quiet home to another with one lady owner and no other pets. He loves being the centre of attention and I spoil him dreadfully. He gets away with murder.' She laughed.

'Have you heard any more about Jean Yorke's teeth?'

'No, but I'm sure I shall. She'll send me the bill for her new ones. I shan't pay it of course.'

* * *

Lizzie broached the subject of a part-time job while she and Raoul were having supper that evening. As she had anticipated he was quite amenable to the idea.

'It won't be easy to find anything in the clerical line,' he said. 'Most of the available jobs are in shops or the hospitality trade.'

'There's one advertised in the latest Ormerey News. It's with a finance company. They want someone who can use Locoscript.'

'What on earth's that?'

'It's a word processing programme. You type into a computer which stores all your work and then prints it out when you need it. It's brilliant!'

'Good Lord! Can you really do that?'

'Don't look so surprised, I used it in my last job. I'm amazed that computers have actually reached Ormerey. There's hope for the island yet!'

Raoul noticed the sarcasm in her voice and smiled. 'You know you'll need a work permit, don't you?'

'Will I?'

'Yes, anyone who's not local needs one to work here. You get them from the States office. You haven't got a police record, have you?' His blue eyes twinkled mischievously.

'Of course not.' She grinned back at him.

'No problem then. I'd no idea I was living with such a high-powered business woman.'

'I've had to make a career for myself. I got married very young, straight from secretarial college. When I found out that John was adamant about not wanting children and we got divorced I had to earn a decent salary to support myself. I've always enjoyed my work.'

There was a sudden commotion in the kitchen and Zapp rushed into the dining room quickly followed by Francesca, red in the face and waving a piece of paper.

'Hello, Frankie.' Raoul tried to stop Zapp from jumping up to the table.

'Sorry to burst in like this but I've had the most awful letter from the Yorkes and a bill for the dentures. Harold Yorke delivered it just now and was very unpleasant. Five hundred pounds! Can you believe it? They're threatening to take me to court if I don't pay it.'

'Calm down.' Raoul took the letter, read it and passed it across to Lizzie. 'The court wouldn't waste its time on something like this. The stupid woman should have kept her teeth in her mouth. I'll go and make some coffee.'

Francesca sank down on to a chair and rested her elbows on the table. She put her head in her hands. Zapp scrambled up into her lap and tried to lick her face.

'Oh, Zapp,' said Lizzie. 'Have you any idea how much trouble you've caused?'

'It's all over the island,' Francesca said gloomily. 'The Yorkes have made sure of that, my name is mud.'

'Rubbish!' said Raoul returning with three mugs of coffee. 'Most people think it's hilariously funny and since when have you ever cared what people think? Just ignore the letter; nothing will come of it I'm sure.'

Chapter 6

The morning of the protest march dawned fine and clear. A stiff north-easterly wind had sprung up overnight, whipping the dry brown leaves off the sycamore trees in Main Square and sending them scurrying in circles over the cobbles.

Theo watched from his living room window in Rachelle House as the crowd began to gather outside. He felt excluded and alone. As the island's president he had to remain strictly neutral and so was unable to take part in the proceedings.

It was Saturday, the day he usually met up with Francesca, Raoul and Lizzie for morning coffee. Now he would have to wait another week before he could spend time with Francesca again. They were definitely making progress, he thought, and he was anxious to ask her out on a date but could not quite summon up the courage. He was too fearful of a rejection. He caught sight of her in the square. She was wearing jeans, which was unusual for her, and a bright red fleece jacket. She was carrying a placard which read "Hands off our Green Belt". He smiled. She turned towards the house and saw him standing at the window. She waved to him and, greatly encouraged, he waved back.

Geoff Prosser, who had acquired a megaphone from somewhere, was trying to rally his troops. Around two hundred people had assembled with banners and placards and were standing around in groups. Children raced about scuffing up the leaves and several dogs were barking in the midst of the general excitement.

Francesca had left Zapp at home much to the disappointment of Belle, Natasha's eight year old daughter. 'Why haven't you brought Zapp, Miss Saviano, I wanted to hold his lead on the walk.'

'There are too many other dogs here, he might get into a fight,' said Francesca. 'Walk with me instead. I'd like to hear how you're getting on in your new class.' She was fond of Belle whom she thought was a lonely child living in the hotel with her mother. Natasha was often working and her grandparents seemed indifferent to her existence. She took Belle's hand and they made their way to the bottom of Main Street where Geoff and Natasha were preparing to lead the march.

The crowd made its way slowly up the street. Shoppers and passers-by stopped to stare and people leaned out of first floor windows shouting encouragement. Val and Bill were outside The Lord Nelson watching the noisy procession. They remained strictly neutral, mindful of the fact Ruth and Simon Brockenshaw were amongst their regulars and that not all of their customers were against the new hotel.

Prunella Soames and her cronies peered out from the Ormerey Supermart, disappointed that they could not join in. The protesters consisted mainly of local islanders but Francesca was pleased to see how many English settlers were lending their support. She noticed Jean Yorke and her husband in the crowd, together with Josie Cleghorn and several members of the Ormerey Ladies Guild, and felt more kindly towards them.

As they walked across the fields towards Yaffingales the chatter and laughter of the crowd rose up to join the trilling of the skylarks high above them. The long dry grass stalks rustled like pattering raindrops as the wind whipped through them. The mood was positive; everyone was entering into the spirit of the occasion. Events like this did not often happen on Ormerey.

Geoff and Francesca were still leading with Belle but Natasha dropped back to where Lizzie was walking with Raoul and Henri. She touched Lizzie's arm.

'Could I have a quick word with you?'

Lizzie was surprised. She had not seen Natasha since the incident at the hotel on her first night on the island. Before she had a chance to speak Natasha rushed on.

'I want to apologise for the awful way Mother spoke to you and Raoul that night. It was so embarrassing. What must you think of us?'

'It's quite all right, Natasha, it's not your fault. I know the reason behind it; Raoul's told me the whole story.'

'Oh, I'm so relieved! I was worried you'd hate us all. My parents are very controlling. They wanted me to marry into an old island family but you need to be in love to get married, don't you? I've always been a disappointment to them.'

Lizzie did not know what to say. Fortunately Natasha continued, hardly pausing for breath. 'I'm glad Raoul has found someone at last. He deserves to be happy. I do hope you'll like it here.'

'I'm sure I shall.' Lizzie smiled into Natasha's friendly face and decided she liked her.

'Mummy! Mummy!' Belle rushed towards them and tugged at her mother's hand. 'Geoff wants you, we're here now. Come on!'

'It's been so nice talking to you, Lizzie, why don't we meet up for coffee sometime and have a proper chat?' Natasha smiled and looked down at her daughter. 'All right, Belle, I'm coming now.'

'I'd really like that,' said Lizzie.

They had reached the Yaffingales field. Geoff perched himself on top of the wooden gate with Francesca and Natasha standing on the grass on either side. He raised his megaphone.

'Well, here we all are! Have we any States members present?' He counted five raised hands. 'Good! I hope that we have demonstrated how vitally important this issue is to the people of Ormerey. On Monday morning we shall hand our petition to the President. We have nearly one thousand signatures, including every single member of the Ormerey Museum Society. I would like to thank everyone who has signed the petition, all those who have worked so hard to collect signatures and all of you who have turned up today.'

A cheer rose from the crowd.

'It's been a good turn out,' said Francesca to Raoul, linking her arm through his.

'Yes, well done Frankie. I see one or two reporters are here, we'll be in the Guernsey Evening Press now, and hopefully on the Radio Guernsey news in the morning.'

'Geoff, Natasha and I have all been interviewed,' Francesca said proudly. 'Let's hope we've really made a difference.'

* * *

Lizzie was having morning coffee with Natasha at the Rock Café; it was the third time that they had got together in the week following the protest march. Each had found in the other a sympathetic listener and a warm friendship was developing between the two women. They sat outside enjoying the warm September sunshine and sipping their cappuccinos.

Natasha was telling Lizzie about her troubled marriage. 'My parents have never forgiven me for marrying Danny. He was the first man I fell in love with.'

'What was he like?'

'Tall, fair and very handsome with blue eyes. That's where Belle gets her colouring from.'

'I remember Raoul saying he was from Jersey.'

'Yes, he was a fisherman. Not nearly good enough for my parents of course. They just could not leave us alone. They wanted us to live in the hotel but Danny wanted us to rent a house of our own which is what we did. Mother said Danny should give up commercial fishing and work at the hotel. Naturally he refused; fishing was his way of life. He loved the sea. Things went from bad to worse. I thought Mother would come round when Belle was born but she interfered more than ever, finding fault with everything and telling me that I wasn't looking after the baby properly. I had the most awful post-natal depression and Danny couldn't cope. I was crying all the time, Belle was difficult and fretful and Danny couldn't understand what was going on. We were always arguing. In the end he'd had enough. He went back to Jersey and we got divorced.'

'That's dreadful,' said Lizzie. 'Post-natal depression is an illness. Didn't you get any help from your doctor?'

'Not until it was too late. It was back in 1982, and you must have noticed how behind the times this island is. The only doctor here was well past retiring age. I don't think he'd ever heard of post-natal depression. I certainly hadn't, all I knew was how tired and ill and miserable I was all the time. Everyone kept telling me to pull myself together. It wasn't until Doctor Pointer arrived and explained what was wrong and put me on anti-depressants that I started to feel normal again.' Natasha sighed. 'It was a dreadful time.'

Lizzie was sympathetic. 'It must have been. Are you still in touch with Danny?'

'Yes, he's married again and has two little boys. Belle often goes to visit and sometimes they all come over here. She loves her little brothers.'

The waitress approached their table. 'The gâche has just arrived from the airport. Would you like some?'

'Yes please,' said Lizzie, 'and two more cappuccinos if that's all right.'

The waitress smiled and took their empty cups. 'Won't be a tick,' she said.

Natasha brightened up. 'Enough of all my woes. How are things with you?'

'I don't seem to be able to get a work permit,' said Lizzie.

Natasha frowned. 'Have you been to the States office?'

'Yes, and the Clerk said I couldn't apply for a work permit myself; I had to have a job and then my employer would apply for one for me. I found that odd because I've applied for a job and when I phoned them to check if they'd got my application they said they couldn't consider me because I didn't have a work permit. What am I supposed to do?'

'It sounds like a typical Ormerey conspiracy to me,' said Natasha. 'Someone somewhere doesn't want you to have a job. They think that if you can't work you'll have to leave the island. I've seen it all before, too many times.'

'But why should people want me to leave?' Lizzie was puzzled. 'I know the women in the Ormerey Supermart can't stand the sight of me but surely the government can't have anything against me. Perhaps they think the incomers shouldn't take jobs away from the locals. Is that it, do you think?'

'Possibly,' Natasha was thoughtful for a moment, 'but it's more likely to be personal. There are people here who are very jealous of Raoul and the St Arnaud wealth. You do know, don't you, that Prunella's husband George Soames is the Clerk's brother. That's why the Supermart gang are so influential; they've got a direct hot line to the most senior civil servant. You wouldn't believe some of the things that go on.'

'Raoul calls them the Ormerey mafia.'

'He's right. What does he think about your difficulty in getting a work permit?'

'He just says "never mind love, don't let these people get you down".' Lizzie sighed. 'I don't understand why I need a work permit; these islands are British after all.'

'The Channel Islands are Crown Dependencies, they are not part of the UK or the EU. They each have their own government and make their own laws. Geoff will tell you all about it; he's very knowledgeable about the history and politics of the islands.' Natasha flushed slightly and Lizzie smiled.

'You like Geoff, don't you? I've noticed the way you look at him.'

'Is it that obvious? Oh dear, for God's sake don't tell anyone. I'll feel such a fool; he isn't remotely interested in me.'

'Are you sure? You seem to get on very well. Maybe he's just shy.'

'Geoff? Don't make me laugh! He's the most up-front bloke on the island; he's always voicing an opinion on something or other. No, he's not interested. I don't think he's ever had a regular girlfriend since he came here. He's a bit of a loner.'

'Perhaps he's never met the right girl. Maybe he needs a bit of encouragement.'

Natasha looked horrified. 'I couldn't. Promise me you won't say anything. You know how gossip flies round the island.'

'I promise. I won't breathe a word to a soul.'

'Not even to Raoul?'

'Not even to Raoul,' Lizzie was emphatic. 'It isn't something he needs to know. Talking of Raoul, I must go and think about lunch. He still hasn't got over the shock of it not being on the table on the dot of twelve.'

Natasha laughed. 'Once an Ormerey man, always an Ormerey man! He won't change you know.'

'No, but he'll get used to it in time,' said Lizzie with a laugh.

* * *

While Lizzie and Natasha had been having coffee Raoul and Henri had spent a productive morning sanding down the rusty patches on Henri's Toyota pick-up and painting them with a rust inhibitor.

'That's a good job done,' said Henri. He looked at his watch. 'Lunch time already.'

Since his wife had left him Henri had lived with his widowed sister, Sophie, and had acquired the use of his late brother-in-law's large garage and extensive collection of tools. He wiped his hands on a greasy rag, said goodbye to Raoul and went indoors.

Raoul walked the short distance back to The Sycamores dodging the fast moving traffic as he went. It was 11.55am when the whole island was on the move in the rush to get home in time for the mid-day lunch. The Ormerey rush-hour Lizzie called it and Raoul smiled to himself. He was glad she appeared to be settling down at last and was making friends. Perhaps she would go off the idea of getting a job. He hoped so; he enjoyed having her around the house which had been so empty since the death of his father the previous year.

Raoul had never experienced paid employment; he had never needed to. The St Arnauds were a wealthy family owning several properties and parcels of agricultural land which they rented out. After leaving school at sixteen, Raoul had helped his father with the maintenance of the houses, all of which were at least a hundred years old and in constant need of decoration and repair. It had been a happy and relaxed way of life until age and infirmity had overtaken his parents and Raoul found himself in the role of carer as well as being responsible for the properties and their tenants. Lizzie's arrival in his life had opened a whole new chapter.

Raoul sat down at the kitchen table to read the Guernsey Press and wait for Lizzie. It was nearly one o'clock when she appeared.

'Sorry I've been so long.' She started to rummage around in the freezer which wobbled precariously on the uneven floor. 'Is pizza all right? It's a bit late to start cooking now.'

Raoul sighed. 'I suppose when you're working we'll have to have dinner at night like the English do.'

'Don't worry about it, I very much doubt if I'll ever get a work permit never mind a job.' Lizzie put the pizzas in the oven and told Raoul what Natasha had said about a conspiracy.

'She could be right, though it does sound a bit far-fetched. Look Lizzie, I've been thinking.'

'What?' Lizzie took some tomatoes and a lettuce out of the fridge and started to prepare a salad.

'Why don't you work for me?'

'Isn't that what I am doing?' She smiled and waved the knife at him.

'I mean a proper job. You know how I hate paperwork and I've got so behind with it all that I just can't face tackling it. I've let it slip since Dad died and I haven't even given it a thought since you came, not until now that is. I'll pay you of course.'

Lizzie stared at him. 'You don't need to pay me, Raoul, I'll do it anyway. I'll be glad to. What I need is something to do, something I can get my teeth into. I don't need the money.' She thought for a moment. 'If I'm helping you with your business for no remuneration then I don't need a work permit, do I?'

'No, so that solves that problem.'

'May I use the spare room as an office?'

'That's a good idea, and I'll buy you one of those computer things so you can get properly organised. It will be a huge load off my mind I can tell you.'

Chapter 7

In October it started to rain; heavy west-country rain that fell in sheets pulling the dead brown leaves off the trees and leaving puddles all over the common. Gulls splashed and bathed in the fresh water and flocks of starlings wheeled and swooped against the leaden sky.

The harbour was almost empty; the visiting boats had all departed for their winter berths in calmer waters.

'It will be like this until next Easter,' said Raoul staring at the few local craft that remained, rocking and straining at their moorings. 'Ormerey is dead in the winter.' They were sitting in the pick-up staring out at the grey sea. It was too wet to go for their usual walk.

'It's beautiful,' said Lizzie. 'I like the wildness and the desolation; it's such a contrast to the summer.'

Raoul squeezed her hand. 'Ormerey is always beautiful, Lizzie, in all its moods and colours. No two days are ever the same. That's why it's so popular with photographers and artists.'

They sat and watched as five oystercatchers stepped daintily across the grass, their red bills caked with earth as they probed for earthworms.

'You know winter's arrived when you see the oystercatchers on the common,' said Raoul. 'Curlew feed here too and occasionally I've seen a bar-tailed godwit. The gannets will be gone soon; they leave around mid-October.'

'Where do they go?'

'They spend the winter at sea and then come back to the gannetries in the spring to breed. It's a big day on Ormerey when the gannets return.' Raoul was pleased that Lizzie appeared to be settling down at last. He started up the engine to continue their drive around the coast.

Lizzie was settling into a routine. The spare bedroom at The Sycamores had been redecorated and turned into an office. A new desk and an office chair had arrived on the boat from Guernsey and an Amstrad computer had been flown over from England. Lizzie had started the mammoth task of sorting out Raoul's paperwork and filing it neatly in a second-hand filing cabinet they had managed to acquire from Henri.

'Probably from the tip,' said Raoul. 'It's a bit battered but it will do.'

Lizzie worked for Raoul three mornings a week. On Tuesdays she had coffee with Natasha in the Rock Café and on Saturday mornings she and Raoul had their regular date with Francesca and Theo. The afternoons were spent either walking or going out for a drive depending on the weather. Lizzie was developing a keen interest in the island's fauna and flora and Raoul enjoyed teaching her, recalling the happy times he and Francesca had spent at Yaffingales under the tutelage of Edwin Draycott when he and his wife had owned the little house in the valley.

Raoul had taken over the task of food shopping and cooking lunch on the mornings that Lizzie was working. This suited them both; Lizzie was spared the misery of shopping in the Ormerey Supermart and Raoul could choose what he wanted for lunch and what time they ate.

This change had not gone unnoticed by Prunella. 'We don't see much of your girlfriend these days,' she simpered at Raoul as he piled his purchases on to the counter.

'No, she's busy and she doesn't enjoy shopping in here,' he replied mildly. Raoul had an air of easy self-assurance that Prunella found disconcerting. She looked at him warily out of her pebble-like eyes trying to think of a suitable reply to this remark.

Raoul continued. 'You really ought to do something about sprucing this shop up and giving the whole place a good clean. It's no pleasure shopping in here. Everything's covered in dust. I wanted some candied peel but I notice that it is four months out of date. You shouldn't be selling that. You need to pull your socks up, Prunella. This shop's a disgrace.'

Prunella had regained her composure and snorted angrily. 'You've got very fussy since that woman arrived.'

'It's got nothing to do with Lizzie; it's a question of hygiene.' Raoul kept his tone even. 'You'll be in a fine pickle if the Environmental Health people from the States of Guernsey come over and make an inspection. I've a good mind to ring them up and complain. It's time somebody did.'

He smiled at Prunella and left her fuming behind her till.

'Really!' she said to Pauline, one of her colleagues. 'How dare he speak to me like that. Raoul St Arnaud is so up himself these days. It's ever since that ghastly woman arrived. They think they're so posh.'

'They may think they are,' sneered Pauline, 'but they're still living in sin.'

* * *

Theo was miserable. He sat at his desk in the small room at the back of Rachelle House that he used as an office and stared out at the rain-soaked garden. The trees, bereft of leaves, traced a delicate pattern against the grey sky but Theo was oblivious to their beauty. He shuffled morosely through the pile of papers that had arrived in the morning post from the States of Guernsey but he was unable to concentrate. His thoughts kept drifting to Francesca and the problem of Yaffingales.

He got up and made himself a cup of coffee, his second that morning, and spread a copy of the plans for the new hotel out on his desk. Personally Theo thought that the hotel would be an asset to the island bringing work and, ultimately, more tourists which the local economy badly needed. As President of the States Theo had to remain neutral, he could not influence the Planning Committee in any way and it was their decision as to whether or not the plans should be approved. He wondered if any of them had been swayed by the protest march or the petition. There had been a lot of publicity in the Guernsey Evening Press and on the local radio station. Only time will tell he thought wryly. He felt unable to discuss his opinion on the matter with anyone for fear of Francesca getting wind of it, and that would ruin his chances of any sort of relationship with her. Gossip spread like a forest fire through the Ormerey population; once an opinion was voiced out loud it was impossible to keep it a secret.

Theo had decided that he wanted to marry Francesca. He had thought long and hard about where his life was going and realised that it was going nowhere. He was fed up with being the island's President. He was tired; the work load was getting heavier and he felt as though he was drowning under all the paperwork. He had thought of retiring in December when his present four year term of office came to an end. But what then? He saw his days stretching endlessly ahead in monotonous mediocrity, rattling around in a house that was far too large for him and contained so many unhappy memories. He thought how nice it would be to move into Puffin Cottage with Francesca, living in companionable comfort for the rest of his days and then he remembered Zapp. Theo did not like dogs and had a particular aversion to Francesca's snappy little basenji. He knew that he could never ask her to part with it. He toyed with the idea of talking things over with Raoul; he might ask him out for a drink sometime but maybe that wouldn't be appropriate. He sighed, racked with indecision. He had no clear idea of how to move things forward.

His reverie was interrupted by the shrill ringing of the telephone. It was one of his clients, Ian Warrington, the proprietor of the Imperial Hotel.

'I need to see you a.s.a.p, old man. When would be convenient?'

'Now is as good a time as any,' said Theo. He did not care for Ian Warrington whom he considered to be an insufferable snob but on an island as small as Ormerey one could not be too fussy about whom one accepted as clients. 'An income tax matter is it?'

'No, no! We need to discuss this Yaffingales business. We don't want another big hotel on the island, do we?'

'Sorry, old man,' said Theo. 'You know I can't discuss that. As President of the States I have to remain strictly impartial.' He smiled to himself as he replaced the receiver and felt a little happier.

***

'I see you've got your new teeth at last.' Josie Cleghorn's booming voice reverberated around the elegant dining room of the Imperial Hotel where three stalwarts of the Ormerey Ladies' Guild were having morning coffee.

Jean Yorke scowled and Natasha, who had just brought their coffee to the table, tried to keep her face straight.

'Hush dear!' Emily Platt patted Josie on the arm and turned to Jean. 'They look very nice, Jean, are you happy with them?'

'Yes, now I've got used to them but it's been a great inconvenience. We've asked Francesca to pay for them of course; five hundred pounds.'

'Goodness!' said Emily, 'they never cost that much surely?'

'Well no, but there were our air fares to Guernsey and the taxis, and Harold thought I needed a treat after all the trauma I've been through so we had lunch at the St Pierre Park Hotel.'

'You don't expect Francesca to pay for your lunch, do you?' Emily was shocked.

'Of course she should pay. It's her fault we had to go at all. It will teach her to keep that dog under control.'

'Is there anything else I can get for you, ladies?' Natasha was hovering within earshot. She could not wait to relay details of the conversation back to Lizzie.

'No thank you,' Jean gave her a dismissive look.

'I can't see Francesca Saviano paying up,' said Josie helping herself to a slice of gâche and spreading it liberally with butter.

'She'd better or she'll find herself in court. Harold is adamant on that point.'

Emily, always the peacemaker, pushed a strand of wispy grey hair that had fallen in front of her glasses back into place and helped herself to more gâche. 'I don't think going to court would be a good idea, Jean. After all you might lose and think of the publicity. Either way it will be reported in the Ormerey News.'

'No it won't! Harold will see to that, he's on the board of governors of the Ormerey News. He's the chairman and what he says goes. Anyway I shan't lose!'

'You'll look a complete fool if you do,' said Josie bluntly. 'Do you really want that? Surely it would be better to just forget the whole thing and put it behind you.'

'Harold will never let it go; he's determined Francesca should pay.'

'Well she won't, you know how stubborn she is,' Josie retorted, 'and Raoul will back her up. He'll pay for a good Guernsey lawyer if she has to go to court. Is Harold prepared to pay for a lawyer? The whole thing could end up costing you a fortune.'

Jean snorted derisively. 'Well, we shall see, won't we?'

Emily sighed with resignation.

Chapter 8

On the last Sunday in October Lizzie awoke to an unpleasant odour of drains. It had rained heavily all night and showed no sign of abating. She lay in bed for a few moments watching the raindrops careering down the window pane, joining one another to make rivulets on the glass, and then she got out of bed. Raoul was still asleep. She put on her dressing gown and slippers and made her way downstairs. The smell was stronger in the hall and it was with trepidation that she opened the door into the kitchen.

The floor was completely underwater. Lizzie stared in horror. It came up almost to the level of the step she was standing on. She wondered what on earth had happened and then saw water pouring down the walls. The roof was leaking.

She rushed upstairs and shook Raoul. 'Wake up! The kitchen floor is flooded. Come and look.'

Raoul rolled over sleepily. 'Don't panic, I expect the drain's blocked that's all.' He closed his eyes.

'Please get up!' Lizzie shook him again.

He sat up. 'For God's sake, Lizzie, it's only a bit of water. Take the cover off that drain in the corner and give it a poke with something. It'll soon drain away.'

'You come and sort it out, it's three inches deep against the back wall and the roof is leaking like a sieve.'

'It always does when we have a lot of heavy rain and if the drain's choked up the water can't run away. Just put your wellies on and deal with it.' He lay down again. 'God preserve me from helpless women.' He put the pillow over his head.

Lizzie lost her temper. She snatched the pillow and threw it across the room. 'You deal with it, it's your bloody kitchen!' she screamed.

'Oh, for God's sake!' Thoroughly awake now Raoul got up and followed Lizzie downstairs. He stood on the hall step and peered into the kitchen.

'What a fuss over a little bit of water,' he muttered as he paddled across the floor and lifted the rubber cover off the drain. He removed the grating. 'Pass me Dad's walking stick.'

Lizzie, refusing to step into the murky water, leaned forward and handed it to him. He poked and prodded for a few minutes. 'It's blocked,' he said. 'It needs a plumber. I'll call Joe tomorrow.'

'Tomorrow!' Lizzie shrieked. 'What's wrong with now?'

'It's Sunday, no one works on Sundays.'

'Surely a plumber will come in an emergency?'

'Not Joe,' said Raoul. 'It's hard enough to get him to turn up on a weekday.'

'Then call another plumber.'

'We always have Joe, he's family. He'll be offended if I call someone else.'

'Well, if he's family he can do you a favour and sort this out today.'

'No chance! I'm not ringing him at this time on a Sunday morning. Just calm down, Lizzie, it's not the end of the world.'

'It's all very well to tell me to calm down,' Lizzie took a deep breath and tried to speak evenly. 'What about the roof?

It looks as though the whole thing needs replacing.' She looked upwards to the corrugated plastic sheeting which was discoloured and covered with moss. Water was still running down the walls.

'Rubbish!' said Raoul. 'It's only leaking where it joins the wall; Joe can fix that.'

'If he ever comes,' said Lizzie bitterly. 'We're still waiting for him to put in that tap you found in your bunker. How on earth do you expect me to cope in this awful kitchen in the winter? I'll freeze to death for one thing; there's no heating in here, and I'll have to live in my wellies.'

'Oh stop complaining! You've done nothing but moan about this kitchen ever since you got here. If it's not good enough for you then I suggest you go back home. You know where the airport is.'

Lizzie stared at him aghast. It was a common phrase on Ormerey "you know where the airport is" along with "your face doesn't fit here." She'd had both those comments flung at her in the Ormerey Supermart and from some of the locals in the pub but she never thought she would hear those words from Raoul. She fled upstairs, dressed hurriedly and rushed out of the front door.

Ten minutes later Lizzie was banging on the door of Puffin Cottage. Francesca, still in her dressing gown, opened it and Lizzie stumbled across the threshold in tears.

'Whatever's happened?'

'I've had a dreadful row with Raoul; he's told me to go home.'

'I'm sure he didn't mean it,' said Francesca soothingly. 'You know how grumpy he can be first thing in the morning. Come in and have some breakfast.'

She led Lizzie into the cosy kitchen. Zapp, ecstatic at the sight of an early visitor, leapt on to Lizzie's lap the moment she sat down at the pine table. She hugged the little dog and put her face against the short soft fur on his neck. He tried to lick the tears off her face and Lizzie relaxed. She looked round Francesca's sparkling kitchen with its colourful Quimper pottery and gingham curtains at the window and could not help contrasting it with the one she had just left.

Francesca made coffee and toast and Lizzie relayed the happenings of the morning. 'I don't know what to do,' she said miserably.

'Do nothing,' said Francesca. 'He'll calm down. He knows very well that he should have done something about that kitchen years ago and that's why he's cross. It'll blow over.'

Lizzie was doubtful. All her feelings of alienation and homesickness which had diminished over the past few weeks came flooding back.

'Maybe I should go home to England. Perhaps my face doesn't fit here after all.'

'Rubbish!' said Francesca briskly. 'Stay here with me today and give Raoul some space. As soon as it stops raining we'll take Zapp out for a good walk.'

The phone rang. Francesca smiled, 'that'll be Raoul.' She reached for the receiver.

'Hello Frankie, is Lizzie there with you?'

'Yes she is; we're just having breakfast.'

'We've had a bit of a row.'

'She's told me all about it. I'm not taking sides; I'm sitting firmly on the fence. I've suggested to Lizzie that she spends the day here. It will give you both a chance to calm down.'

'Bless you, Frankie.'

'If you'll take some advice from your older and wiser cousin, Raoul, you'll do something about that bloody awful kitchen of yours.'

Raoul laughed. 'Careful, Frankie, you're slipping off the fence!'

* * *

The early morning rain storm gave way to a mild, windless day. A weak sun shone low in the afternoon sky, casting its mellow light over the landscape creating long cool shadows.

Francesca, Lizzie and Zapp set out along the airport road towards the cliffs. The pastel coloured houses of the town were soon left behind as they reached the wide open farmland and the pungent smell of fresh manure assailed their nostrils. Zapp flattened his ears and dived between the wooden bars of a gate.

'No, Zapp, I'm not having you rolling in anything disgusting today,' said Francesca, tugging hard on the lead. Zapp shot backwards through the gate into Francesca's legs. 'You know what a fuss you make when you have to have a bath.'

The low sunlight caught the thousands of spiders' webs strung between the dead grass stalks giving the fields a silvery sheen. They could see the sea on the horizon, flat calm like a huge, shimmering lake. Lizzie felt the beauty of the scene steal into her and her spirits lifted. Her argument with Raoul seemed trivial now and she felt sorry she had made such a fuss.

The two women and the dog left the road and turned on to the grassy track that led over the cliffs and down on to the beach. They could see Fort Jackson below, surrounded by water except for the concrete causeway which snaked across from the mainland in a graceful curve. The tide had just turned and the rocks and shingle were wet and glistening. Zapp, free at last, rushed on to the beach.

The sea shone like glass and the seabirds resting upon its barely moving surface looked like ethereal creatures from another world. The only sounds were the sharp cries of the wheeling gulls and the soft shushing of the waves caressing the shore. Lizzie and Francesca sat side by side on the edge of the causeway. The tide was retreating fast and Zapp splashed about happily in the shallow rock pools nibbling at seaweed.

It was Francesca who broke the silence. 'Raoul would be devastated if you left, you know. He's happier now than I've seen him in years.'

'You wouldn't say that if you'd heard him today. He said I was always finding fault with the kitchen and if I didn't like it I should go back to England.' A defiant note crept into Lizzie's voice. 'I still think he should be firm with the plumber.'

'It wouldn't do much good. The Ormerey workman is a law unto himself. If the weather's good for fishing he'll be out on the rocks and if it's bad he'll be in the pub. It's the island way. You can't win I'm afraid.'

Lizzie sighed. 'Am I doomed to spend the rest of my life in that dreadful kitchen?'

'Cheer up,' said Francesca, 'but Raoul does have a point, you know. You do find fault with a lot of things.'

'I suppose I have been moaning a lot,' said Lizzie, 'and I had a very undignified row with Mrs Cleghorn in the paper shop yesterday when she jumped the queue. Oh dear!'

'Never mind about her,' retorted Francesca, 'she's an appalling woman, no manners at all.'

She shivered. 'Time to get moving I think.' She called to the dog and they all set off along the coastal path towards Saline Bay.

'I'll tell you something about Raoul,' Francesca continued. 'He likes fiery women. That's one of the things he likes about you, you can stick up for yourself. He's proud of you. The island no longer sees him as the man whose wife ran off after a few weeks of marriage. He's now half of a couple.'

Lizzie smiled, comforted by her friend's words. 'Now he's seen as the man who's been grabbed by a gold digger.' She laughed. Her heart was lighter than it had been all day.

There was a damp chill in the air and the sea had changed to the colour of pewter. The low grey clouds over the horizon were tinged with pink. Francesca put Zapp on the lead, he had a habit of terrorising the cat and poultry at Rock Cottage. Fortunately the chickens were in a small coop on the front lawn. Zapp strained towards them, nearly choking himself, and did not notice the cat on the cottage window-sill, all fluffed up and glaring at him. They passed safely without incident. It was almost dark by the time they reached Francesca's front door.

'Come in and have a cup of tea. I've got some fresh doughnuts.'

Lizzie reluctantly refused. She was anxious to get back to Raoul. She hugged Francesca.

'Thanks Frankie, what would I do without you?'

'Oh, go on with you!' Francesca returned the hug. 'I'll see you tomorrow.'

The smell of the drain hit Lizzie as soon as she opened the back door. The water had seeped away leaving a small puddle around the grating. She tiptoed across the muddy flagstones and went into the sitting room. Raoul was watching television. He looked round as she entered.

'You'll be pleased to know that Joe is coming first thing tomorrow to sort out the drain. We'd better go out for tea; I can't stand the smell in the kitchen.' He grinned at her. 'Feeling better?'

'Yes thanks, and Raoul, I am sorry.'

'So am I, love. Don't worry about it. We'll soon be back to normal.' Raoul hesitated, looking rather sheepish.

'What?'

'Well, in order to persuade Joe to come I had to tell him what a hard time you were giving me, nagging and carrying on. He feels so sorry for me now that he's promised to drop everything else and come. I'm really sorry.'

'There's no need to be,' Lizzie laughed, 'I don't care what you said as long as it gets him here. Let's hope he actually turns up.'

* * *

Much to Lizzie's surprise Joe did turn up the next morning at eight o'clock sharp. Mindful of what Raoul had said to him about her the previous day, and because she was so relieved to see him, Lizzie decided to be nice.

'Would you like a cup of tea, Joe, or would you prefer coffee?'

'Ta, Mrs St Arnaud, coffee please, milk and two sugars.'

'I'm Mrs Bayley, Joe, not Mrs St Arnaud, but please call me Lizzie. I gather you and Raoul are related.'

'Yes, my mother and Raoul are first cousins.' He smiled at her. She doesn't seem so bad after all he thought and wondered how his own wife, Kate, would have reacted in similar circumstances. Not well he thought wryly. He sat down at the kitchen table.

A few minutes later Raoul appeared. 'Hi Joe, good to see you.' He was brisk. 'I think Lizzie had better go out for the morning while you and I tackle this job. You've brought your rods I take it.'

'In the van,' said Joe gulping his coffee.

Lizzie grabbed her jacket and her binoculars and shot out of the door into the fresh air. Yesterday's mild calm weather had lasted overnight and the morning was bright and clear. She headed for the airport, the only place on the island that would be open so early in the morning where she could get some breakfast.

A light breeze ruffled Lizzie's hair as she made her way up the short hill to the airport. The wind sock was hardly moving. It was quiet inside the terminal building. The red eye flights to Guernsey and Southampton had already departed and there was a lull before the next scheduled arrivals. Lizzie ordered coffee and two toasted teacakes from the buffet.

'You're early today.' Judy, the small middle-aged woman behind the counter, fixed Lizzie with a beady stare. 'Meeting someone are you?'

'No,' said Lizzie, not wanting to be drawn into a conversation. 'I'm going birdwatching.'

Lizzie took her breakfast outside and sat at one of the tables. She had a good view over a small wooded valley where she could hear a robin singing his autumnal song; so different from his exuberant trilling in the spring, the mournful notes falling out of the tree like teardrops. A plump cock pheasant waddled into view alongside the perimeter fence, the sun glinting on his colourful plumage. He was followed moments later by his hen and four well-grown young. Lizzie watched the little family until they wandered back into the wood. She took her crockery inside and set off on her walk. She decided to go to Yaffingales and, if there was nobody around, sneak into the terraced garden overlooking the sea. It was so quiet and peaceful and there would be plenty of birds.

Joe and Raoul meanwhile had unblocked the drain and scrubbed the flagstones down with hot soapy water and disinfectant. 'That should please your new lady.' Joe surveyed the glistening floor with satisfaction.

'Yes,' said Raoul. 'Could you take a quick look at the roof while you're here? It's leaking quite badly; I think the flashings round the edges need replacing.'

Joe got his ladder and inspected the kitchen roof. 'Bad news I'm afraid, Raoul, the whole roof needs replacing. You'll need a builder for this job.'

'Surely not!' Raoul was disbelieving. 'Can't you patch it up?'

'It's way beyond patching up. I'm surprised it hasn't fallen in on you; the only thing holding it together is the moss. The plastic's all cracked. You need to start again from scratch.'

Raoul groaned. 'It'll have to be done then. Who on earth am I going to get to do it before the winter sets in?'

'I suggest Fords, they're expensive but they'll do a good job and they'll do it quickly if you tell them it's an emergency.'

'I'll give them a ring,' said Raoul. 'By the way I've been meaning to ask you, how's Aunt Mary?'

'Gran? Oh she's fine! Kate and I went to Guernsey for a day last week and there she was in the Wimpey Bar with three of her mates. She's quite amazing for her age.'

'And your parents?'

'They're both well. You should take Lizzie over there to meet them; they'd be so pleased to see you.'

'That's a good idea,' said Raoul. 'We could spend a week in Guernsey while the roof's being done.' He had temporarily forgotten how irritating his cousin Felicity could be.

Chapter 9

Joshua Ford, who owned the largest building firm on the island, together with his two sons, came round himself to inspect Raoul's kitchen roof and to give him an estimate. A taciturn man, he kept his feelings to himself when he saw the state of it, and promised to make a start the following day.

Raoul telephoned his Aunt and told her that he was bringing Lizzie over to Guernsey for a few days and suggested that he brought her along to introduce her to the family. His Aunt Mary was delighted.

'It's over a year since we saw you, Raoul, at your father's funeral. I'll ask Felicity to arrange a get-together so we can all meet your girlfriend. When are you coming?'

'Tomorrow,' said Raoul. 'We've booked into Moore's Hotel in the Pollet. I'll ring you from there.'

Aunt Mary was Raoul's father James St Arnaud's younger sister. She had moved from Ormerey to Guernsey in 1926 when she married Colin Gardner. Now a spritely eighty six year old widow she still lived in the large family home in the Vale where she had lived with her husband and brought up her only daughter, Felicity. Aunt Mary felt the loss of her adored elder brother keenly and had an especially soft spot for Raoul who was like his father in so many ways, inheriting not only his fair colouring and good looks but also his easy-going personality and his inherent kindness. She was looking forward to seeing him.

Raoul and Lizzie took a taxi from Guernsey airport to St Peter Port and deposited their luggage at Moore's Hotel before walking to Creasy's department store where they were meeting Aunt Mary for coffee. They found her seated at her favourite table in the window area of the coffee shop with its magnificent view over the harbour and the islands of Herm, Jethou and Sark. She stood up to greet them, a tall slim woman, smartly dressed with beautifully permed white hair and immaculate make-up. She gave Raoul a hug, then took Lizzie's hand and kissed her warmly.

'It's lovely to meet you, my dear; we'd no idea Raoul had found himself a girlfriend until yesterday when he phoned.' She turned to Raoul. 'You are a dark horse. How long have you known each other?'

'Just over a year,' said Raoul, 'but she's only been with me on Ormerey for a couple of months. We met quite by chance in London when I was over there. What are we having? Three coffees?'

'Yes please, dear ,and some gâche would be nice.'

They were soon tucking in. 'Felicity's arranged for us all to have Sunday lunch round at her house so Lizzie can meet the family,' Aunt Mary dabbed her lips delicately with a paper napkin.

Raoul groaned inwardly. He was not keen on Felicity who was five years his senior and who had been a spoilt bossy child, making family visits a torment for himself and Francesca. Now she's an insufferably bossy woman he thought but he kept his feelings to himself. It would be interesting to see what sort of impression she made on Lizzie, and it would be nice to see Julian, Felicity's husband, who could be quite interesting to talk to if one could ever get him on his own. He smiled at his Aunt. 'That will be lovely,' he said.

Felicity lived at Fort George with her husband in a house that was too large for them now that their three sons had left home. Julian Rockdale was a quiet dignified man, over six feet in height with thick iron grey hair, who was enjoying a busy yet relaxed retirement. He left the running of his luxurious home and his social life to his wife who was a born organiser and ran both their lives with clockwork efficiency. This regime had worked well while Julian was working and he had no desire for changes now. He had occupied a senior position at one of the large offshore banks in St Peter Port. The work had been stressful at times but the substantial salary had enabled Julian to buy the large house at Fort George alongside several of Guernsey's millionaires. Thanks to his wife's support, and her willingness to take on all the family responsibilities leaving him free to concentrate on his job, he had reached retirement age with his health intact and now enjoyed bridge, sailing and golf. He was looking forward to the family get-together.

Sunday dawned bright and sunny. Julian joined his wife in the kitchen as she prepared the lunch. 'It's a pity Joe and Kate can't make it,' he said sniffing appreciatively. A delicious aroma of roast beef permeated the kitchen.

'Hm!' snorted his wife. 'I expect Lizzie's met them already.'

It was a source of disappointment to Felicity that her eldest son was a plumber and, even worse, lived on the uncivilised outpost that was Ormerey. She had been horrified when Joe had announced that he was to marry an Ormerey girl, a situation for which she held her Aunt and Uncle responsible; all those visits to the northern isle during the school holidays, not to mention the summer beach parties where inhibitions were shed and teenage pregnancies resulted. 'It isn't that I dislike Kate,' Felicity often said to Julian, 'it's just that Joe could have done so much better.'

'But we wouldn't have those adorable grandchildren, would we?' Julian always replied and Felicity was forced to agree.

Their second son William was a chartered accountant and lived with his wife Rosemary in a small house in the Vale, quite close to Aunt Mary, and the youngest, Jamie, had followed his father into the bank and resided in a smart flat in St Peter Port.

The Rockdale family were already gathered in the conservatory when Raoul and Lizzie arrived. Introductions were made. Lizzie was struck by the strong physical resemblance between Raoul and Felicity; they could be brother and sister she thought. The second Rockdale son, William, had also inherited the St Arnaud good looks, his blonde wavy hair brushed back from his forehead, his blue eyes warm and friendly.

'Hello,' he said to Lizzie. 'You're a surprise; what a crafty old dog Uncle Raoul is.'

Lizzie laughed. 'You are all quite a surprise to me,' she said.

William's wife Rosemary was sitting with Jamie and Aunt Mary. 'What do you think of her?' she asked, nodding towards Lizzie who was still talking to William.

'She looks nice,' said Jamie. He turned to his grandmother. 'You've met her already, haven't you?'

'Yes,' replied Aunt Mary. 'She is nice and they seem very happy.'

Felicity was pleasantly surprised by Lizzie. She had not been sure what to expect but now she noted with approval

Lizzie's smart appearance and attractive speaking voice. No trace of some ghastly accent she thought as she welcomed the visitor warmly and kissed her on both cheeks. 'I'm so glad you could come,' she said. 'We seldom get together as a family; we should do it more often.'

Lizzie tried to visualise the Rockdale family sitting down to a meal at The Sycamores and failed. She was rather overawed by Felicity and her luxurious home.

Lunch was a jolly meal. Roast beef and Yorkshire pudding were followed by lemon meringue pie and the conversation was lively and flowed easily.

'What brings you over to Guernsey?' Julian asked Raoul.

'I'm having a new roof put on the kitchen. We had a flood last time it rained heavily. Fords are working on it now so we thought it would be nice to have a short break over here, and it would be a good opportunity for Lizzie to meet you all.'

'How awful to have a flood in the kitchen; it must have made life very difficult,' said Aunt Mary. 'I remember that kitchen from years ago; I can't imagine what it's like now.'

'Joe came and unblocked the drain and cleaned the floor up for us,' said Lizzie finishing off a second helping of lemon meringue pie.'

'It's good to know he does work occasionally.' William's tone was sarcastic and Lizzie smiled.

When the meal was over Felicity hustled Raoul into the kitchen to help her with the coffee. Raoul gazed around the large modern kitchen-breakfast room with its Aga and numerous gleaming appliances and hoped that Lizzie would stay in the dining room.

'Well,' said Felicity to her cousin. 'Are you and Lizzie planning to get married?'

'No, we're not. Why?'

'Mother does not approve of you living together and, quite frankly Raoul, neither do I. There's the St Arnaud good name to consider. How do you think it reflects on the rest of the family? You can't keep a mistress, you know, it's just not done.'

'I can do what I bloody well like,' snapped Raoul, 'and don't refer to Lizzie as my mistress; it's insulting. A mistress is a woman kept by a married man in a separate establishment. Lizzie is my partner. Lots of couples live together these days.'

'Not people of our generation,' said Felicity, 'not in the islands. Maybe there are a few youngsters cohabiting but not people like us'.

'People like us!' said Raoul. 'What a snob you are, Felicity.'

He marched out of the kitchen and saw Lizzie in the garden with their host who was showing her his late-flowering roses. He joined them. Julian noticed Raoul's firmly compressed lips and his frown and guessed that he and Felicity had been having one of their inevitable spats. He smiled to himself. 'Jamie's got a day off tomorrow,' he said. 'The two of us are taking the boat over to Herm. Would you and Lizzie like to come with us?'

'Thanks,' said Raoul. 'We'd love to.'

'We usually have a leisurely lunch at The Mermaid and then take a walk round the island. This weather's set to last for a few more days. I can't remember when we last had such a glorious Indian summer.'

Lizzie was admiring a border of Michaelmas daisies in varying shades of blue, mauve and crimson. She watched the colourful butterflies gathering nectar in the warm sunshine and recognised red admirals, peacocks and small tortoiseshells.

'Coffee's ready!' Felicity called from the French windows. She was all smiles. Raoul was relieved. One good thing about Felicity he thought, squabbles soon blow over – she doesn't bear grudges – and I don't have to see her very often.

* * *

The Indian summer lasted into the first week of November and was brought to an abrupt end by strong westerly gales and driving rain. Raoul and Lizzie flew back to Ormerey on a plane buffeted hither and thither by the wind which Lizzie found unnerving. She clung on tightly to Raoul and shut her eyes as the bright runway lights loomed closer through the rain and the plane tilted sideways as it made a sharp turn in order to approach the runway from the eastern end. The passengers applauded as the Trislander touched down safely. The pilot turned and grinned.

'Safe on terra firma!' he said.

Raoul was surprised to find Joe waiting to give them a lift back to The Sycamores. 'Wait till you see the new kitchen', he announced as he loaded their bags into his car. 'You'll love it!' Lizzie was doubtful but she smiled politely.

The town was deserted as they drove through the wet cobbled streets, the only building lit up and showing any signs of life was The Lord Nelson. There were few street lights on Ormerey; most of the island lay in inky blackness and Lizzie found herself once again comparing the island with Guernsey with all its modern trappings of civilisation. She shivered and wondered how she would cope with the long dark winter evenings when, even in town, the streets were empty.

Both Raoul and Lizzie were amazed at the transformation when they entered their kitchen.

'It's been repainted,' said Raoul.

'Yes, Frankie helped me with that, she chose the colours. I hope you like it.'

'It's lovely,' said Lizzie, 'so bright and cheerful.'

The dull cream walls had been painted white and the cupboard doors and other woodwork were pale yellow instead of the dark blue they had been previously. Raoul looked up at the roof.

'No more leaks then?'

'No, Fords have done a really good job. They've used that new three-layered polycarbonate sheeting; it's a good insulator, you'll need blinds for when it's sunny or you'll be too hot.'

'What's this at the back here?'

'I got that new carpenter from Guernsey to make that. It's a plinth to put your appliances on so that they are level instead of rocking on the sloping floor.'

'You are clever Joe.' Lizzie was delighted. 'We've got a new fridge freezer coming on the next boat.'

'God knows what the total bill for all this will come to,' said Raoul, 'I'll need a few stiff drinks to get over the shock.'

Joe laughed and winked at Lizzie. 'Did you have a good time in Guernsey? How are the folks?'

'We had a lovely time and I really like your family. They made me very welcome, and we had a marvellous day on Herm with your father and Jamie. I found some beautiful shells on Shell Beach. Raoul's promised to take me to Sark next year.'

***

Theo had decided to ask Francesca, Raoul and Lizzie to have dinner with him at the Imperial Hotel. He mentioned it to them during Saturday morning coffee at the Rock Café. Francesca giggled.

'Daphne Warrington won't like that; she hates Raoul.'

'She turned us away on my first evening here,' said Lizzie.

'She won't know,' said Theo with a broad grin. 'I'll book a table for four in my name and give her a surprise. She won't argue with me.'

Theo was as good as his word and booked a table for that same evening. Francesca fussed over what to wear and sought Lizzie's advice.

'What about this red cocktail dress?' Lizzie was rummaging through Francesca's wardrobe.

'Oh that! I've hardly worn it. Don't you think it's a bit too dressy?'

'Not for the Imperial Hotel. It's nice to dress up occasionally. You want to impress Theo don't you?'

Francesca blushed. 'I don't want to overdo it.'

'No danger of that; he's obviously mad about you.'

'You think so?'

'Oh yes! It's a pity he's so shy. The two of you should be having a dinner date on your own.'

'Mmm! I don't know. Perhaps it's better to keep things as they are – just friends.'

'You never know how things are going to turn out. Wear the red dress,' said Lizzie.

Theo was waiting in the bar when the other three arrived at the hotel. 'Our table's ready,' he said. 'We'll go straight through.' He turned to Francesca. 'You look nice, that colour suits you.' Francesca blushed.

The dining room was emptier than Lizzie had ever seen it; fewer visitors now summer had ended she supposed. She looked for Daphne Warrington and saw her talking to Harold and Jean Yorke. Smart in a black cocktail dress, she stiffened when she saw Raoul and Lizzie and pursed her lips in annoyance.

Natasha showed them to their table. 'Don't worry,' she whispered to Lizzie. 'Mother won't say anything, you're with the President.'

Belle approached with a basket of bread rolls which she handed round.

'That child should be in bed,' Daphne Warrington swept up to their table. 'She'll be too tired for school on Monday.'

'It's half-term, Mother, I did tell you.'

'Well, I hope you've got something organised; I don't want her under my feet all day.'

Belle stared stonily at her grandmother. 'I'm going to stay with Daddy in Jersey.'

'Good, I'm glad to hear it,' Daphne snorted and stalked off without acknowledging the presence of Theo and his little party. Natasha and Lizzie exchanged a look.

Theo looked across at the Yorkes. 'What's the latest in the teeth saga?' He grinned at Francesca.

'It's not funny, Theo, they've threatened to take me to court.'

Theo gave a bellow of laughter. 'It'll never come to that; the woman will make a complete fool of herself.'

'That's what I think,' said Raoul. 'Stop worrying, Frankie.'

It was an enjoyable evening. Theo was a good host, self-assured and confident in his presidential role and its familiar environment of entertaining. The food and wine were excellent.

'The Warringtons certainly know how to run a good hotel,' said Lizzie, 'this is on a par with the mainland.'

'Don't sound so surprised.' Theo gave her a sardonic smile. 'We're not completely uncivilised.'

Belle appeared with a dish of after dinner mints.

'Thank you my dear.' Theo reached for his wallet and extracted a pound note. 'Here's a tip for the waitress.' Belle beamed with delight.

'You've made a friend for life there,' said Francesca. 'It's been a lovely evening, thank you Theo.'

'My pleasure.' Theo beamed round at them all.

Chapter 10

By the middle of November a soft drizzle was falling steadily over Ormerey. The last leaves had dropped off the trees and the colour of the bracken had deepened to burnt sienna. The island sighed gently and shuffled itself into the winter.

Francesca's summons to appear in the Ormerey Court arrived early on a Tuesday morning. She took it straight round to The Sycamores. Raoul and Lizzie were having breakfast in the kitchen.

'Just look at this,' Francesca said furiously. 'Jean Yorke's suing me for a thousand pounds, that's double the amount she asked for originally.' She threw herself into an empty chair and put her head in her hands.

Raoul took the letter from her. 'I don't believe it, the woman must be mad.'

Lizzie placed a mug of fresh coffee in front of Francesca. 'Here you are, drink this and you'll feel better.'

'Thanks love,' Francesca smiled at her. 'I can't stay long; I have to be at school in less than an hour.'

'Don't worry about that, I'll run you down in the pick-up. We need a plan Frankie; we can't take it for granted that you'll win this case. It will depend on which Jurats are sitting on that day.'

'I don't care if I do lose,' Francesca was defiant. 'I shall refuse to pay a single penny to that woman.'

'I thought you'd say that,' Raoul looked at her, his face serious. 'That's why we must prepare in advance. You know the Court has the power to freeze your bank account if you can't or won't pay. Have you got any money in a savings account?'

'Yes.'

'Well, I suggest you go to the bank at lunch time and transfer your savings into your current account. Then write me a cheque and I'll pay it into my account today. Then at least you'll have access to your funds if the worst comes to the worst.'

Lizzie was horrified. 'Can the Court really do that, freeze people's bank accounts? How do they live without access to their money? What about their standing orders and direct debits? How do they pay their bills?'

'With difficulty,' said Raoul, 'they have to rely on family or friends or go back to the Court to beg for some of their own money. I've seen it happen more than once, it's humiliating.'

'Could they freeze my bank account in England?'

'Not without going through an English court. I thought you'd moved your account over here.'

'I haven't got round to it yet but after hearing this I don't think I will. I'll leave my money safely in England.'

Francesca was still worried. 'Won't the bank think it's odd if I withdraw all my savings?'

'It's none of their business what you do with your money; you're perfectly entitled to withdraw your savings if and when you want.' Raoul got up from the table. 'Come on, Frankie, time we were going if you're not going to be late for school. I'll engage a good advocate from Guernsey to represent you in court. Don't worry about it.'

He turned to Lizzie. 'Are you having coffee with Natasha this morning?'

'Yes, I'll be back in time to get lunch. I'll see you then.'

* * *

Lizzie had already attended the Ormerey Court once with Raoul to listen to a drink driving case. It was all part of getting to understand how things on the island were done Raoul had explained; the government and the justice systems had their origins in France and were very different to England. Lizzie had misgivings about the way the Ormerey Court was conducted and she voiced these to Natasha in the Rock Café.

'I gather the Jurats have no legal qualifications,' she said, 'yet they take on the role of a judge or magistrate, and a jury as well in criminal cases. The Jurats are just ordinary members of the public who have been appointed to sit in judgement on the rest of us.'

'It's a very prestigious appointment,' said Natasha. 'You have to have some standing on the island in order to be made a Jurat. A recommendation is made to the Home Office in London and they have the final say about who is appointed. They don't pick just anybody; it has to be somebody who is well respected in the community, someone with integrity. The Jurats have to take a solemn oath when they take up their appointment. The Greffier, he's the Clerk of the Court and a qualified Guernsey advocate, is there to advise them on the law.'

'Hm,' said Lizzie. She was not convinced. 'How can the Jurats possibly be impartial on an island as small as this where everybody knows each other and there is so much malicious gossip? In England you are not allowed to sit on a jury if you know the defendant or if you are connected to them in any way.'

'Well, this isn't England,' said Natasha, a note of irritation in her voice. 'Historically the islands are French and we still do a lot of things the French way.'

Lizzie was silent. She did not want to get into an argument with Natasha who had been born on the island and was therefore local even though her parents were English. The islanders have such a fierce loyalty to their homeland she thought. Raoul and Francesca were right when they told her that she would be happier if she accepted the way things were done on Ormerey instead of constantly comparing the island with England.

* * *

The Ormerey Court was held in the large room on the top floor of the Island Hall, the same room in which the States' meetings were held. It was an imposing chamber decorated in cream and pale blue with a lush red carpet covering the floor. Lizzie looked around at the portraits hanging on the walls, large oil paintings depicting island dignitaries and past Presidents of the States. A Pietro Annigoni portrait of Her Majesty the Queen hung behind President's carved wooden chair.

'That must be Theo's father,' said Lizzie studying a fine oil painting of Pierre Rachelle, 'but it could be Theo. Aren't they alike?'

Raoul looked up at the picture. 'Yes, he was always known as Young Pierre, and that one next to it is Theo's grandfather, Pierre Rachelle senior, Old Pierre, who had that quarrel with Grandpa after Frankie's father was killed. The family likeness is very strong isn't it?'

'He looks formidable.'

'He ruled the island with a rod of iron, few people dared to cross him. Theo's father was a complete contrast; a mild man who was well liked but completely dominated by an overbearing wife.'

'And Theo, do you think he's a good president?'

'Oh, Theo's a pussy cat, he gets walked over if he's not careful but he's popular.'

'Do you think he and Frankie will ever get married?'

'Who knows?' said Raoul. 'Look, the place is really filling up. It's a good thing we got here early.'

Jean Yorke's case had provoked considerable interest and the public gallery was full with people standing at the back of the room.

'See that young woman in the black suit?' Raoul nodded to where a smartly dressed woman with dark hair scraped back into a roll sat studying a sheaf of papers in front of her. 'That's Miss Simmonds, our advocate from Guernsey. She flew in yesterday and spent the evening with Frankie. I have every confidence in her.'

The Greffier asked for silence and everyone stood while the six Jurats, four men and two women, entered the chamber, resplendent in their blue robes and quaintly shaped hats. The Greffier opened the proceedings.

'Ladies and Gentlemen, today's case has been brought by the Plaintiff, Mrs Jean Yorke, who is seeking one thousand pounds in damages from the Defendant, Miss Francesca Saviano, as compensation for the destruction of her dentures by the Defendant's dog.'

There was a titter from the public gallery.

'I will have silence in the court.' The Chairman of the

Jurats, Gordon Taylor, stood up and glared round the room. 'Mrs Yorke, are you represented in court today?'

'My husband, Harold Yorke, is representing me.' Jean simpered at the Jurats.

'Miss Saviano?'

'Miss Simmonds from Slater and Pollock,' said Francesca.

The Chairman nodded at Miss Simmonds and turned his attention to Harold Yorke. 'Please describe to the Court the circumstances that have brought us all here today, Mr Yorke.'

In the public gallery Geoff Prosser whispered in Natasha's ear. 'She'll lose with that buffoon representing her; this is going to be fun.'

Natasha smiled. 'Don't be so horrid,' she said, 'but I hope you're right.'

Harold Yorke explained what had happened to his wife's dentures at the Ormerey Ladies' Guild coffee morning.

Mr Taylor leant his elbows on the bench in front of him and placed his fingertips together. 'Perhaps you would be good enough to explain to the court exactly where you wife's dentures were when the dog grabbed hold of them.'

Harold looked across at Jean. 'They were on a coffee table under a saucer.'

'What were they doing there?'

'My wife was finding them uncomfortable and removed them so she could eat a slice of gâche.'

There were more supressed titters. Gordon Taylor glared in the direction of the public gallery which subsided into silence.

'Hm,' he said, 'was the dog running loose in the room?'

'Yes,' replied Harold Yorke.

The Chairman turned to Miss Simmonds. 'Perhaps you could explain how the dog came to be running about out of control.'

'It was an unfortunate accident, Sir. The dog had been tied up all morning. Miss Saviano was just about to leave the room when the dog saw some gâche on the low coffee table. He made a dash towards it and in doing so jerked the lead out of Miss Saviano's hand. She tried to retrieve the dog but it was too late. He had already grabbed the dentures. It all happened very quickly; he must have mistaken the dentures, which were wrapped in a tissue, for something edible.'

'Miss Saviano is not denying what happened?'

'No, Sir. She fully admits it happened and she has apologised to Mrs Yorke. I would like to point out that had Mrs Yorke not removed her dentures this incident would never have occurred. Miss Saviano feels that it is unjust that she should be expected to pay for replacement dentures, and we feel that the sum requested in court today is excessive.'

'Thank you Miss Simmonds. Is there anything that you would like to say in reply, Mr Yorke?'

'We do not consider the sum requested to be excessive. My wife has suffered considerable distress and has been traumatised by this incident. She should be compensated for that. The dog was out of control. We have an independent witness who can testify to the fact that Miss Saviano has very little control over the animal.'

A worried frown creased Raoul's brow and he leaned forward in his seat. Francesca stared in surprise as her next door neighbour walked over to the witness stand.

'Could you give us your name, please?' Gordon Taylor smiled encouragingly at the elderly woman who stood nervously in front of him.

'Miss Susan Cottingham.'

'Thank you, Miss Cottingham. Please take the Oath.'

Miss Cottingham muttered under breath.

'Could you speak a little louder please, Miss Cottingham, so that the Court can hear you.'

In a trembling voice Susan Cottingham read the words on the card that had been handed to her.

'Thank you, Miss Cottingham. Were you a witness to the incident described?'

'Yes, I was there and it happened exactly as described, but there is something else that I wish to tell the Court about the dog.'

'Please proceed.'

'I live next door to Miss Saviano, and her dog, Zapp, barks a lot. Sometimes he barks all night and keeps me awake. You would think Miss Saviano would make an effort to stop her dog from barking but she is obviously unwilling or unable to do so. Sometimes it barks all day while she is out at work, I am driven nearly mad by the noise. She has no control over the animal at all.'

Harold Yorke smirked at his wife.

Gordon Taylor continued with his questioning. 'Have you complained to Miss Saviano about the nuisance her dog is causing?'

Miss Cottingham hesitated, looking uncomfortable. 'Well, er… no. I don't like confrontation of any kind.'

'Had you thought of reporting the nuisance to the Police?'

'No.' Miss Cottingham fiddled nervously with the handle of her bag.

Miss Simmonds rose to her feet. 'May I ask Miss Cottingham a few questions, Sir?' Gordon Taylor nodded.

'Miss Cottingham, are you sure that the dog you can hear barking is Zapp?'

'I'm quite sure.'

'You couldn't be mistaken? Maybe it's some other dog that lives close by?'

Miss Cottingham looked nervously across at Harold Yorke and swallowed hard. 'I'm quite sure it's Zapp.'

'Would you please describe the bark, Miss Cottingham?'

'Pardon?'

'What kind of bark is it? Is it deep like the noise made by a German shepherd dog or yappy like a Yorkshire terrier?'

'Oh, it's yappy, a continuous yapping. It drives me mad.'

The faintest hint of a smile passed over the advocate's face. 'What if I were to tell you, Miss Cottingham, that the dog that you have heard yapping cannot possibly be Zapp? Zapp is a basenji, a breed of dog which does not bark.'

Miss Cottingham's mouth fell open. She went pale and stared at Miss Simmonds. There was a collective gasp from the public gallery.

Gordon Taylor spoke. 'Is this correct, Miss Simmonds?'

'Yes Sir. The basenji is well known as a barkless breed. The noises these dogs make have been described as howls or yodels. This can be confirmed by the Guernsey Dog Club. One of their members breeds basenjis. I believe Zapp came from there.'

'I see.' Gordon Taylor addressed Miss Cottingham. 'You are obviously mistaken, Madam, it must be some other dog that you have heard yapping.'

Animated whispering broke out amongst the onlookers.

'Quiet please! The Jurats will now retire to deliberate. Do you have invoices to support your wife's claim, Mr Yorke?'

Harold Yorke passed a sheaf of papers to the Greffier who handed them to the Chairman. Everyone stood while the Jurats filed out into a small ante-room adjacent to the Court.

Raoul turned to Lizzie and grinned broadly. 'They've blown it! That idiot Harold should never have brought in Susan Cottingham.'

'Do you think she really had heard a dog barking?'

Raoul shrugged. 'She's very friendly with Jean Yorke so Harold may have put her up to it. We'll never know.'

'But if she's lied under oath that's perjury,' said Lizzie.

'It can't be proved. People lie in court all the time and get away with it.'

The Greffier gave a sign and everyone stood up as the Jurats entered the court and took their seats.

'That was quick,' Geoff whispered to Natasha.

The Chairman spoke. 'After a short deliberation this court is unanimous in finding against the Plaintiff in this case. It is the opinion of the court that what happened was a very unfortunate accident, and whereas it could be argued that Miss Saviano should have kept a tighter hold on her dog's lead to prevent him from running loose, she was not aware that the dentures were on the coffee table. The dentures would not have been damaged if Mrs Yorke had not left them lying about. Her dentures are her responsibility and I suggest that in future she takes better care of them.'

Gordon Taylor looked across at Jean Yorke who flushed with embarrassment and lowered her eyes. He turned to Francesca. 'Miss Saviano, I suggest you learn from this unfortunate episode and make sure that you keep a tighter hold of your dog in public places to make sure that it does not misbehave.'

Francesca nodded. 'I understand, Sir.'

'It is the opinion of this court that the damages claimed by the Plaintiff are excessive and far exceeds the cost of replacement dentures, which one assumes would be insured under the Plaintiff's general household policy anyway. This case has been a waste of court time and I order the Plaintiff to pay all the court costs and the Defendant's costs as well.'

There was a horrified gasp from Harold Yorke as the court stood once again and the Jurats left the chamber. Raoul managed to grab Francesca's arm as everyone made for the door.

'Isn't it great? Well done, Frankie.'

'Well done, Miss Simmons,' said Francesca, 'it was well worth getting an advocate and the Yorkes are going to have to pay her bill.' She laughed delightedly. 'Thank God it's over.'

They went out into the square. Francesca was soon surrounded by a group of people offering their congratulations. Theo appeared and took Raoul to one side.

'You must all be very pleased,' he said,' but I'm afraid Frankie's euphoria will be short lived; Brockenshaw's plans for the hotel have been passed by the Building and Development Control Committee. Nothing can stop it from going ahead now.'

Chapter 11

News of Francesca's victory soon spread around the island.

'I won't be able to hold my head up in public,' Jean wailed. 'I have been made to look such a fool, and Susan didn't help by talking about the wrong dog. The stupid woman!'

'It's your own fault,' said Josie unsympathetically. 'I told you to drop the matter; it should never have gone to court.'

Jean, Josie and Emily were sitting in the Yorke's large modern kitchen drinking tea. 'It's Harold's fault.' Jean was on the verge of tears. 'He just wouldn't let it go and now it has cost us even more money. Trust Raoul St Arnaud to get an expensive advocate from Guernsey, and we have to pay for her. It's so unfair.' She sniffed loudly.

'It'll blow over in a few days,' Emily patted Jean on the arm soothingly while Josie poured them all a second cup of tea.

'I wouldn't be too sure,' said Josie. 'What about the court report in the next Ormerey News? I saw that new editor, Janine Briggs, sitting in the press box taking notes.'

'It won't be printed.' Jean sniffed again and recovered her composure. 'Harold will make sure of that. He's already had to reprimand her several times over things she insists on reporting that the Board didn't approve of. He never had any trouble when Marie Teesdale was the editor.'

'That's because Marie always did as she was told,' said Josie tartly. 'She was past it; she should have been pensioned off years ago. This new girl's a breath of fresh air.'

'You shouldn't be unkind about poor Marie,' said Emily. 'She did her best.'

Josie snorted. 'I wouldn't get your hopes up,' she said to Jean.

The Ormerey News, a fortnightly publication, was owned by its Board of Governors of which Harold Yorke was the chairman. It was a genteel little magazine which reported the States' and People's meetings, charity events, sports fixtures and other snippets of island news. The Ormerey News had always taken what Francesca called a saccharine approach to island events. Anything likely to upset the upper echelons of Ormerey society was banned by the Board of Governors who had the power to override editorial decisions.

Lizzie, who read the Ormerey News avidly from cover to cover, remarked to Raoul that it was hardly a free press. 'So much is left out,' she said, 'it's hardly worth buying. There was nothing about that drink driving case we sat in on, and that fight outside the pub where those two lads ended up in the police court didn't get a mention either.'

'That's because one of them is the son of a States member, and the man in the drink driving case is one of Harold Yorke's cronies.'

'So we won't read about Frankie's case then as it involves Harold Yorke's wife.'

'No. He and his board are sure to veto it.'

'That's appalling!' said Lizzie. 'They should report all the court cases or none at all.'

'I agree,' said Raoul. 'It's very biased. It all depends on who you are whether you get a good or bad press or none at all. Loads of local news gets left out, but it's improved since the new editor took over.'

'Another Ormerey mantra,' said Lizzie with a touch of irony. 'It all depends on who you are.'

Raoul grinned. 'Another branch of the Ormerey mafia runs the Ormerey News. Cross them at your peril.'

To the consternation of the Board of Governors and the delight of the readership, the court case was reported in full. Under the headline "A Victory for Common Sense" Janine Briggs had written a detailed and amusing account of the proceedings. Jean Yorke's humiliation was complete.

'You can't stay indoors for ever,' said Josie when Jean telephoned her to say that she would not be going to the Imperial Hotel for coffee. 'You should come out and hold your head up as if nothing has happened; people will think more of you if you do.'

Jean, however, could not be persuaded. Harold was furious. He stormed into the tiny office of the Ormerey News where Janine and one of her reporters were packing up copies of the magazine to send to Guernsey. Several outlets on the larger island had sold out and asked for more to be sent over.

'How dare you print an account of my wife's court case. You were asked specifically not to do so.'

Janine was unperturbed by his outburst. 'It's island news,' she said, 'and this edition has been so popular we've sold nearly three times as many copies as usual. The Board should be pleased.'

Harold's florid complexion deepened to purple. 'You have deliberately disobeyed an order,' he spluttered.

Janine drew herself up to her full height, which was a good three inches taller than Harold Yorke, and tossed her long blonde hair out of her eyes. 'May I remind you, Mr Yorke,' she said coldly, 'that I am the editor of this magazine. I have been employed to edit it and that is what I do. I decide what material is printed and I will not be dictated to by anyone. Now if you will excuse me, I have to get this parcel to the airport in time for the lunch time flight.'

'You mark my words, young lady! Remember the Board hired you and the Board will fire you. I'll have you drummed off this island.'

Janine laughed and held the door open for him.

* * *

In addition to the court case, the latest edition of the Ormerey News carried a notice announcing a public display of the new plans for Yaffingales. It was to be held in the Island Hall the following Saturday.

Raoul and Lizzie went along with Francesca and Theo after their morning coffee in the Rock Café. Francesca looked mutinous and Theo took her arm as they made their way into the crowded room.

'It's not as bad as you think,' he said gently. As the President, Theo had already seen the final plans which had been passed by the Building and Development Control Committee and he had been pleasantly surprised.

Francesca glowered at him. 'How can it not be?'

They had to wait for a few moments while the crowd moved away from the display boards where the architectural plans and an artist's impression of the finished hotel were exhibited.

'Look, Frankie,' said Raoul. 'They are not pulling the house down after all.'

Francesca stared in amazement. Theo smiled and gave her arm a squeeze. Simon Brockenshaw, who was standing close by ready to answer questions from the public, drew Raoul on to one side. He was a short, balding man with glasses; he looked older than his forty five years.

'I know how distressing this business is for your cousin', he said, 'but we've decided to keep the cottage and use it for self-catering holidays. It will have to be gutted and modernised, of course, and we shall restore the gardens. I do hope that will be of some comfort to her.'

'I'm sure it will be,' said Raoul. 'Your hotel looks splendid, Mr Brockenshaw. Will your guests have access to the gardens?'

'Oh yes, we'll reinstate the path down to the beach, put some proper steps in and a hand rail. I'd like to make the bunker into a bird hide; it's an ideal spot. What do you think?'

'I think that's a very good idea. It has been used as a bird hide in the past, by the previous owners and by Francesca and myself. But Mr Brockenshaw…'

'Please call me Simon.'

'Simon, you do know that you'll still have a lot of opposition even though you've modified your plans for the hotel. It's the violation of the green belt that's the problem. The island is so small, every inch is precious, and the green belt hasn't been touched for years until now. People are worried that it's the thin end of the wedge; it will open the way for further development. That's why Geoff Prosser and his friends are so up in arms. You've also got the locals to contend with, most of them hate any kind of change. They want the island to stay the same.'

'You've got roads, electricity and running water. Did the locals protest when those were put in?'

Raoul detected the bitterness in Simon's voice. 'The Germans put those in,' he said. 'Before the war we had dirt tracks and our water came from wells or the town pump. Most of our infrastructure was built during the occupation. The islanders were presented with a fait accompli when they returned.'

'But they didn't rip it all out!'

'No.' Raoul laughed. 'Once your hotel is up and running people will see how much it is doing for the island economy; it will be accepted.'

'Will it? I'm not sure that my wife and I will ever be accepted here. We've made lots of acquaintances but few friends, even among those who support our venture. Ruth isn't happy here, you know, she's finding it hard to settle.'

'I'm sorry to hear that. We need more people here, especially people like you who are willing to invest in the island. It's such a pity that you bought land in the green belt and not in the building zone.'

'Yaffingales and its field were for sale. It's a beautiful location; Ruth and I fell in love with it. We've been in the hotel trade for over twenty years. We were sure we could make a success of it here, but now I don't know…' his voice trailed off.

Raoul felt sorry for him. He thought of Lizzie and her difficulties; how much worse it must be for Ruth

Brockenshaw finding herself in the middle of a controversy fuelled by local islanders. He knew from his own experience how vicious and spiteful some of them could be.

* * *

'Let's go for a walk after lunch,' Raoul said as he and Lizzie made their way up Main Street back to The Sycamores. 'It's a beautiful day, we could ask Frankie to join us. Where is she by the way?'

Lizzie turned and looked back down the street. 'There she is. Hi Frankie!'

They stopped and waited while Francesca caught up with them. She was flushed and out of breath. 'I need to ask you two for a favour. Could you possibly take Zapp out for me? Theo's taking me to lunch and I don't know what time we'll finish.'

'Is he now?' Raoul smirked. 'A date at last, eh?'

Francesca's flush deepened. 'Not really! We're only going to the pub. Theo wants to talk about Yaffingales.'

'So he says!' Raoul chuckled.

Lizzie gave him a poke. 'Of course we'll take Zapp,' she said to Francesca. 'Can he wait till we we've had some lunch?'

'Yes, he's already been out once this morning. Thanks ever so much.' She turned and hurried back down the street to join Theo.

After lunch Raoul and Lizzie walked round to Puffin Cottage. Zapp was asleep on the settee in the sitting room, snuggled amongst the cushions in a patch of sunlight. 'That dog is completely spoilt,' said Raoul. He tapped on the window. 'He sleeps everywhere except in his own bed.'

'He likes the sun,' said Lizzie, 'he sleeps wherever the sun is.'

Zapp leapt off the settee and rushed to the front door where he greeted Raoul and Lizzie ecstatically, his curly tail wagging in delight. Lizzie found the extending lead and attached it to his collar.

'Let's go out to Fort Jackson,' said Raoul, 'we can let him off the lead on the causeway.'

They walked along the airport road until they came to the headland overlooking the fort. It was a glorious afternoon, sunny and mild with hardly a breath of wind. They sat down on a bench and Zapp jumped up and positioned himself between them. The tide was high; small waves lapped at the edges of the causeway.

'Look at all those shags,' said Raoul, 'there must be at least a hundred of them. Did you bring the binoculars?'

Lizzie handed them to him. 'Is that a grey heron on the beach?'

'Yes, and there are several mallards swimming just offshore – see?'

'I thought they were a fresh water species.'

'There are always a few here in the wintertime.'

A flock of oystercatchers which had been resting at the water's edge suddenly flew up into the air uttering shrill cries. Two Dalmatians ran on to the beach followed by a short woman in a Barbour jacket.

'That's Ruth Brockenshaw,' said Raoul. 'Simon says she's not happy here, she's finding it hard to make friends.'

'Oh dear, the poor woman, I do sympathise with her.'

They got up and walked down the zigzag path to the beginning of the causeway. Ruth caught sight of them and put her dogs on the lead. She smiled politely as she approached them and Raoul and Lizzie smiled back.

'What beautiful dogs,' said Lizzie. Raoul shortened Zapp's lead; he was straining towards the Dalmatians.

Ruth beamed. 'Thank you,' she said. 'This is Blizzard and this one is Storm, he's got more spots, and this must be Zapp the famous denture-chewing basenji.'

'Don't come too near,' said Raoul. 'He gets defensive when he's on the lead and tends to snarl if other dogs come too close.'

'He looks so smart with that foxy face and neat curly tail. Do you show him?' Blizzard and Storm were sitting quietly beside Ruth, an exemplary example of canine obedience.

'No,' said Raoul. 'He's far too badly behaved, aren't you Zapp?'

They said their goodbyes and continued with their walk.

'How sad she looks,' said Lizzie. 'I feel so sorry for her. Where do the Brockenshaws live?'

'In one of those bungalows overlooking the harbour. They've had a huge amount of work done to it.'

'They must have pots of money.'

'They own a hotel in Eastbourne and Simon's brother owns one in Worthing. They have a thriving family business.'

They walked along the causeway to the fort which rose up grey and forbidding in front of them. Raoul let Zapp loose and he raced ahead, chasing a few loitering herring gulls which flew up indignantly, then wheeled above him, their raucous cries sounding like human laughter. The sun was setting in a blaze of orange and scarlet. They watched it disappear below the horizon. Raoul took Lizzie's arm and they walked back along the causeway with the darkening sea splashing gently on either side.

Francesca was waiting for them at Puffin Cottage. 'I've put the kettle on,' she said. 'Would you like some toasted crumpets?'

'Yes please.' Raoul took his coat off. 'How was your lunch date?'

'I told you, it wasn't a date. We were discussing Yaffingales.'

'And?'

'Well, I am coming round to the idea of the hotel now that I know the house won't be pulled down and the gardens are going to be restored. Theo says the hotel will be open to non-residents for meals and cream teas on the terrace. It could be really nice.'

'Yes, it could,' said Raoul, 'I'm glad you're happier about it, Frankie.' He gave her a hug.

* * *

Janine Briggs, the editor of the Ormerey News, had been sacked. The first Raoul and Lizzie heard of this was during breakfast the following day while they were listening to BBC Radio Guernsey's Morning Report.

'This is very sudden,' the interviewer was saying. 'Were you expecting it?'

'Yes,' Janine replied. 'The Chairman of the Board of Governors told me I'd be fired. He had asked me not to publish the report about a court case involving his wife, but as the editor of the magazine I made the decision to run it.'

'The case of the dog and the dentures?'

'Yes, that's the one. The Board of Governors tried to supress it. It's not the first time they've tried to override editorial decisions.'

'What will you do now? Will you stay on Ormerey?'

'Mr Yorke has threatened to have me drummed off the island but I have every intention of staying. I refuse to be bullied. He can't make me leave.'

'What about work? Do you think you'll find another job?'

'I hope so. In the meantime I've got some freelance work to keep me busy, most of it in the UK. Nobody here can interfere with that.'

'Thank you, Janine Briggs. I wish you the very best of luck.' The interview ended.

'Good for her,' said Lizzie.

'Yes,' said Raoul, 'you have to stand up to the Ormerey mafia. I've told you that before.'

Chapter 12

'We need to think about Christmas,' said Raoul. 'It's December already.'

'What do you usually do on Christmas day?' Lizzie was sitting at the kitchen table sticking stamps on envelopes.

'Last year was my first Christmas on my own. I went to Frankie's for lunch and spent the rest of the day round there. Before that she used to come round here and cook for Dad and me. I thought we might invite her here this year, give her a rest from all that cooking. How do you feel?'

'Fine, it's a good idea. We could ask Theo as well, if he hasn't already arranged something himself.'

A large shape appeared behind the frosted glass of the back door.

'Good Lord!' said Raoul. 'It's Sophie. What on earth can she want?' He opened the door. 'Hello, Sophie, how nice to see you.'

Sophie's bulk filled the doorway. She glared at Lizzie out of small black eyes which were set like currants in her flat pudding face. She lumbered in and turned to Raoul, ignoring Lizzie completely. 'It's Henri', she said bluntly.

Lizzie gathered up the letters off the table. 'I'll just go and post these,' she said. 'Please excuse me.' She darted into the hall and out through the front door. Sophie made her feel uncomfortable; she oozed dislike and disapproval from every pore. Lizzie had never seen her smile.

'What's wrong with Henri?' Raoul was suddenly alarmed. 'Is he ill?'

'The stupid fool's gone and got himself stuck on the roof. He needs to be got down.'

'Why is he on the roof? He can't stand heights.'

'Loose ridge tiles.' Sophie set her mouth in a thin line. 'Are you coming or not?'

'Of course I'm coming.' Raoul grabbed a jacket, slammed the back door and, with difficulty, heaved Sophie into the passenger seat of the pick-up. He could guess what had happened; Sophie, reluctant to pay a builder, had urged her brother to fix the tiles.

Henri was sitting astride the roof ridge clutching the chimney, white faced and trembling.

'It's all right,' Raoul called. 'We'll soon have you down.'

'I can't move,' moaned Henri. 'I've gone all dizzy. I told Sophie I couldn't do it.'

Raoul swore under his breath and shinned up the ladder. 'Swing your leg over and slither down on your stomach towards me.'

'I can't!'

'Of course you can. I'll catch hold of your feet and guide them on to the ladder.' Raoul's tone was calm and reassuring. 'Trust me.'

Henri hesitated for a few moments and then did as instructed. Soon they were both safely on the ground. Henri collapsed on to a wooden crate, still shaking. 'Me legs have gone!'

'It's the shock,' said Raoul. 'Sophie, he needs hot sweet tea. Now!'

He glared at her retreating back as she plodded into the kitchen and turned to Henri. He knew he had him at a disadvantage but he could not help himself. 'Henri,' he said, 'why don't you and Sophie like Lizzie?'

'What?'

'You heard. Sophie was positively rude to Lizzie this morning, and you're not much better. What has she ever done to you?'

'Well…' Henri looked uncomfortable.

'Well what?'

'She's so English, isn't she, and posh. I find her hard to talk to. She's not the right sort for you at all.' Raoul glared and Henri, recovering his composure, blundered on. 'You're just having a mid-life crisis. You always did like posh birds. Your wife didn't stay long, did she? She was English as well. You'd do better with a local woman.'

'Like you did, you mean?'

'Mine was Guernsey, nearly local. Not English at any rate.'

'And where is she now? Back in Guernsey. You're a fine one to talk!'

Henri sighed. 'I don't mean to be rude to your Lizzie; she makes me feel awkward that's all. She looks down on people like me and Sophie.'

'That's nonsense! Lizzie's not a snob. It's not fair to tar her with the same brush as some of those rich retired English settlers. Just give her a chance.'

Henri sighed again. He was still pale and shaking. 'Look mate, I don't want us to fall out over this. I'll have a word with Sophie and we'll make more effort. OK? Thanks for rescuing me by the way.'

'A pleasure! You'll need to get Fords to look at those ridge tiles; they've done an excellent job on my roof.'

'Get this down you.' Sophie appeared with two mugs. 'We'll have no talk of Fords. Daylight robbery.'

'She'd rather see me splattered all over the yard.' Henri took a noisy slurp of tea.

* * *

Francesca found herself to be at the centre of island gossip in the run-up to Christmas as she accompanied Theo to several official functions and private parties.

Jean Yorke was back at the helm of the Ormerey Ladies Guild, presiding over the December get together. They had been busy decorating the Island Hall in preparation for Christmas and, task completed, had stopped for some well-earned refreshments.

'Do you think Francesca and Theo are an item?' she asked, patting her hair. Jean had taken Josie's advice, put her humiliation in court to the back of her mind, and treated herself to a new hairdo.

'No,' said Emily. 'Francesca says they are just friends. Most of Theo's invitations are addressed to "The President and Guest". It's nice that he's found someone to accompany him instead of always turning up on his own like he used to.'

'Well, I can't see her as a President's wife,' sniffed Susan Cottingham. 'She's hardly the type.'

Emily rounded on her. 'That's a very unkind remark, Susan, just because you were made to look such a fool in…' She stopped hurriedly; she had promised Jean that she would not mention the court case. Susan glared at her.

Josie quickly intervened. 'You know Theo is having Christmas lunch at Raoul St Arnaud's this year?'

'Really!' A buzz went round the room. There was a keen rivalry among the Ormerey ladies when it came to inviting the President to Christmas lunch.

'Yes, you've all been pipped at the post.' Josie laughed. 'You should just see your faces!'

'Well!' said Jean. 'I am surprised; we didn't invite him because he came to us last year. Fancy him going there. Raoul and that woman still aren't married.'

'So what?' said Josie. 'Raoul and Francesca are cousins, don't forget, they always spend Christmas together.'

'Even so,' sniffed Jean. 'Theo Rachelle is the President and he has a position to maintain in Ormerey society. He shouldn't be seen to be condoning an adulterous relationship.'

'What rubbish you talk, Jean. Raoul and Elizabeth are both single. Neither of them is committing adultery. How they choose to live is their own business.'

Jean stared at Josie in surprise, hurt that her friend should disagree with her so vehemently in public. She sat down and rummaged in her handbag to cover her embarrassment.

* * *

Lizzie's and Francesca's ears should have been burning as they wandered around the Ormerey Pharmacy looking for Christmas presents. Francesca was also looking at make-up, something she had never had much use for in the past.

'My life is a social whirl,' she remarked as she tried several tester lipsticks on the inside of her wrist. 'I'm really enjoying it; I've never had such a busy Christmas.'

'This colour would suit you,' said Lizzie. 'You can wear bright red with your dark colouring.'

'You don't think it's too bright?'

'No. It would go beautifully with your red dress.'

'We're going to a posh do tonight.' Francesca selected the lipstick and put it in her basket. 'Drinky-poos at the Bardsleys. All the States members will be there. Are you and Raoul going?'

'No, we haven't been asked. I don't really know the Bardsleys.' Lizzie thought for a moment. 'I know who they are though; they live on the hill near the Brockenshaws. Raoul knows them.'

As soon as she got home Francesca telephoned Raoul. 'It's the Bardsleys' party tonight. Lizzie says you weren't invited. You usually go, don't you?'

'I was invited,' said Raoul tersely. 'The invitation didn't include Lizzie. I tore it up and threw it in the bin. She doesn't know so you won't mention it to her, will you?'

'Of course not. How rude of them not to invite Lizzie. They would have done if she was your wife,' she added tentatively.

'I'm well aware of that,' Raoul snapped. 'I'm not getting married just to please the likes of the Bardsleys.'

Francesca hastily changed tack. 'Have you been invited anywhere else?'

'We're going to the party Joshua Ford always holds for his regular customers. It's in the Island Hall on Saturday, and on Christmas Eve we're having tea with Joe and Kate and the children.'

'That's nice. Theo and I are really looking forward to Christmas day. It will be lovely to relax while someone else does all the cooking.'

* * *

Joshua Ford held his annual Christmas party in the Island Hall. It was a grand affair to thank his clients for their business and to ensure their continued good will.

The room was already crowded and very noisy when Raoul and Lizzie arrived. Joshua and his wife Pam met them at the door. Pam, resplendent in midnight blue with her platinum hair in a French roll, looked at Lizzie curiously as they shook hands; so this was the woman at the centre of so much disapproving gossip.

Raoul and Lizzie made their way into the hall. 'The Christmas decorations are better than usual this year,' said Raoul, 'a vast improvement on the tatty old things that we've had in the past. I should think those dated back to just after the war.'

Lizzie smiled as they negotiated their way through the crowd. People were huddled in little groups talking animatedly. One or two people nodded to Raoul before turning away and Lizzie felt uncomfortable under the scrutiny of so many stony stares. She looked round desperately for a friendly face, hoping to see Natasha or Geoff Prosser but there was no sign of either of them.

'Look, there are the Brockenshaws,' said Raoul. 'Come on.' He steered Lizzie towards a corner table where Simon and Ruth were sitting on their own. 'May we join you?' he asked.

'Please do,' said Ruth, her face lighting up. 'It would appear no one else wants to talk to us.'

'Nor to us either,' said Lizzie.

'We're *persona non grata* because we're not respectably married.' Raoul laughed.

'It's not funny, Raoul,' Lizzie frowned at him. 'I can't get over how rude people are here. You're supposed to circulate at this type of party; it's an opportunity to mix and get to know people. It's bad manners to deliberately ignore other guests and turn your back on them.'

'I agree.' Ruth whispered in Lizzie's ear. 'Don't you find some of the people who live here are just plain ignorant?'

'Yes, or downright snobs!'

'Girls, girls!' said Simon. 'Lighten up and have a drink, then we'll go and get some food. We might as well enjoy ourselves while we're here.'

Raoul did not need asking twice. They made their way to the buffet table. Harold and Jean Yorke fixed Raoul with a malevolent glare.

'If looks could kill I'd be dead!' he said to Simon with a grin.

'I wish I'd been in the court that day. Ruth said it was as good as a pantomime.'

'Josie's got a new purple rinse,' said Lizzie. 'It looks very bright under this strip lighting.'

'Miaow!' said Raoul. He turned to Simon as they sat back down at their table and tucked into to a sausage roll. 'Have you started work at Yaffingales? We haven't been up there for a while.'

'We've levelled the field,' said Simon. 'We'll start digging the foundations for the hotel after the New Year.'

'What about the cottage?' said Lizzie.

'We're leaving that until after the hotel's finished. We're hoping to be open by next August.'

'That's ambitious; I doubt if you'll make it. It'll all grind to a halt when you get to the plumbing stage.' Raoul winked at Lizzie.

'Ford's got all his own people. He'll bring men over from Guernsey if necessary. We won't be using independent tradesmen from here; the work needs to be co-ordinated.'

'Fords have done a splendid job on our place,' said Ruth. 'You must come over sometime.'

'Yes, come and join us for a nightcap later,' said Simon. 'We've left the car at home so we can all walk down together. You can see what we've done to the bungalow.'

'We'd love to,' said Lizzie.

'Hello! I hope you are all enjoying yourselves.' Pam Ford placed a plate of mince pies on the table. 'There's coffee over there if you'd like some.'

'Thank you, it's a delightful party.' Raoul beamed at her. Lizzie was about to snort and hastily changed it into a cough. Raoul nudged her under the table. Simon exchanged a look with his wife and tried, unsuccessfully, to hide a smile.

* * *

'The Brockenshaws are nice, aren't they?' Raoul said later, after they had left their hosts in their luxury bungalow and were walking back up the hill towards the town.

'Yes, they are. Thank goodness they were at that awful party or we wouldn't have had anyone to talk to, so many people turned their backs on us.'

'It's not Pam's fault that her guests are so ill-mannered.'

'I know, but I hope we haven't been invited to any more cocktail parties.'

'We haven't,' said Raoul. He was glad he had not told her about the Bardsleys.

It was a cold clear night, bright with stars. Lizzie shivered. 'I'm glad you brought the torch. I keep forgetting there are places with no street lights; it's hard to see where we're going.'

They both jumped as a large pale shape flew soundlessly across the road in front of them.

'A barn owl!' Raoul laughed. 'There's a pair that nest in that ruined building over there. You should hear the noise the chicks make in the spring; it's a hissing sound, really eerie, and frightens people to death if they don't know what it is. Come on, it's cold.' He tucked Lizzie's arm through his. 'You'll enjoy Christmas here, Lizzie. There's carol singing in the square tomorrow and Santa brings presents for the children. And don't forget we're going to Joe's on Christmas Eve.'

'I'm looking forward to that. I've bought a Lego bus for Archie. Kate says he's mad on Lego, and I got a cuddly gannet for Abi.'

'You are clever. I never know what to buy for kids.' He squeezed her arm. 'What would I do without you?'

Lizzie was silent. Her conscience was pricking her. Christmas was a time for families and she really ought to have done something about visiting her father. She was sorry she had fallen out with him. He had made no secret of the fact that he disapproved of her move to Ormerey and they had parted on bad terms.

Chapter 13

Ormerey pulled out all the stops for Christmas. Coloured light bulbs were strung diagonally across Main Street and the large Christmas tree in the square twinkled with fairy lights. The shops had decorated their windows; even the drab Ormerey Supermart had a few strands of tarnished tinsel draped over its shelves, and colourful tins of sweets and biscuits stood precariously in every available space.

On Francesca's advice Lizzie had done her shopping early. 'Everything sells out quickly. None of the shops like to overstock in case they have stuff left over. You need to check the dates on everything in case they're last year's, especially those.' Francesca indicated the festive tins. 'I'm really looking forward to spending Christmas with you and Raoul, Lizzie.'

'And Theo? Don't forget him!'

Francesca blushed. 'I'm not sure how I feel about that. I'll have to leave Zapp at home and he's used to having titbits from the Christmas table.'

'Never mind, we'll make him up a doggy bag.' Lizzie giggled and looked at Francesca. A frown creased her forehead. 'It could be a problem, couldn't it? Theo not liking dogs?'

'I'm not going to worry about it now. Let's just enjoy Christmas.' She tucked her arm through Lizzie's. 'Have you got everything you need?'

Lizzie surveyed her shopping trolley. 'Yes, I think so. I can easily pop back if I've forgotten anything.'

Lizzie was nervous about cooking Christmas lunch for Francesca and Theo. Francesca was known throughout the island for her culinary skills. By the time Christmas morning arrived she was beginning to panic.

'Stop worrying,' said Raoul. 'You'll be fine. I'll help you. You did most of the preparation yesterday anyway.'

He was as good as his word, vacuuming the living and dining rooms and flicking a duster over them before peeling potatoes and preparing the Brussels sprouts.

Lizzie was amazed.

'I used to do all the housework before you arrived and cooked for myself as well. Frankie helped a lot when my parents were still alive. She was brilliant; bringing round meals and cakes and things, and helping with the caring when they became frail. They both stayed at home right up until the very end.'

What a remarkable man he is, Lizzie thought. She put her arms round him and hugged him. 'I love you, Raoul, you make me so happy.'

Raoul was touched. 'I love you too. You're the best thing that's happened to me for years. You've changed my life.' He kissed her. He looked at the dining table, set with the best Doulton china and sparkling with crystal. 'Everything looks lovely, you've done me proud.'

Francesca arrived with a huge box of chocolates and was followed five minutes later by Theo who handed Raoul a bottle of champagne. 'Time to celebrate!' he said with a smile.

'I wonder if there's going to be an announcement,' Raoul said later as he joined Lizzie in the kitchen where she was struggling to take the turkey out of the oven. She found it difficult to balance on the sloping floor.

'I don't think so, it's much too soon.' Red in the face, she pushed her hair out of her eyes and looked at Raoul. 'They haven't even been out on a proper date yet.'

'Well, not as far as we know! I do wish they would stop pussy-footing around each other. They are neither of them getting any younger.'

'Shh! They'll hear you.' She giggled suddenly. 'I can't see Theo putting up with Zapp, can you?'

'No, I can't! It'll be a case of "me or the dog". Poor Frankie! Seriously though they really should get married. They're made for each other.'

In spite of Lizzie's misgivings the lunch was a great success. Theo had long since lost his shyness with the other three and was the life and soul of the party. He raised his glass.

'Merry Christmas everyone! Here's to us all – and to a happy and successful 1991. May all our dreams come true!' His dark eyes rested for a moment on Francesca and she glowed as she took a sip of champagne.

Lizzie handed round the chocolates. 'Where did you spend Christmas last year, Theo?'

'With the Yorkes. It was a very nice meal but not nearly so much fun as this. Thank you all. I can't remember when I enjoyed a Christmas so much.'

Raoul smiled. 'You're very welcome, Theo. I hope it's the first of many.' He leaned back in his chair and stretched. 'Let's go and put our feet up in the living room.'

Lizzie was feeling light-headed. 'We ought to go for a walk; it's a lovely afternoon. I need some fresh air and poor Zapp has been shut in all this time.'

Raoul grinned at her. 'You go; I'm much too comfortable here.' He sank into an easy chair beside the fire and motioned Theo into the opposite one. 'We'll just have a nice little snooze while you and Frankie take the dog out.'

'We'll be back in time for the Queen's speech,' said Francesca tartly. 'You'll have to wake up then!'

* * *

Lizzie was overcome by a sudden wave of homesickness as she took the Christmas decorations down and put them away. She re-read all her cards and letters from England, including a card from her father and step-mother which she had not expected to get. Thank goodness she had sent them one. She wondered if her friends missed her as much as she missed them. She doubted it; they all led busy lives.

'Why the glum face?' Raoul entered the room with an armful of logs for the fire.

'I was just thinking about home.'

'You mean England?'

'Yes, it seems like years since I was there.'

'Oh Lizzie, you don't regret coming here, do you?' His brow furrowed with anxiety.

'Of course not, but sometimes I just…'

'What?'

'I just feel homesick for all the people and places I used to know. It's hard to explain. Living here is like living abroad; different government, different laws, different way of life. I feel so cut off from everything I know.'

'Oh sweetheart!' He put his arms round her. 'A lot of English people feel like that when they first come here. You'll get used to it.' He laughed. 'Funny how a few miles of sea can have that effect. We islanders like feeling cut off, out of the way of the rest of the world.'

'Perhaps I'll go back to Tonbridge for a visit. I really ought to try and make things up with Dad and Cynthia. You know how things are between us and every time I phone he's curt and offhand. I was surprised to get a Christmas card from them. It's going to be awkward seeing them but I can't put it off for ever.'

'Of course you can't.' Raoul's heart sank. He was afraid that if she went she would be even more unsettled on her return. 'Why don't you wait till the spring? The weather will be better then. The flying's so iffy at the moment with all these gales and cross winds.'

Lizzie remembered the bumpy flight back from Guernsey. 'You're right. Perhaps it would be better to go then; a few more weeks shouldn't make any difference.'

Raoul found it hard to understand Lizzie's difficulties with her father. His own relationship with his parents had been so good. 'Don't worry so much, Lizzie. You have the right to choose how you live your life; your father shouldn't try to control what you do.'

'It's all down to Cynthia. Ever since they got married Dad's let her walk all over him. She was the one who said I should think of my father in his old age and that it was extremely selfish of me to move so far away. He agreed with her like he always does.'

'I'm sure it will all come right eventually.' Raoul gave her a quick hug. 'Henri wants me to go fishing with him this morning. We thought we'd just have a couple of hours at Saline Bay while the tide's right. He's gone off fishing from the rocks since he got stuck on his roof. I'll be back for lunch. Sure you're OK?'

She smiled. 'I'm fine. I must go to the shop and restock the larder. See you later.'

Feeling more cheerful Lizzie finished putting the decorations away and went across the street to the Ormerey Supermart. This shop is worse than ever, she thought as she mooched around unable to find several of the items she wanted. She found Francesca staring gloomily at the few shrivelled vegetables on display.

'We've had no boat for three weeks,' she said to Lizzie. 'Christmas day fell on boat day this year, so did New Year's Day and then there was that horrendous gale. We'll have to wait another week.'

'Couldn't the boat come on a different day?'

Francesca rolled her eyes. 'You must be joking! Ormerey Shipping change their schedule? I don't think so! The freezer cabinet is completely empty. I shall have to make do with tinned vegetables.'

She found a tin of peas covered with dust at the back of a shelf. 'This has probably been here for years! We had two boats in the week before Christmas and everyone stocked up then. January is always a bad month, I should have warned you.' She picked up a pint of milk. 'Thank goodness for the island farm; we never run out of dairy produce.'

Pauline was on the till, red-faced and flustered.

'Where's Prunella today?' asked Francesca.

'She's got 'flu. So's Julie, I'm on me own.' Pauline glared belligerently. 'It's no good moaning about empty shelves; it's not my fault!'

'No one said it was,' Francesca smiled sympathetically. 'There seems to be a lot of 'flu about at the moment. I hope they soon get better.'

'Come and have a coffee,' said Lizzie as they left the shop. 'When do you start back at school?'

'Tomorrow.'

They went through the yard into the kitchen. Lizzie put the kettle on. 'Sorry about the mess. I've been taking all the Christmas stuff down and haven't got round to clearing up in here.' She moved the breakfast crockery off the table into the sink.

Francesca sat down. 'Where's Raoul?'

'He's gone fishing with Henri. I hope he doesn't catch anything.'

'Why?'

'I hate it when he brings fish home; he expects me to gut them. He called me a wimp when I told him I couldn't do it.'

Francesca laughed. 'Oh Lizzie! Gutting fish is easy. There's nothing to it. I'll show you how.'

'No thank you!' said Lizzie firmly. 'I don't want to know.'

* * *

By the middle of January Lizzie realised what people had meant when they had warned her about the Ormerey winter. January and February were the months in which many islanders took their annual holidays; consequently several shops were shut and those that were open closed up at lunch time. Many establishments, including the Rock Café, found that it was not worth opening when there were so few people about. Fortunately, for those who remained on the island, The Lord Nelson and the Imperial Hotel were functioning as usual.

Lizzie walked down Valmont Road to the harbour. It was a mild sunny day with a promise of spring in the air.

She noticed the bright green leaves of three-cornered garlic which had sprung up under the sycamore trees at the side of the road. There was a strong smell of damp earth and she stopped for a moment to watch a blackbird picking through the leaf litter, his yellow bill contrasting with his shiny black plumage. As soon as she reached the coast the wind lifted her hair and blew it in all directions. She felt scruffy and dishevelled by the time she reached the Imperial Hotel and went straight to the ladies' cloakroom to tidy up before meeting Natasha for coffee in the restaurant. Ian and Daphne Warrington were on holiday in Barbados and had left Natasha in charge.

Natasha, looking stunning in a turquoise cowl-neck sweater and black velvet trousers, greeted Lizzie warmly. 'I love it when they go away,' she said. 'I wish they'd go more often.'

'Have you any guests staying?' Lizzie felt uncomfortable in her jeans and sweatshirt and wished she had worn something smarter. The room was busy with several elegantly dressed women enjoying coffee and cakes. She noticed Jean Yorke and her friends from the Ormerey Ladies' Guild.

'Only two couples but the restaurant is quite busy; so many places are closed.' Natasha sat down and poured the coffee. 'I've got some exciting news! You haven't met my brother Hugo, have you?'

Lizzie, her mouth full of chocolate éclair, shook her head.

'He's moving back to Ormerey, and you'll never guess what! He's opening a new shop here.'

'What sort of shop?'

'A supermarket!' Natasha's green eyes sparkled with excitement. 'He's always worked in retail and when he was over here at Christmas he went to look at those two empty shops at the top of town and he's taken out a lease. He's hoping to be open in time for Easter. Isn't it marvellous?'

'Wonderful!' said Lizzie. 'I'll never have to go in the Ormerey Supermart again. They won't like it, will they?'

'They'll have to pull their socks up or they'll go out of business. Hugo reckons he's on to a winner.'

'I can't wait,' said Lizzie, 'but it will cost a fortune to convert those two shops and fit them out as a supermarket. It's a big risk to take.'

'Father's putting up the money; Hugo's putting in the expertise. It will be another family business.'

'The Warrington empire grows and grows.' Lizzie smiled. 'How's Geoff these days? I haven't seen him for ages'

A faint flush crossed Natasha's alabaster skin and tinged her cheeks. 'I haven't seen much of him either; I've been so busy since my parents went away. He did call in for a drink in the bar last night. I told him about the new shop. He was very pleased.'

'I expect everyone on the island will be.'

The room had filled up while they had been chatting. 'You're very busy today,' Lizzie remarked as she looked around.

'We're the only place open for morning coffee at the moment, and we've got a big party booked in for lunch. Josie Cleghorn's having her 80th birthday bash; seventeen people.'

'Some of them are here already,' said Lizzie looking across at the group of Ormerey Guild ladies chatting and giggling at a corner table, 'and they look as though they've already been at the sherry!'

'Oh, God!' said Natasha. 'Heaven help us when that lot get tiddly.'

* * *

Janine Briggs was perched on a bar stool in The Lord Nelson reading the latest edition of the Ormerey News. Following her dismissal the previous editor, Marie Teesdale, had been persuaded to come out of retirement until a replacement for Janine was appointed.

'That rag's not worth buying these days.' Geoff Prosser seated himself on the stool beside her. 'It's as boring as it was before you came. Fancy a proper drink?' He eyed her empty coffee cup.

'No thanks. I need to keep a clear head; the Guernsey Evening Press has asked me to do something for their Ormerey page and they want it by 5pm today. If they like it they'll give me a permanent slot.'

Geoff ordered a pint of lager and took a slurp. 'What are you going to write about?'

'Hugo Warrington's new shop.'

'Excellent! Would you like my thoughts on it?'

'Oh, yes please!' Janine rummaged in her briefcase for her notebook. She had interviewed Geoff before and found him interesting and very knowledgeable about the island.

'That's great! Thanks very much,' she said when she had finished writing. 'I've got a couple more people to see and then I've got the makings of a good article.'

'How are you managing now you've lost your job?' He grinned at her. 'You've got a lot of public support, you know, people admire the way you stood up for yourself.'

She laughed. 'I've been surprised by that, after all I am a stranger here and I have managed to upset a few people. I've got my freelance work to keep me busy and I've found another job typing manuscripts for someone. I'm being well paid for that. Oh…' she looked anxious suddenly.

'It's all right! I won't let on. I'm guessing you don't have a work permit for that?'

'I know I should have one now I'm employed. I didn't need one before; journalists are in the exempt category like doctors and vets. I'm afraid Harold Yorke will scupper my application somehow or other. He wants me off the island!'

'Take no notice of that; the man's a bully and a pompous old fool as well. I'll tell you what to do. Ask your employer to apply for a work permit for you when the Yorkes are away on holiday. They always spend the whole of February in the south of France. One of their daughters lives there. That will give you time to get your application processed. It will be all done and dusted by the time they get back.'

'That's brilliant! You're a real pal, Geoff. Must fly now and get this thing written.' She waved her notebook at him. 'Thanks again!'

'My pleasure.' He watched her walk out into the street. She carried herself well; a tall elegant figure in tight blue jeans with her long blonde hair tied back in a scarlet ribbon. He smiled and wondered about asking her out. The woman he had hankered after for years was way out of his league and he was tired of being alone. The years were slipping by and he wasn't getting any younger. He finished his lager and walked purposefully out of the bar.

Chapter 14

Francesca stared out of the window at the rain beating against the glass like small sharp daggers. She could not remember a wetter February. It had rained almost continuously since the beginning of the month and her mood was as dark as the clouds that raced overhead.

She was worried about Theo; she had neither seen nor heard from him for over a fortnight and could not help wondering if she had upset him in some way. They had been getting on so well and suddenly he was ignoring her. She was filled with a horrible sense of foreboding, memories of her desolation after their earlier estrangement crowding in on her. She had been disturbed by dreams for the last few nights; dreams of a young Theo avoiding her; of Claudine Rachelle screaming and trying to push her into the sea. She had woken to find her face wet with tears.

Francesca shook herself briskly. She was letting her imagination get the better of her. Theo was probably just busy. January was the start of the new tax year in Guernsey and he had all his clients' tax returns to sort out. She decided to go and see him. It was Saturday, the day they used to meet up for coffee before the Rock Café closed for the winter.

'I'm going out,' she announced to Zapp. 'Just be good while I'm gone!'

Zapp was curled up in an armchair with his nose buried in his tail. He opened one eye and looked balefully at his mistress. She had already shooed him outside once this morning. He hated getting wet; his short sparse coat, so well adapted to the African sun, was no protection at all against the cold European rain.

Francesca donned her mac and sou'wester and headed outside into sheets of rain that were being driven almost horizontal by the furious southerly gale. There'll be no flying today she thought as she battled her way through the outskirts of town, eventually arriving at the top of Main Street. It was deserted except for traffic driving at speed and sending up sheets of water on both sides. The cobbles gleamed like wet fish scales.

From long experience Francesca knew exactly where to tread to avoid being drenched by the water pouring from broken downpipes on to the pavement, and which doorways to jump into to escape being splashed by passing motorists. She made her way carefully down the street, past the bank where two window boxes of winter-flowering pansies lent a splash of colour to the drab scene. She noticed one or two people chatting in the bread shop, otherwise the town was empty. Skirting the puddles in the square she pushed open the white wooden gate of Rachelle House.

She hesitated, suddenly filled with doubt about her mission. She wondered if it would be better to turn round and go home; she had never visited Theo at his house before. As she stood there, trying to make up her mind, Theo's front door opened and Dr Pointer, the island's GP, stepped out into the rain. Francesca stared in horror, her stomach gave a lurch and she caught her breath. What had happened? Was Theo ill? Had there been an accident?

'Ah, Francesca!' Dr Pointer approached her briskly. He was a chubby, middle-aged man from the north of England, down to earth with a friendly cheerful manner. 'I'm glad I've caught you. I was going to ring you as soon as I got home.'

'Is Theo ill?'

'He's had a bad dose of 'flu. He's over the worst now but he's been very poorly indeed.'

Francesca looked stricken. 'I didn't know. Who's been looking after him?'

'He's been on his own except for his cleaning lady, Mrs Evans, who's been calling in every day. She phoned me because she was so worried; she's been doing her best but as you know she's no spring chicken and she's exhausted. I've sent her home until Monday. He refused to let me call anyone else but I insisted. He suggested you.' The doctor looked at her enquiringly. 'You're a friend of his I take it?'

'Yes. Oh dear! I feel so bad. I should have called round sooner or phoned…' her voice trailed off. She was near to tears.

'There, there,' the doctor said kindly. 'You're here now.' He led her into the porch out of the rain. 'I must warn you though, Mr Rachelle is very depressed; not himself at all. The 'flu can leave you feeling like that. I'd be much happier if someone could come and stay here in the house with him for a while. It would cheer him up no end and would aid his recovery.'

'I don't know if he'd want me,' said Francesca doubtfully. 'Anyway I work full-time at the school and what about Zapp?'

'Zapp? Oh, your little dog. I'm sure someone could be found to look after him.' He took her by the elbow and ushered her into the hall. 'I shall insist that Mr Rachelle has someone in the house to look after him, otherwise I shall put him in the hospital.' He grinned at her. 'That should do the trick!'

'But I can't take time off work,' Francesca protested.

'Don't worry about that. Mrs Evans has promised to keep coming in on weekday mornings and giving him a snack for lunch. He'll be all right on his own for a couple of hours until you get back from school.'

'You seem to have got it all worked out,' said Francesca weakly. She felt as though she had been run over by a bulldozer. Everything was happening so fast. Only this morning she was worried she'd been given the cold shoulder and now it would appear she was moving into Theo's house with him. She felt panicky; her life was getting out of control. She looked round the dingy hall with its sombre oil paintings, the heavy gilt mirror and the threadbare carpet. Her heart sank.

She followed the doctor into the sitting room, a large room overlooking the square. Theo was sitting in an armchair by the fire. He started up when he saw Francesca and smiled. 'Frankie! You've come!'

'Of course I've come! You should have called me sooner. Dr Pointer says you need someone to stay in the house with you until you're better. Would you like me to?'

'Would you, Frankie? I'd be so grateful.' His eyes filled with tears. 'I've been feeling so low; I don't seem to be able to do anything and work's piling up. Bertie Soames has been on and on at me about it.'

'Never mind about that,' said the doctor. 'It can either wait until you're fully recovered or someone else will have to do it. I sometimes wonder what we pay our civil servants for! You are to have complete rest, Mr Rachelle, I can't stress that enough.' He smiled at Francesca. 'I'll leave him in your capable hands.'

* * *

Raoul and Lizzie were just finishing lunch when the back door was flung open and Francesca burst in accompanied by a flurry of rain. She tore off her sou'wester, shrugged herself out of her raincoat, dropped both garments on the floor and burst into tears.

'What on earth's happened?' Raoul was alarmed. He sat Francesca down on a kitchen chair and picked up her wet clothes.

'It's Theo! He's ill.' She poured out the whole story. 'You should see him. His face has gone thin and he looks so old and sad. I can't bear it. He's lost weight too. How come none of us knew he was ill? What sort of friends are we?' She lapsed into fresh sobbing.

Lizzie put the kettle on. 'I thought we hadn't seen him around for a while.'

'I should have phoned or gone round sooner. Have you got any tissues?' Francesca sniffed loudly.

Raoul handed her the box of tissues Lizzie kept on the top of the fridge. 'It's not your fault,' he said gently. 'Some people find it very hard to ask for help. Theo's always been independent and he's a very private person when he's not being Mr President.'

'I know,' said Francesca miserably, 'but I still feel bad. Now he's got this awful depression; Dr Pointer was thinking of sending him to hospital if there was no one to look after him.'

Raoul looked at his cousin thoughtfully. 'This is a big thing you're taking on, Frankie. Are you sure you're up for it?'

'Of course I'm up for it.' She took a deep breath and wiped her eyes. 'Although it depends on whether I can find someone to have Zapp for me. I can't possibly take him with me; Theo would probably have a relapse.'

'We'd love to have him,' said Lizzie.

Francesca brightened immediately. 'That would be wonderful, he knows you two so well. Are you sure though? You know what a handful he is sometimes.'

'I shall endeavour to instil some discipline into that dog; it's time somebody did. You won't know him when you get him back.' Raoul grinned. 'Now that's settled, let's go in the living room and have a cup of tea. We can't hear ourselves properly in here with that rain drumming on the roof.'

'It can make as much noise as it likes as long as it doesn't come in.' Lizzie carried the tea tray into the sitting room.

Raoul put a match to the fire. It flared up immediately, brightening up the room. 'That's better! Now Frankie, you'd better decide what you need to take to Theo's and then I'll run you home to collect it. We'll bring Zapp back here so you can settle him in, then I'll take you down to Rachelle House. How does that sound?'

'Perfect,' said Francesca. Warmed by the tea and the fire she relaxed and felt more optimistic about being able to cope with this sudden and unexpected turn of events.

* * *

The miserable weather was affecting everyone. Josie, feeling rather flat after the excitement of her 80th birthday party, was tired of being stuck indoors with only the TV for company. She phoned Emily.

'How do you fancy a cream tea at the Imperial? My treat! I'm going stir crazy.'

'So am I! That would be lovely.'

'I'll come and pick you up. I'll only be about ten minutes.'

Feeling more cheerful, Josie backed her ancient Mini out of the garage and set out for Emily's little terraced cottage on the other side of town.

'You'll never guess what I've just seen.' Josie leaned over and held the passenger door open for Emily.

'What?' Emily had never understood why Josie, who was a large woman, had such a small car. She squeezed herself in with difficulty.

'I have just seen…' Josie paused for maximum effect as she let out the clutch and the car bounced over the cobbles, 'I have just seen Francesca and Raoul going into Rachelle House with two large suitcases and a holdall. It looks as though she's moving in.'

Emily's jaw dropped. 'Surely not?'

'As sure as I'm sitting here. What do you make of that?'

'I'm surprised at the President. You would think he'd marry her before moving her into his house.'

'They go back a long way. I remember hearing that they were engaged once but Claudine Rachelle put a stop to it.'

'Claudine Rachelle was a formidable woman.' Emily was relieved when Josie pulled up in the hotel car park.

'I shall ask Natasha,' said Josie briskly. 'She'll know. Come on.'

They made a dash through the rain to the hotel's main entrance and hung their coats in the cloakroom before settling themselves in the cosy lounge where afternoon tea was served. Belle appeared. 'Good afternoon Mrs Cleghorn and Mrs Platt. Have you come for tea?'

'Two cream teas please, dear.' Josie smiled at the little girl and thought how pretty she looked in her red pinafore dress and white sweater. 'Please tell your mother I would like to see her.'

Belle went through to the dining room where Natasha was laying the tables for dinner.

'That child has charming manners,' said Emily as Natasha appeared. 'She's a credit to you.'

'Thank you.' Natasha flushed with pleasure. 'What can I do for you?'

'Natasha dear,' Josie spoke in hushed tones, 'do you know anything about Francesca moving in with Theo?'

Natasha's eyebrows shot up. 'What?'

'I've just seen Raoul taking Francesca into Rachelle House with two large suitcases and a holdall. You're so friendly with Elizabeth; we thought you might know what's going on.'

'I know nothing about it. Lizzie hasn't said anything to me – and even if she had,' Natasha added hastily, 'it really wouldn't be my place to say.'

Belle wheeled in a trolley with two cream teas, a coffee and walnut cake and a chocolate gateau. 'Enjoy your tea, ladies.' Natasha, her mind in a whirl, returned to the dining room.

'I don't think she knows anything,' said Emily.

'No.' Josie was thoughtful. 'It's odd though. I thought she and Elizabeth were close. You can't tell me that Elizabeth doesn't know what's going on. She and Francesca are as thick as thieves.' She poured out two cups of tea and relaxed back into her armchair. Conversation ceased for a few moments while the two women tucked into scones spread liberally with cream and jam.

'I wonder if the new hotel will be as good as this one.' Emily gazed out of the large window at the rain pounding the sea, roughening the surface into millions of tiny ripples. A few herring gulls hovered above it, facing into the wind, their wings hardly moving.

'If it is,' said Josie, 'I do wonder if the island can support two top quality hotels. They will be in direct competition with one another. I know Ian and Daphne are worried. Now which sort of cake would you like?'

'The coffee and walnut, please. Yaffingales will be lovely in the summer but I can't see people driving out there over that rough track in this kind of weather. It would be so much easier to just pop down here.'

'Oh, they will have to put in a proper road,' said Josie. 'Soon the island will be so built up it will be quite spoilt.'

* * *

'That was delicious,' said Theo finishing off the last of the scrambled eggs and grilled tomatoes that Francesca had prepared for their supper. He smiled across at her. She was seated in the armchair opposite him on the other side of the fireplace. He thought how at home she looked, and how pretty with the firelight glinting on her dark curls.

'Would you like anything else? Some more bread and butter or a yogurt?'

'A yogurt would be nice. This is the first time I've felt like eating for ages. I'm so glad you're here, Frankie. I've been feeling so miserable and alone. There seems to be no point to anything.'

Francesca was surprised and touched by the admission; Theo rarely opened up to anybody. 'I can stay for as long as you want me to,' she said gently and patted his shoulder on her way to the kitchen to find the yogurt.

'Raspberry or blackcurrant?'

'I don't mind.'

'You need building up,' she said as she passed him the raspberry yogurt before sinking back into her chair. 'You'll soon be feeling better. It's awful being on your own when you're ill.'

'It's awful being alone,' he said sadly.

Francesca was determined to lighten his mood. 'Would you like a game of Scrabble or would you prefer to watch TV while I go upstairs and unpack? It won't take me long.'

'I'm quite happy in front of the TV. What's on?'

Francesca riffled through the Radio Times which she had brought with her. 'There's a game show or a repeat of Dad's Army.'

'I'll watch Dad's Army.' He smiled at her. 'I'm feeling better already.'

Francesca climbed the wide staircase which opened out on to a large landing. She found her suitcases had been placed on the bed in the room next to Theo's. She shivered; it was bitterly cold and the room smelt musty and damp. She located the bathroom where there was a large linen cupboard containing towels, sheets and blankets. She selected the bedding she needed; that too felt damp. She suddenly realised, to her dismay, that Rachelle House had no central heating. This had not occurred to her before when she was preparing supper. The kitchen was warmed by the large Rayburn stove.

She examined the whole of the first floor and found a small one-bar electric fire in Theo's bedroom. She switched it on and drew the thick shabby curtains across the window, shutting out the sight of the rain-soaked square. She noticed a telephone by Theo's bed and called Raoul. 'Hello, it's me. Could you possibly do me a huge favour and go home and pick up my electric blanket, also a sheet and my duvet and pillow? Everything here is damp. There's a small fan heater in the cupboard under the stairs. Could you bring that too? I'm in danger of freezing to death here.'

'No wonder Theo's so ill,' said Raoul. 'Give me half an hour and I'll be with you. Anything else you want?'

She thought for a moment. 'My electric kettle would be useful. Thanks so much, I'm sorry to bring you out again in this weather.'

'No problem!'

The ringing of the front door bell woke Theo who had fallen into a doze.

'It's all right, it's only Raoul with some things I forgot.' Francesca poked her head round the living room door on her way through the hall.

Raoul greeted Theo and took Francesca's things up to her room. 'I thought it smelt musty in here when I brought your luggage up.' He plugged in the fan heater. 'Not that this will make a lot of difference in a room this size but it's better than nothing. The living room fire's getting low, I'll fetch you some more coal in.'

They went down to the kitchen. 'Ah, this is better!' Raoul examined the Rayburn. 'This runs on oil and I presume it heats the water.'

He went outside, checked the oil tank and found the coal house. He filled the scuttle and took it into the living room, then replenished the log box. 'There! That will keep you going until I come back in the morning. There's plenty of oil in the tank.'

'This is so good of you, Raoul. Is it still raining?'

'It's eased off slightly.' He looked at her, his brow furrowed. 'It's a gloomy old place, this. Are you sure you're going to be alright?'

'Yes, yes! Don't worry, and thanks again, Raoul. I'll see you in the morning. I hope Zapp is behaving himself.'

'Fast asleep on the settee!' Raoul gave her a hug and disappeared into the night.

Chapter 15

Francesca spent a restless night; in spite of warming up the bed she could not get to sleep. The day's events were chasing around her mind like a greyhound pursuing the hare on an endless racetrack. She worried about how she was going to cope with looking after Theo in addition to her full-time teaching job. The lights in the square filtered through the holes in the curtains giving the room an eerie feel. She could smell the damp, which pervaded the whole house, mixed with the scent of the lavender polish Mrs Evans used on the antique French furniture.

The house had a suffocating feel to it. Boards creaked intermittently; Francesca imagined the ghost of Claudine Rachelle walking the landing, her malevolence seeping through the house room by room. She decided to make a hot drink and read for a while. It was pointless tossing and turning for hours. She tiptoed across the landing. Theo's bedroom door was ajar and she peeped in. Theo was sleeping soundly, one arm flung behind his head, his usually immaculate hair tousled on the pillow. She smiled to herself and, feeling more cheerful, crept downstairs.

The kitchen was warm. Francesca filled her electric kettle and made herself a cup of hot chocolate. She sat down at the heavy oak table in the centre of the room and looked around. The kitchen was quite modern compared with the rest of the house. To her relief there was a Calor gas cooker as well as the Rayburn, and a new microwave oven on one of the formica work surfaces. At least meals won't be a problem she thought as she sipped her drink. She had been worried about cooking on the Rayburn. The hot chocolate warmed her and she felt her feeling of panic subsiding. She opened her book and settled down to read until, overcome by tiredness, she went back to bed and fell asleep.

She was woken by the insistent ringing of the front door bell. Pulling on her dressing-gown she hurried downstairs to find Raoul on the doorstep.

He looked at her with a mixture of amusement and curiosity. 'You're up late! How's Theo?'

'I've no idea!' said Francesca shortly. 'You've just woken me up. I've had a dreadful night.'

'Sorry! But you're not the only one. That dog of yours has been a pain; whining and crying after we'd gone to bed.'

'Oh no! Did he settle down eventually?'

'Only when Lizzie went down and let him out of the kitchen. He shot straight into the living room and jumped up on the settee. He was quiet after that.'

'He's used to sleeping on the settee at home.' Francesca led him through into the kitchen.

'You spoil him!' said Raoul, 'and Lizzie's just as bad giving in to him. I think he should be left in the kitchen; he's got a perfectly good dog bed. Lizzie and I have had words over this. Any chance of a coffee?'

Francesca smiled. 'I wondered why you were here so early.' She made three mugs of coffee. 'I'll just take this up to Theo and see if he's awake yet.'

Theo entered the room as she spoke and sat down heavily at the table. He was surprised to see Raoul.

'I've come round to do the fire and bring some more wood and coal in. How are you feeling this morning?'

'A bit woozy; it's these pills I have to take.'

'I'll make some toast,' said Francesca. 'Would you like some, Raoul?'

'Yes please, I haven't had any breakfast.'

Francesca laughed as she located the breadbin and put two slices of bread in the electric toaster. 'Raoul's escaped! He and Lizzie have had words over disciplining Zapp.'

'Oh dear! I don't want to cause trouble.' Theo looked miserable and Francesca was immediately contrite.

'It's not your fault. Anyway, their little squabbles are never serious are they, Raoul?'

Raoul, tucking into toast and marmalade, grinned. 'No, but I just feel I need to make a stand. That dog is taking over the house. He's getting very territorial over the settee.'

'That's Zapp, I'm afraid. He's only making himself at home. You might as well give in now.'

The telephone rang. Francesca went through to the study to answer it and Theo called after her. 'If that's Bertie Soames tell him I'm unavailable.'

'Surely it's not the Clerk at 9.30 on a Sunday morning?' said Raoul.

'It will be. Soames is driving me insane,' said Theo as Francesca returned.

'It is him! He's being very insistent. He says he must speak to you personally. It's urgent.'

Theo banged his fist on the table. 'Tell him to go to hell! Tell him I'm ill! Tell him I'm dead! Tell him anything you bloody well like!'

Francesca exchanged a glance with Raoul and went back to the phone. 'I'm sorry, Mr Soames. The President is too unwell to speak to you this morning. Can I take a message?'

'To whom am I speaking?' Francesca detected the irritation in the Clerk's reedy voice.

'Mr Rachelle's live-in carer,' she replied icily. 'I must insist that you stop bothering Mr Rachelle about work. He will not be returning until Dr Pointer gives him the all-clear. I hope I've made myself plain, and that the President will receive no further calls at his home.' She replaced the receiver without waiting for a reply.

Raoul was laughing when she returned to the kitchen. 'That's our Frankie,' he said to Theo. 'Now I must see to the fire and get home before Lizzie lets that dog wreck the house!'

* * *

The sky cleared around mid-day and the light from the weak wintery sun glistened on the roof tops and cobbled streets of the town. The wind had calmed to a gentle breeze, hardly ruffling Lizzie's hair as she took the rubbish out into the yard after lunch.

'Let's go and see how the work at Yaffingales is getting on,' she said to Raoul. 'Zapp needs a walk.'

They set off up Main Street, Zapp straining at his lead trying to jump up at a black and white cat staring at him superciliously from a window sill.

'It's so mild.' Lizzie took her gloves off and stuffed them into her pocket. 'It feels like spring already.'

'Don't be fooled! The winter's not over yet.'

They turned on to the track across the fields that led to the cliffs and then branched off towards Yaffingales. Small grey-green leaves were sprouting on the bare honeysuckle stems that twined through the hedges, and the silky seed heads of Old Man's Beard gleamed silver in the light of the low-angled afternoon sun. Somewhere a thrush was singing.

'There's Simon's Land-Rover,' said Raoul, squinting into the sun, 'and what on earth's all that?'

'What?'

'Something in the field; I thought they'd levelled it.'

They hurried towards the Yaffingales field to find Simon and Joshua Ford staring at vast piles of rubbish strewn over the muddy churned-up earth. 'How did all this get here?' Raoul looked with horror at the heaps of rusty metal, old kitchen appliances, mattresses, broken furniture and black plastic sacks which the gulls had been tearing apart, leaving the contents scattered.

Simon shrugged, his face hard.

'It was done last night,' said Joshua. 'Someone's been to the tip and carted all this stuff here. I recognise that old settee; I saw it there last week.'

'What do the police have to say?' Lizzie tugged at Zapp who had his nose in a plastic bag.

'Not much!' Simon shrugged again. 'I don't think they're that interested. It's unlikely they'll find the culprits. I'm guessing it's someone against the new hotel who's behind it; they'll all close ranks so we'll never find out. We were due to start digging the foundations this week now the weather's cleared. God knows how long it will take to return this lot to the tip, or how much it will cost. Ruth's distraught; she wants to pack the whole thing in and go home.'

'I'm not surprised,' said Lizzie.

'You can't give in to these bully boys! That's just what they want.' Joshua lit a cigarette. 'We'll start on the clearing up first thing in the morning and I'll have a word with the States Public Works department about better security at the tip.'

'Good luck with that!' said Raoul. 'The security's non-existent; people go down there when they like and dump stuff, there's never any staff around.'

'The tip is the States' responsibility; they'll have to do something. We can't have this happening again and that's down to the police as well. They can get their fingers out for once.' Joshua climbed into the Land-Rover. 'No point in hanging around here any longer.'

Simon turned to Lizzie. 'I wonder if you'd mind calling in to see Ruth. She needs someone to talk to and she likes you.'

'I'll come tomorrow. Would the morning be all right? I have to walk Zapp in the afternoons; he's living with us while Frankie's at Theo's.'

'The morning will be fine. I'll tell Ruth you're coming.' He smiled at her. 'Feel free to take the dog down into the valley whenever you want.'

Lizzie was surprised and delighted. 'Thank you so much.'

Simon and Joshua drove off and Raoul and Lizzie descended into the valley and let Zapp off the lead in the Yaffingales garden. Primroses, the colour of clotted cream, nestled in the long grass in the old flower borders and clumps of snowdrops graced the edges of the path leading down from the terrace. Tiny white flowers of scurvy grass starred the old matted lawns where a blackbird was hunting for worms.

Zapp chased after a rabbit and came to an abrupt halt as it disappeared into a tangle of brambles. The sides of the valley were dotted with bright yellow gorse which caught the last rays of the afternoon sun.

'Look! The gannets are back; they usually arrive in mid-February.' Raoul watched the long line of birds flying low over the water, their plumage brilliant white against the indigo blue sea.

They sat on the terrace while Zapp snuffled around the garden before digging a hole in the lawn and pulling at roots with his teeth.

'I never cease to be amazed at what that dog eats!' Raoul threw a stick at him but Zapp refused to be diverted.

'His ancestors must have hunted and foraged for food in the Congo; the instinct's still there.'

Zapp came and lay on the terrace beside them and licked the earth off his paws. 'I wish we could keep him,' said Lizzie. 'If Theo and Frankie get married perhaps we can.'

Raoul pulled a wry face and said nothing.

* * *

Francesca and Theo sat on either side of the fire in Theo's living room. Beethoven's Violin Concerto was playing softly in the background and Theo could not remember when he had last felt so content. He had reached a momentous decision.

'Frankie, I've decided. I'm going to resign.'

Francesca was just on the point of nodding off into a doze. She gave a start and stared at Theo in amazement. 'Resign as President you mean?'

'Yes, I've had enough. It's time for me to retire. The work's mounted up to an impossible level since I've been ill and that dratted man Bertie Soames is never off my back.'

'Who on earth will replace you? The post's been filled by a Rachelle for three generations.'

'There'll have to be a by-election. I shall write to the Clerk tomorrow.'

'He won't be a happy bunny! Who do you think will put themselves forward?'

'Oh, someone will want the kudos. Whoever it is will get a shock when he realises how much work's involved.' He paused, 'do you think I'm doing the right thing?'

'Definitely, you deserve to retire after such a long stint. It's time someone else took over. How long has it been?'

'Twenty years and it feels like forever. You've no idea how relieved I shall be to be a free man again.'

* * *

It was another mild sunny day as Lizzie walked down the hill to visit Ruth Brockenshaw. The birds were in fine voice; Lizzie picked out a thrush, a blackbird and a wood pigeon from the medley of songs that surrounded her. She turned left into a narrow lane which ran past several bungalows, all with magnificent harbour views. The Brockenshaws lived in the fifth bungalow along the lane, named Seagulls Rest. It had been modernised and extended into a luxury home.

Ruth and the two Dalmatians, Blizzard and Storm, welcomed her warmly. Ruth led her into the large conservatory overlooking the garden. A delicious aroma of freshly brewed coffee wafted through from the kitchen.

'Make yourself comfy,' said Ruth. 'I'll just fetch the coffee.'

The two dogs leapt on to a long sofa and stretched out in the sun. Lizzie sat down on one of the cane chairs and admired the swathes of snowdrops on the lawn which sloped downhill to an evergreen hedge marking the boundary.

'You've got a beautiful garden,' she said as Ruth returned bearing a tray which she placed on the glass-topped table. 'It was dark when Raoul and I came before and we couldn't see it.'

'Thank you.' Ruth gave a wry smile and Lizzie saw, to her dismay, that there were tears in her eyes. She blinked hastily and indicated the dogs. 'Will you just look at that? Hogging the sofa when we've got company! No manners at all!'

'Zapp's the same; he loves to lie in the sun.' Lizzie took the mug of coffee Ruth handed her. 'Have the police made any progress concerning all that rubbish dumped on your land?'

'No, they say they are unlikely to find out who is responsible and we get the impression that they are not really interested. No crime has been committed.'

'Fly-tipping is a crime, surely?'

'Maybe it is in the UK but not on Ormerey apparently. There's no actual law against it here, and no law of trespass either.' Ruth fished for a tissue as tears spilled down her cheeks. 'It seems as though everyone is conspiring against us. Simon says we have to ignore it and carry on but I've lost heart in the project. I hate Ormerey; I just want to pack up and go back to England.'

'Simon's right! Raoul agrees with him, he says we shouldn't give in to bullies. He's told me that some of the people here can be vicious when things don't go their way. They don't like outsiders coming over here and interfering on what they call their island.' Lizzie paused. 'Some of them really hate me; I see it in their eyes when I walk down the street. Some of them I've never even spoken to and they give me the evil eye.'

'Why don't they like you?'

'Because I'm English! Because I'm with an islander! Because they think I'm after his money! Raoul was married once. His wife was English and she wasn't accepted.'

'That's so sad.' Ruth dabbed at her cheeks and Storm got down off the sofa and laid his head on her lap. She stroked him. 'They hate us because we're building the hotel. We thought it would be good for the island.'

'It will be; people will see that once it's up and running and the tourist numbers increase. Even Frankie's come round to the idea.'

'Francesca was one of the organisers of the protest march.'

'Frankie's emotionally involved and she was egged on by Geoff Prosser. His beef was the violation of the green belt not a new hotel. His quarrel is with the States. Frankie's calmed down now she knows the cottage won't be demolished. It holds so many memories of her father who was killed when she was a child.'

'What happened to him?'

Lizzie related the story of Antonio's murder and the subsequent events leading to Francesca's family being evicted from Yaffingales.

Ruth stared at Lizzie, her own troubles temporarily forgotten. 'And no one knows who killed him?'

'No, and probably never will now. It happened fifty five years ago.'

'But there could be people still alive who know what happened and were part of the cover up.'

'Possibly,' said Lizzie, 'but Raoul thinks it's best left buried in the past. There's no point in raking it all up now when Frankie and Theo are getting on so well.'

Ruth was thoughtful, absently stroking both dogs, one on either side of her chair. 'It makes one realise that what is happening to Simon and me isn't unusual. It's so easy to get away with things on a small island; things get brushed under the carpet.'

'Raoul calls the viciousness and thirst for revenge the black side of the Norman character. He says we should read Flaubert's *Bouvard and Pécuchet* to understand what he means.'

'Have you read it?'

'I started it and gave up; it's heavy going and depressing.'

Ruth gave her a quizzical look. 'Raoul must have Norman blood.'

'Only a little! His mother and three of his grandparents were English. There isn't a spiteful bone in Raoul's body. He doesn't bear grudges. Neither does Frankie, they are two of the kindest people I know. Try not to worry, Ruth. I'm sure it will all come right in the end. There are lots of people on your side.'

'I'd like to know who they are,' said Ruth. She refused to be comforted.

Chapter 16

The Ormerey community, still reeling from the news that Francesca had moved into Rachelle House, were stunned by the President's resignation. Speculation about who would stand as a candidate in the Presidential by-election was rife. Three generations of Rachelles had held the prestigious post since Old Pierre, Theo's grandfather, had been elected in 1920.

The whole island buzzed with gossip and conjecture. People gathered together in the pub, in the shops and in the street, everyone voicing an opinion as to who would, or would not, make a good President.

In the Ormerey Supermart Prunella was in her element, standing with hands on hips and holding forth to her colleagues. 'It's good news if you ask me. Theo Rachelle's not fit to be President now he's moved that woman into his house to live with him.'

Pauline, who had always liked her former teacher, stood up for Francesca. 'She's only there to look after him while he's ill.'

Prunella snorted derisively. 'That's their story! I don't believe a word of it. I think my Georgie should put his name forward for President. He's local; he'd soon sort this island out.'

Julie, the youngest member of staff who was unpacking tins of baked beans, supressed a giggle.

'It is not the role of the President to sort the island out.' Josie Cleghorn's voice boomed out from behind the tall shelf of detergents. 'I do not consider your husband to be a suitable candidate, Prunella. He is the Clerk's brother; it would be too incestuous. It would not do at all.'

Prunella was furious. She stuffed her hands deep into the pockets of her pink overall and glared at Josie. 'Who asked for your opinion? You're an outsider, it's nothing to do with you.'

Josie, who was larger in all directions than Prunella, drew herself up to her full height and looked superciliously down her long nose. 'I would like to inform you, young lady, that I have lived on this island for over forty years. I have every right to an opinion and your husband would be most unsuitable.' She marched over to the till and banged her basket down. 'Service, please!'

Julie, still trying to supress giggles, hurried over to oblige. Josie swept out of the store, her purple curls bobbing. She saw Lizzie on the other side of the street and called across to her. 'Elizabeth! May I have a word?' She crossed over to the opposite pavement. 'There's something I'd like to discuss with you. Can you spare me five minutes? We'll go to the pub.'

Lizzie was too surprised to speak. She found herself being ushered down the street to The Lord Nelson. The bar was crowded and full of smoke. Josie pushed her way between the men standing at the bar and addressed Bill in a peremptory tone. 'A G & T, Landlord, a double if you please.' Josie turned to Lizzie, 'What's your poison?'

'I'll just have a coffee, if that's all right?'

'Oh! Don't we drink?' Josie raised her eyebrows. Bill winked at Lizzie as he handed Josie her glass and turned to put the kettle on.

'Not before lunch; I've got to go home and cook. I can't stay too long.' Lizzie noticed Geoff Prosser and Janine Briggs at the other end of the bar with their heads close together. She wondered if they were an item.

'Cheers!' Josie took a large slug of her G & T. 'Now, dear, I've just heard that George Soames, of all people, is thinking of putting his name forward for the Presidential by-election.'

'Heavens! He's the Clerk's brother. Raoul will have a fit; he says the Ormerey mafia have too much power already.'

'My thoughts exactly! Besides he hasn't the gravitas and he's as thick as a concrete block. We need someone to stand against him.' She leaned closer and whispered in Lizzie's ear. 'Some of my friends and I think that Raoul would make an excellent President.'

Overwhelmed by Josie's expensive perfume, Lizzie sat back and sipped her coffee. 'He's already been asked. He doesn't want to do it.'

'Who asked him?'

'Geoff Prosser. He said he would propose him and Henri would second him to encourage the local vote.'

'An excellent suggestion. Why doesn't Raoul want to do it?'

'He says it's not for him. He hasn't enough knowledge of Ormerey or Guernsey law, and he dreads the thought of public speaking.' Lizzie refrained from saying that Raoul had also said that all the paperwork would bore him stiff and he'd never get round to doing it. 'Anyway,' she added, 'Raoul would never be elected because he's living in sin with me!' She gave Josie a challenging look.

'Tosh! He could always marry you. His family name is one of the oldest on the island. He would be ideal; he has the right background and the bearing.'

'But not the temperament.' Lizzie chose to ignore Josie's remark about marriage. 'He's so laid back he's almost horizontal.'

'Lazy, you mean! That easy going manner is all part of his charm but it would do him good to work at something for a change.'

Lizzie counted to ten under her breath. 'I'm sorry, Josie. Raoul is adamant, he made himself quite clear to Geoff and he won't change his mind.'

'Such a pity! Tell him I suggested him, won't you.'

'Yes, he'll be flattered. Thank you for the coffee.'

'So nice to have a chat with you, dear.' Josie would never have admitted it to the Ormerey Ladies' Guild but she was beginning to like Elizabeth Bayley, a candid woman who was not afraid to speak her mind, much like herself.

* * *

Lizzie rushed home to find Raoul in the kitchen opening a tin of soup.

'I'd given you up! Where have you been all this time? You said you were just nipping out to post a letter.'

'Sorry!' said Lizzie. 'I was press-ganged by Josie Cleghorn and dragged off to the pub.'

Raoul stared in amazement. 'I thought you couldn't stand Josie Cleghorn.'

'She's not such a bad old stick. Anyway I had no choice. She's in a tizzy because George Soames is planning to stand in the Presidential by-election and she wants me to persuade you to stand against him.'

'No way! I hope you put her straight.'

'Yes, I did.' Lizzie started to lay the table. 'She's very disappointed. Aren't you worried about George Soames?'

'No! I'd be very surprised if he put his name forward. He's not popular except with his own cronies. He'd have difficulty finding anybody sensible to propose or second him. I expect it's wishful thinking on Prunella's part; she'd love to be the President's lady.'

Lizzie gave a snort of laughter. 'I can just see her in some awful outfit tottering around on the cobbles in six inch heels!'

'Lizzie, you can be very catty at times.' Raoul tried to look reproving but burst out laughing. 'I've had Henri here this morning trying to talk me into putting my name forward. He says we need an islander like Theo; the locals don't want an English President. The trouble is there isn't another Theo, he was in a class of his own.'

'Who do you think will stand?'

'Ian Warrington's always had delusions of grandeur. I wouldn't be at all surprised if he steps forward, or any one from among the ranks of the rich retired. We'll have to wait and see.'

He ladled the soup into two bowls and sat down at the table. 'Come on, eat up. We've got to take that wretched dog out.'

* * *

There had been more vandalism at Yaffingales. No sooner had Joshua Ford and his men cleared the field of all the rubbish and levelled the land again than more rubbish had appeared and the fencing had been ripped out. Two days later Simon found that all the windows in the cottage had been broken. Someone had entered through the French windows and completely wrecked the kitchen and the bathroom. The washbasin and toilet had been smashed to smithereens and the bath was full of rocks and rubble. The kitchen range had disappeared; all that was left was a gaping hole in the wall.

'Now that a crime has been committed I insist that you do something about it.' Simon Brockenshaw stood in front of the desk in the poky room adjacent to the Island Hall that served as the island's police station and addressed the Sergeant.

Joshua Ford backed him up. 'Surely by now you have some idea of who is responsible? There's obviously more than one person involved. If you'd been keeping a watch on the site since that first spate of vandalism this latest outrage wouldn't have happened.'

The island's Police Sergeant, Malcolm Green, an even tempered man who considered himself to be everyone's friend, bristled. 'The island is patrolled at night; we can't be everywhere at once.'

Joshua was not going to be put off by excuses. 'If that's the case, I fail to see how you could miss a vehicle transferring waste from the tip to Yaffingales, or dismantling and carting away an Aga stove. I assume you've been out to the site and seen the damage?'

The Sergeant looked uncomfortable. 'I'm sending Derek out there this morning. He'll make a report.'

'Fat lot of good that will do,' said Simon bitterly. 'Who's Derek?'

'Constable Peasgood,' said Joshua. 'I suggest that you post a man out there during the night until this business is cleared up, and patrol the island regularly, not just once at midnight. Everyone knows where you'll be and when; you can hear that vehicle of yours approaching a mile off.'

The Sergeant looked annoyed and drew himself up to his full height. 'We haven't the man power, Mr Ford.'

'Get more men over from Guernsey then,' snapped Joshua. 'What the hell do we pay our taxes for?'

'Have you any idea who might be behind it?' Simon asked as they left the police station.

'I've racked my brains; it's obviously someone who doesn't want to see the hotel built.' Joshua rummaged in his pocket for his cigarettes.

'Can't the police interview the people who were on the protest march?'

'They'll never bother to do that! I doubt whether it would get them anywhere. You have to realise that the Ormerey Police are heavily biased in favour of the locals. If you were an islander they'd have got it sorted by now.'

'Ruth and I were wondering if the Warringtons could be behind it. They've made it very clear they don't want a rival establishment on the island.'

'It's not their style,' said Joshua. 'Anyway, I've heard that Ian Warrington's standing for President. He won't want to jeopardise his chances by resorting to criminal activity. No, it's among the locals that we need to look, though I'd leave it to the police if I were you. You don't want to get involved in anything really nasty.'

'I don't think the police are going to exert themselves, and the States have refused to post anyone to keep an eye on the tip.'

'Don't worry,' said Joshua. 'If necessary I'll put one of my own chaps to guard the site at night. The trouble is it will add to the cost of the project.'

'So be it,' said Simon. 'I refuse to be beaten by this.' He wondered miserably how Ruth would react to this latest development.

* * *

Theo was feeling much better. Following his resignation he felt as though an enormous weight had been lifted from his shoulders.

'It's such a relief,' he remarked to Francesca as they strolled up Main Street together. 'I'm sure it was stress that made me so ill, not just the 'flu. I can relax now and enjoy my retirement.'

'What about your business?' Francesca admired a pale green silk blouse in the window of Belinda's Boutique, the more up-market of Ormerey's two clothing shops, and wondered if she was justified in buying it now the party season was over.

'I shall finish all this year's tax returns, and then give my clients notice of my retirement,' said Theo. 'There are several good accountancy firms in Guernsey so it shouldn't be too much of a problem for any of them. Some of them will moan, of course.' He tucked Francesca's arm through his, 'I shall be a gentleman of leisure like your cousin Raoul!'

Francesca giggled. 'I can't see you messing about at the tip and storing rubbish in German bunkers like Raoul and Henri do, and you don't fish either.'

'I could sort out the garden,' said Theo thoughtfully. 'It's in a bit of a state and I quite like the idea of growing vegetables. It will be nice to do the things I want to do for a change without people hassling me all the time.'

Dr Pointer was pleased with Theo's progress when he called on his regular weekly visit. 'I would like you to stay on the medication for a while longer, Mr Rachelle. How are you sleeping?'

'Better than I have done for years; no States business to worry about any more, it was getting me down more than I had realised.'

'It's the most sensible thing you could have done, retiring as President,' said the doctor. 'Time to let someone else have a go. It will be interesting to see who is interested in taking your place.' He scribbled out a prescription and handed it to Theo. 'There you go, come and see me at the surgery in a fortnight. I suspect Francesca has played a large part in your recovery.'

'I couldn't have managed without her,' said Theo, 'I shall really miss her when she goes home.'

Chapter 17

The mild February weather ended abruptly and March was blown in by a bitterly cold north-easterly wind accompanied by flurries of snow. Redwings and Fieldfares, escaping colder climes, joined the oystercatchers and gulls on Briac common. A sizable flock of lapwings landed on the grass at the airport, mingling amicably with the curlew already there.

Zapp went mad in the snow tearing round the garden in circles like a small steel ball flying round a bagatelle board. Lizzie enticed him in with a biscuit and slipped his lead on. 'Come along! Walkies!'

The snow was about an inch deep but had already thawed out in the street where it had been squashed by traffic and tramping feet. Large drips of water fell from roofs and tree branches, annoying Zapp who was already over-excited. He pulled Lizzie down the street and into Main Square where he suddenly spotted Francesca and hurled himself at her in an ecstasy of delight.

'Hello, darling.' Francesca squatted down and hugged the little dog. She looked up at Lizzie. 'I have missed him.'

'Come for a walk with us. It's ages since we had a chat.'

'OK! Hang on a tick while I pop inside for some gloves and tell Theo that I'm going out.'

Zapp tried to follow her but Lizzie shortened his lead and he stood shivering in the snow, whining piteously.

'We'd better get a move on.' Francesca re-joined them, wearing stout boots and thermal gloves. 'He hates the cold but he'll be fine once he's running about.'

Francesca was right. As soon as they were on the move again Zapp stopped shivering and pranced about, sniffing at gate posts and in the grass verges as they turned down Valmont Road and made their way to the sea.

'You should get him a little coat,' said Lizzie.

Francesca laughed. 'I did when I first got him. He threw the most awful paddy and tried to tear it off himself. Once it was off he chewed it up. I'm not buying another. It's a good thing this hill isn't slippery; when we have a lot of snow that packs down into ice it's lethal.'

Briac Common was covered with snow, now churned up by laughing shouting children hurling snowballs at each other and attempting to build a snowman.

'Let's go down on the beach. Zapp will go mad if a snowball hits him.' Francesca disappeared into a narrow gully between the sand dunes that led to the beach.

Lizzie had never seen snow on a beach before. There was little on the sand itself but the shingle at the base of the sand dunes was covered, and the marram grass was bent over by the weight of snow. A mixed flock of turnstones and ringed plover flew up en masse from the water's edge and winged their way to the far end of the bay where they alighted delicately and resumed feeding. Zapp, released from his lead, tore about kicking up wet sand and burying his nose in piles of snowy seaweed.

'When do you think you might be going home?' Lizzie hurled a piece of wrack for Zapp to chase.

'Soon I hope,' said Francesca, 'but I'm dreading telling Theo in case he asks me to stay.'

'Do you think he will?'

Francesca shrugged. 'He's got used to having me around, he likes the company.'

'But you don't want to stay?'

'No. I hate that gloomy old house; it's so cold and damp and I feel as if Theo's mother is haunting the place.'

'Oh Frankie!' Lizzie shrieked with laughter.

Francesca gave her a stern look. 'It's not funny! I can't wait to get back to Puffin Cottage and all my own things. Theo can manage on his own now he's so much better and Mrs Evans has agreed to come for two hours every weekday morning to clean and cook for him.'

'You have got him well organised. Has he quite recovered now?'

'He's got to stay on his medication for a while longer but he's fine. He's so much happier now he's retired; he's got all sorts of plans.'

'That's nice!' Lizzie wondered if Francesca figured in any of Theo's plans.

Francesca gave her a sly smile. 'I know exactly what you're thinking! You're wondering if Theo and I are going to get married.'

Lizzie blushed. 'Well, are you? Raoul hopes you are, he thinks you are both very well suited.'

Francesca snorted. 'Raoul can put his own house in order. I don't know if Theo wants to marry me or not,' she added gently. 'He hasn't said anything other than he likes having me around.'

'Hardly a declaration of love,' said Lizzie, 'but you know how reticent Theo can be. From the way he looks at you sometimes I'd say he was mad about you. Do you love him?'

'Yes, I do. I always have but I'm not sure that I want to marry him.'

'Why not?'

'Oh Lizzie, at our age we're both so set in our ways, and I can't possibly live in that awful house.' She sighed. 'I'm not sure that he'd want to move into Puffin Cottage, it's so small, and what about Zapp?'

Hearing his name, the dog ran up to them, looking hopeful.

'No treats,' said Francesca. 'You've had quite enough seaweed.' She threw a kelp stalk into the water and Zapp raced after it. He stopped short at the water's edge and watched the stalk bobbing away on a retreating wave. Both women laughed.

'He never goes in further than his ankles,' said Francesca. 'I can't wait to have him back home again.'

'We'll miss him,' said Lizzie. 'We've loved having him.'

* * *

Under the island's constitution a Presidential election was held every four years, but owing to the fact that no-one had come forward to stand against Theo Rachelle since 1971, he had continued in office unopposed since that date. The next election was due to take place in December, but as a result of Theo's sudden and unexpected resignation, a by-election had been called.

The local islanders grumbled amongst themselves, moaning that Theo could have waited until December instead of resigning nine months early, thus giving them too little time to field a candidate of their own. They did not want an English president.

Francesca found herself defending Theo at every turn. 'Theo has resigned for health reasons,' she told everyone who accosted her. 'He's not well enough to continue right through till December.'

The whole island was gripped by election fever. Ian Warrington, the proprietor of the Imperial Hotel, was the first person to be proposed and seconded. To Prunella's annoyance George Soames decided not to stand, fearing a humiliating defeat if it was a straight race between himself and Warrington. The electorate waited with bated breath to see who else would come forward.

Lizzie was disappointed not to have a vote.

'You have to reside here for a year and a day before you can be put on the electoral role,' Raoul explained. 'You'll be able to vote in the Ordinary and the Presidential elections in December.'

The Ordinary elections were held every two years when half the complement of States members came to the end of their term and could, if they wished, put themselves forward for re-election. This arrangement built some continuity into the system and at the same time made way for new blood. Six of the twelve States members were due to end their term of office in December and Lizzie was looking forward to being able to vote. It would make her feel she really was part of the island community at last.

To everyone's disappointment there was no by-election after all. No one came forward to stand against Ian Warrington who walked in unopposed, the first English President in the island's history.

Ian Warrington was popular among many of the island's business community and English settlers but not with the majority of local islanders who still regarded him as an outsider even though he and his wife had lived on Ormerey since 1950.

'You should have put your own man forward.' Geoff Prosser had joined a group of grumbling locals in The Lord Nelson.

'No one was prepared to stand.' Emile Duvall, elder brother of Henri and Sophie, leaned against the bar puffing at a cigarette. A retired fisherman with bright blue eyes in a wrinkled sunburnt face, he fixed Geoff with a forbidding look. 'You've always got a lot to say for yourself, haven't you? You forget you're not one of us.'

Geoff ignored the jibe and carried on. 'It's no use grumbling! You've got the rest of the year in which to select someone, preferably someone young and dynamic who's prepared to put in the time and effort to learn the system.'

Albert, who once crewed on Emile's boat, snorted with derision. 'The younger fellows are all too busy raising families and earning a living. They haven't the time.'

'What about you, Henri?' a voice shouted from the back of the room. 'You're not working!'

Henri guffawed with laughter. 'Who me? I haven't the brains or the know-how. We tried to persuade Raoul, me and Geoff, but he didn't want to know.'

'He'd be just the man,' said Albert. 'He's local and well-heeled. What does he do all day anyway?'

'Get's Henri down off his roof,' laughed Emile. 'Eh, Henri?'

Henri shuddered dramatically. 'I still feel dizzy when I think about it.'

Sid, one of the younger fishermen, chipped in. 'Raoul St Arnaud's got that English bird in tow. Can any of you see her as the President's lady?'

'She's posh enough!' said Albert, 'but they ought to be married first.'

'Lizzie's a nice woman,' said Geoff. 'Anyway there's no point in speculating; Raoul is adamant he won't do it.'

'What about you?' Emile fixed his piercing gaze on Geoff again. 'Why don't you put your money where your mouth is?'

'You've just told me I'm not one of you.'

'You're nearly local,' said Sid.

'I'll take that as a compliment!' Geoff, who was seated near the window, had just seen Janine outside. 'Excuse me, chaps! Things to do; people to see.' He drained his glass and headed for the door.

* * *

Jean Yorke arrived back on Ormerey after six weeks in the south of France refreshed and in high spirits. After several heart-to-heart talks with her elder daughter, Sarah, her depression had lifted and she was full of optimism about the future of the Ormerey Ladies' Guild.

Sarah Yorke, a high-powered business woman, rented an apartment in a smart block near the coast with its own extensive gardens and a swimming pool. She invited her parents to stay for several weeks every winter. Nothing would induce her to visit Ormerey.

'You look tired, Mother,' she had said when she picked Jean and Harold up from the airport. 'What's been happening on Ormerey?'

On hearing the saga of the dentures and Jean's subsequent humiliation in court, she had taken her mother on one side and spoken to her firmly. 'You really must not let Father push you around so much, Mother. You should never have gone to court. You should stick up for yourself. Put your foot down. Father's a bully, you know, everyone can see it except you.'

'I can see it,' Jean had replied. 'It's just easier to go along with what he wants; otherwise there's a row. He never backs down.'

'Just keep calm and go with the flow. Let him rant on and then do your own thing. You should have refused to go to court.'

'I know.' Jean had smiled at her daughter. 'When did you get to be so sensible?'

'I have to deal with conflict all the time at work. I learned lots of techniques at business school. I want you both to relax while you're here and enjoy yourselves. No rows!'

Jean had relaxed. Harold had taken himself off to play golf most days and she had sat by the pool, wandered round the shops and swam every day. She had loved this time on her own; it had given her plenty of time to think. She still smarted when she recalled Francesca's criticism of the Ormerey Ladies' Guild. *"It's not a proper club. It's just an excuse for gossip and tittle-tattle."* Following further chats with Sarah she had resolved to make some changes when she returned home.

Harold Yorke also returned from his holiday feeling relaxed and rejuvenated but his good mood did not last for very long.

'That bloody woman's been given a work permit,' he spluttered as he returned from the bakery with fresh croissants for breakfast.

'Please don't swear, dear.' Jean took the bag from him and popped the croissants into the microwave. 'Which woman?'

'That Briggs woman that I sacked from the Ormerey News. She's now writing for the Guernsey Evening Press. Can you believe that? And she's working for that English author who lives up by the airport, typing his latest book apparently. I turn my back for five minutes and…'

'Do calm down, dear, you know what that French doctor said about your blood pressure.' Jean handed him a cup of freshly percolated coffee. 'That reminds me, I must make an appointment for you with Dr Pointer.'

'And another thing!' Harold carried on as if his wife had not spoken. 'We weren't here for the Presidential by-election. That's your fault; you insisted on staying in France for an extra fortnight.'

Jean, mindful of her daughter's advice, did not challenge him as once she would have done. 'There wasn't an election. Ian was unopposed.'

'Precisely! Had we been back in time I would have put my name forward; then there would have been an election and I might have won.'

The island's had a lucky escape, Jean thought to herself with a smile.

* * *

Francesca and Theo sat side by side on a bench in a sheltered corner of the churchyard. It was a bright sunny day with a fresh breeze. Small round clouds drifted across the sky, reminding Francesca of the clouds her pupils drew in their pictures. The lush grass between the graves was dotted with daisies, celandines and primroses.

'I'm glad the States never mow the grass until the spring flowers are finished,' said Francesca. 'It's so pretty here.'

'And peaceful,' said Theo.

A robin perched on a nearby gravestone and fixed them with a bright black eye before trilling a few notes of song. Francesca had brought flowers for her parents' grave. It was her father's birthday. He would have been eighty one this year. She wondered how he would have looked as an old man. Her memories of him were still clear; a swarthy man with thick black hair, his eyes as dark and merry as her own.

Theo watched as she arranged her freesias in a jam jar and placed it on the green chippings that covered the grave. He wished she wasn't going home. He wanted to ask her to stay and marry him but he could not find the words. He was afraid of an outright rejection. It was still too soon.

'I'm going to miss you, Frankie,' was all he managed to say as she returned to her seat next to him. 'You will come and see me, won't you?'

'Oh Theo!' She took his hand in hers. 'I'm only five minutes away, of course I'll come and see you, and you can visit me at Puffin Cottage whenever you like.'

He smiled and squeezed her hand. 'Thank you, Frankie.'

Raoul called for Francesca that afternoon. He piled her luggage into the pick-up, watched by Jean Yorke and Josie Cleghorn who had just emerged from the church where they had been arranging the flowers.

Francesca gave Theo a peck on the cheek before she left. 'Take care of yourself,' she said. 'Remember I'm only a phone call away.'

Theo said nothing. He opened the front door for her and stood in the porch while she climbed into the pick-up.

He raised his arm and waved before turning back indoors, ignoring the small crowd that had gathered in the square agog with curiosity, as Raoul drove Francesca away.

'No proposal then?' Raoul negotiated his way up the narrow street, lined on both sides with parked cars.

'Shut up!' said Francesca sharply.

Raoul glanced sideways and saw that her eyes were glistening with tears. 'Sorry, love.' He spoke gently. 'I thought you wanted to go home.'

'I do.' Francesca sniffed and fumbled for a tissue. 'Theo looks so bereft; I do hope he'll be all right.'

'Of course he will,' said Raoul reassuringly. The man's a complete idiot, he thought.

Lizzie had walked Zapp back to Puffin Cottage. They were waiting in the front garden when Raoul and Francesca arrived. Zapp hurled himself at his mistress, his curly tail wagging. They all trooped inside. Raoul took Francesca's suitcases up to her bedroom and nearly fell headlong as Zapp careered past him down the stairs.

'At least we'll have some peace at home now,' he said to Lizzie as Francesca disappeared into the kitchen to put the kettle on.

'I'm going to miss Zapp. Couldn't we get a dog, Raoul?'

'No, not yet anyway.' He grinned at her. 'I've got a funny feeling that we might end up with this one!'

Chapter 18

As the days lengthened Ormerey gradually awoke from its winter torpor. Shops resumed their normal opening hours; a trickle of visitors, mostly naturalists and birdwatchers, arrived at the airport; the Rock Café reopened and the staff arranged tables and chairs on the terrace in the expectation of good weather.

March, which had roared in like a lion, looked set to frolic out like a lamb. The weather was sunny and mild. Flowers burst into bloom all over the island and the gardens were full of daffodils. Briac Common was yellow with buttercups and up on the headlands the gorse blazed gold, and delicate white flowers covered the dark wind-sculptured blackthorn bushes.

Raoul took Lizzie up to the high cliffs at the western end of the island to see the wheatears, the first of the spring migrants. They watched the colourful little birds flying from rock to rock, their white rumps flashing in the sun. A flock of linnets and meadow pipits flew up in front of them, alighting father off to feed in the short rabbit-cropped grass.

Lizzie took some photographs of the spectacular rugged scenery; the steep cliffs and rocky islets covered with nesting shags and gulls; the narrow ledges where the fulmars nested and, far below, the aquamarine sea frilled with white where it churned and tumbled against the rocks.

A small path took them down into a deep valley through which a stream trickled on to a narrow stony beach. Raoul helped Lizzie across and they struggled through the boggy ground, thick with dark green sedges, buttercups and red campion. A few stunted sycamore trees were breaking into leaf and a chiffchaff was singing, his notes high-pitched and sharp above the squawking of the gulls. The climb up to the next headland was steep and Raoul and Lizzie were both out of breath when they reached the top.

'You get a good view of the airfield from here.' Raoul collapsed on to a bench. 'There's a plane just taking off. Look.'

The yellow Trislander roared over their heads and Lizzie experienced the stab of longing she always felt when she saw a plane heading for England.

The coastal track led round the perimeter of the airfield and on to Yaffingales in its sheltered valley on the south side of the island. The field was now a busy building site. Joshua Ford was leaning against a fence post, a cigarette hanging from his mouth, his eyes on the horizon far out to sea. He started when Raoul spoke to him.

'I see the work is progressing well; I take it you've had no further problems out here?'

'I've got a man out here twenty-four seven.' Joshua indicated the blue Portacabin in the corner of the field. 'I'm not expecting trouble here but the Brockenshaws have received some vicious hate mail. The police are looking into that.'

'They won't get anywhere,' said Raoul.

'No, they won't,' agreed Joshua. 'I despair of this island sometimes. People come here with the best of intentions to improve life for everyone, and all they get is hostility from a small segment of the community. Remember the Collingwoods?'

'Who were they?' asked Lizzie.

'A young English couple who came over here and started a moped hire business,' said Joshua. 'It was a good idea and popular with the holidaymakers.'

'What happened?'

'One of the cycle hire companies really had it in for them – put sugar in their fuel tanks and God knows what else. They cut their losses and left after only one season.'

'The woman was expecting a baby,' said Raoul, 'and was really upset by the hate mail, abusive phone calls, dog mess pushed through the letter box, all that sort of thing. They decided Ormerey wasn't the place they wanted to bring up a child and who can blame them?'

Lizzie was silent. She slipped her hand into Raoul's and he gave it a reassuring squeeze. 'It looks as though the Brockenshaws will ride out the storm,' he said to Joshua.

'I hope they do. This is the best contract I've had for years.' Joshua lit another cigarette. 'I've had to take on extra lads and I've got two new apprentices. I wish more people would see the positive side. There are limited opportunities for work here; it's not easy for the youngsters to find jobs.'

'There will be lots of jobs in the new hotel.' Lizzie turned to Joshua. 'Are you local?'

'Me? I'm Guernsey!' He grinned at her. 'Pam's local. She didn't want to leave Ormerey so we settled here and our kids are local. It's been good for all of us.'

Lizzie gazed across the valley to the horizon, where the dark sea met the pale sky. It's good for the locals, she thought, but not so good for us strangers.

* * *

Ian Warrington's first public appearance after being sworn in as President of the States of Ormerey was the opening of his son's new shop. It was a bright, breezy morning and a large crowd had gathered at the top of Main Street to witness the grand opening. The shop windows, under a smartly painted sign saying "Hugo's Emporium" were festooned with posters indicating products new to Ormerey and special offers.

'Special offers!' said Raoul, 'we've never had those here before!'

Ian Warrington stood on a crate and called for silence. 'Thanks to my son, Hugo, we now have a modern supermarket on Ormerey which, I am sure you will all agree, will benefit the whole island. Please come and enjoy a glass of wine and sample a selection of our delicious cheeses.'

Daphne Warrington, dressed for the occasion in a chic purple suit with cream accessories, cut the scarlet ribbon across the entrance of the shop. 'I now declare Hugo's Emporium officially open,' she announced. A cheer rose from the crowd and people surged forward into the store.

Raoul and Lizzie were joined by Francesca and Theo. 'We're waiting until the first mad rush is over,' said Lizzie.

'Good idea!' Theo, who had his arm tucked through Francesca's, beamed round at everyone.

'How are you, Theo?' Raoul noticed the former President had lost the grey look he had worn for so long; his face had filled out and there was a healthy colour in his cheeks. He was wearing a dark green fleece and jeans instead of his habitual business suit and looked ten years younger.

'I'm fine now, thanks to your cousin and her excellent care.'

Francesca blushed. 'Come on, I can't wait to explore this new shop.'

Natasha joined them. 'There's still an awful crush in there, I'd wait a bit longer if I were you.'

They stood and watched as people drifted out of the store, many with loaded carrier bags. Josie Cleghorn stopped on her way past. 'A lovely store; so much choice and so clean. I shan't be using the Ormerey Supermart again.'

'Neither shall I!' said Lizzie emphatically.

'Oh, do come on!' Francesca was growing impatient. 'There'll be no wine left at this rate.'

Natasha laughed. 'Don't worry, there's plenty for everybody.'

Daphne Warrington, who was standing at the door greeting people, pointedly ignored them as they entered.

Francesca giggled. 'No need to be polite to you, Theo, now you're no longer the President.'

'It would pay her to be civil to everyone,' said Theo. 'We're all potential customers.'

Lizzie was amazed at the size of the new store. 'I never imagined it would be so huge.'

'It's two adjacent shops made into one,' said Natasha, 'and we've opened out the storerooms at the back. Do you think the white walls look too clinical?'

'No,' said Lizzie. 'It's nice and bright and the lighting's good, we can actually see what we're buying.'

'The staff look smart,' said Raoul admiring the blue and white striped shirts worn with navy skirts or trousers.

'Mother's grilled them about good customer service; they must be polite at all times.'

Lizzie snorted. 'Daphne should practice what she preaches,' she whispered to Francesca.

There was a large array of fresh greengroceries. Francesca gave a squeal of delight. 'Look at this brilliant selection of fruit and veg. Think what I'll be able to cook with this lot.'

'These are the first non-bendy carrots I've seen on this island.' Lizzie helped herself to a plastic bag and filled it with carrots.

Hugo Warrington, tall, dark and extremely good looking, smiled at them both. His likeness to Natasha was striking. 'Miss Saviano, how lovely to see you! ' He kissed Francesca on both cheeks. 'Please take a glass of wine; we've got red, white or rosé. Help yourselves to cheese.' He handed round a tray with cubes of different cheeses speared on cocktail sticks. 'Enjoying your retirement, Mr Rachelle? Father's got a hard act to follow.'

'I'm sure he'll make an excellent President,' Theo replied generously. Privately he considered Ian Warrington to be too inexperienced in the political field but he was prepared to give him the benefit of the doubt. Time will tell, he thought. 'What a splendid venture this is, Hugo. I wish you every success.'

'Thank you.' Hugo turned to speak to Harold and Jean Yorke who were trying to catch his attention.

'Your brother's very handsome,' Lizzie whispered to Natasha. 'Is he married?'

'No, his coming back here has caused quite a flutter among the female population. Watch this space!'

'You've got a lovely delicatessen counter,' said Francesca, 'and a great selection of frozen foods.'

'We're not doing fresh meat or bread,' Natasha explained. 'We don't want to take business away from the local butcher or baker.'

'But you don't mind upsetting Pink Prunella?'

'Not at all! That place is so appalling it deserves to lose business.'

* * *

The last week in March brought Easter and the school holidays. Francesca was glad of the break; she had found the winter term, combined with looking after Theo, exhausting. 'Three whole weeks off,' she said to Lizzie as they walked along the beach at Saline Bay. 'What bliss!'

'I'm going to England for a visit next week.' Lizzie struggled to walk in the soft sand. Saline Bay faced north into the English Channel and caught the full force of the wind. The beach shelved steeply. Zapp danced about playing 'chicken' with the huge waves that thundered in, hitting the shore with a thud before rolling back, dragging the loose sand and pebbles back into the swirling foam with a sinister sucking sound.

'It's always very rough here,' said Francesca. 'It's dangerous for swimming; there's such a strong undertow. Do be careful, Zapp, I'm not going in there if you get caught by a wave.' She turned to Lizzie. 'How long will you be away for?'

'Only a week.' Lizzie threw a piece of kelp up the beach for Zapp and he chased after it.

'Are you going back to your flat in Tonbridge?'

'Yes, I need to check up on it. Kent is beautiful at this time of year; full of blossom. It seems like forever since I was there. There are so many people I want to see, I hope I can fit them all in.' She paused. 'And I must go and see my father and try to make things up with him. I find it so hard going back to that house since Cynthia ruined the garden.'

Francesca patted her arm sympathetically. 'Raoul will miss you.'

'I'm sure he'll survive for a week!' Lizzie changed the subject. 'You and Theo are getting very cosy these days.' She watched the flush creep up Francesca's face and wondered how far their relationship had progressed but she did not like to ask.

'We are spending a lot of time together. I'm cooking him an authentic Italian meal tonight. I've managed to get all the right ingredients thanks to Hugo's Emporium.'

'The new shop is such a boon, I do hope it's doing well.'

'It is according to Hugo, but not as well as he'd hoped. Apparently some of the locals are boycotting it and staying loyal to the Ormerey Supermart.'

'Really?' Lizzie was surprised.

'Well, it's what they're used to; you know how they resist anything new. Prunella's very smug about it.'

Lizzie steered the conversation back to Theo. 'You know that we'd always have Zapp if you and Theo want to be together.'

'I don't know what Raoul would think of that idea.' Francesca looked doubtful.

'He'd be so pleased to see you and Theo settled I'm sure that he wouldn't mind. You could always live together, properly I mean, like Raoul and I do. You don't have to get married if you don't want to.'

'It's the living together that's the problem, not marriage. There are practical difficulties like where we would live. You know how I hate Rachelle House. I can't see Theo agreeing to move; it's been his family home for generations.'

Francesca looked bleak, her hands thrust deep into her pockets.

'But you're not happy with things as they are,' said Lizzie gently. 'Surely you and Theo could come to some kind of compromise. We've had to; if I want to be with Raoul I have to live here.'

'Oh Lizzie! I thought you were happy here.'

'I am. I'm very happy with Raoul. He's the love of my life but I still feel out of place here and I get so terribly homesick. I wish I didn't but I can't seem to help it. Raoul says it will pass.'

'I'm sure it will,' said Francesca comfortingly.

* * *

Natasha stood in the dining room of the Imperial Hotel and gazed miserably out of the large window. It was a lovely day outside. Hotel guests were making their way down on to the beach, well wrapped up against the cold wind. She was exhausted. There had been so much preparation to do in the new shop leading up to its grand opening, and before that she had borne the responsibility of coping with the hotel while her parents were on holiday. Even after their return they had left her to cope; too busy establishing themselves as the President and his lady. She had lost count of the number of new outfits her mother had bought.

She saw Geoff Prosser's battered old Ford pull up outside and watched as he and Janine Briggs clambered out. Janine, chic in a red wool coat with a black fur collar; Geoff looking as scruffy as usual in a faded blue anorak, jeans and trainers. She hoped they were not coming into the hotel for coffee and sighed with relief when they walked on down the road which skirted the harbour. They must be an item, she thought as she watched them, everyone's talking about them. Janine was laughing at something Geoff was saying to her and Natasha felt a fierce stab of jealousy. It was an unpleasant feeling. That should be me out there she thought miserably.

'Natasha! What are you doing gazing into space like that? We've got guests for morning coffee.' Daphne swept into the room in a haze of perfume, closely followed by Jean Yorke, Josie Cleghorn and Emily Platt. Natasha jumped, startled out of her reverie.

Daphne showed the three women to a table before hissing in her daughter's ear. 'Do buck up! You've got a face like a wet weekend, and bags under your eyes! I don't know what's the matter with you these days.'

Natasha sighed. 'I'm tired, Mother, I need a holiday.'

Daphne snorted.

Jean Yorke had invited her two friends for coffee in order to outline her new ideas for the Ormerey Ladies' Guild. 'We need to put our little group on an official footing,' she said, 'with a proper committee.'

'We thought you had given up with the Guild,' said Emily. 'We haven't had a meeting this year.'

'Well, I've been away, haven't I?' said Jean. 'While I've been away I've had a good think. Francesca had a point when she said we were just a gossip group. We need to up our profile.'

Josie and Emily stared at her in amazement. Josie finally broke the silence. 'What did you have in mind?' she asked weakly.

Jean hesitated while Natasha poured out the coffee and placed a plate of buttered gâche on the table.

'Ooh lovely!' Josie looked up at Natasha. 'You look tired, my dear, you work too hard.' Natasha smiled, momentarily cheered by the older woman's sympathy.

'We need a chairperson, a secretary and a treasurer,' said Jean briskly, 'and I suggest that each member pays an annual subscription. The present system of paying a pound at the door each month is too hit and miss. We need to cover the cost of room hire as well as refreshments. We could have a speaker sometimes, and we could run fund-raising events to help local charities. What do you think?'

'I think it all sounds splendid.' Emily helped herself to a slice of gâche.

'I agree,' said Josie, 'and I think we should write to people and invite them to join. It would be nice to have Francesca back with us and perhaps she could bring Elizabeth.'

Jean raised her perfectly groomed eyebrows in surprise. 'I thought you and Elizabeth didn't get on. I heard you pushed in front of her in the Ormerey Supermart on her first day here.'

'Oh I may have done,' said Josie airily, 'I must have thought she was a holidaymaker. It's all forgotten now. We get on quite well,' she added, 'she's a very sensible woman.'

Jean and Emily exchanged amused looks.

'We do miss Francesca's cakes,' said Jean, 'but all dogs will be banned! Excuse me for a moment, girls.' She got up and headed in the direction of the ladies' cloakroom.

'I wonder where all this has come from,' said Josie thoughtfully. 'Jean's very bright and bushy-tailed after her holiday. Do you suppose she's had a love affair?'

'Jean?' Emily shrieked with laughter and helped herself to the last slice of gâche.

Chapter 19

At the beginning of April Lizzie took her long awaited trip to England. The red-eye flight which should have left Ormerey at 8.15am was delayed for two hours by thick fog. Lizzie left Raoul on a damp, murky island and stepped off the plane at Southampton into the full glory of an English spring.

Flying over the New Forest Lizzie marvelled at the varied shades of soft green, dusky pink and brown below her; the trees clothed in their new foliage contrasting with the dark green evergreens. The River Itchen sparkled in the sunshine and, as the Trislander flew lower, Lizzie could pick out details of life on the ground; traffic queuing at roundabouts; children playing in a school playground; cows in the fields, and even tiny black and white specks on the grass which were crows and seagulls.

The moment her feet touched the tarmac Lizzie had an overwhelming feeling of having come home. Full of happy anticipation she collected her luggage and walked to the small station. Once on the train she removed her jacket and relaxed back into her seat, watching the Hampshire countryside flashing past the window. Each stop brought her closer to London; Basingstoke; Woking; Clapham Junction and finally Waterloo. Far from being intimidated by the frenzied bustle of the concourse after eight months on a tiny island, Lizzie drank in the atmosphere with relish. She made her way to Bonaparte's, ordered a coffee and sat outside watching the people rushing by.

She recalled with a smile the very first time she had met Raoul. It had been on a train pulling in to Waterloo East station. She had been standing behind a tall blonde man who had turned to her in confusion. 'How on earth do I get this door open? There's no door handle.'

'This is one of the old carriages. You need to open the window and lean out, like this.'

He had stepped aside and Lizzie had pulled the window down, stuck her arm through and opened the door using the handle on the outside.

He had grinned sheepishly. 'I feel such a fool.'

'We all get caught out the first time,' she had said returning his smile.

'I've got to catch a train to Southampton Airport,' the man had continued. 'Can you point me in the right direction? I haven't a clue where I'm supposed to go.'

'You need the Waterloo mainline station. Come with me.'

They walked up the slope, along the long passageway, crossed the road and entered the mainline station.

'I'm sorry to be such a nuisance. Am I holding you up?'

'Not at all. Are you new to London?'

'I haven't been here for years. I don't know England well. I live on a small island called Ormerey.' He grinned at her. 'Do you know where that is?'

'The Channel Islands, isn't it?'

'Spot on.' The man had smiled at her again and Lizzie had thought how charming he was.

'You need platform 9,' she had said looking up at the departure board. 'That train stops at Southampton Airport Parkway.'

'I don't need to go yet; my flight isn't till 5.30. You've been so helpful; please let me buy you a coffee or something.'

She had taken him to Bonaparte's. They had sat outside and talked for two hours. That was how it had all started.

Lizzie smiled at the recollection, finished her coffee, walked across to Waterloo East and boarded a train for Tonbridge. Leaving the suburbs behind the train passed through the North Downs and into the Weald. Lizzie's heart lifted at the sight of the familiar farms and oast houses, lambs in the fields and blossom on the trees. A flock of lapwings rose from the grassy expanse of Tonbridge sports ground situated between the encircling arms of the River Medway. She glimpsed a pair of mute swans, wings raised in elegant arches over their backs. She was home.

* * *

Watching Lizzie's plane take off and soar over the western cliffs left Raoul with a flat, empty feeling. Lizzie had been unable to contain her excitement while they had sat in the cramped airport lounge waiting for the fog to lift. She was full of what she was going to do in England; see her friends; visit art galleries and museums; go shopping. All the things she can't do on Ormerey he thought miserably as he drove back to town. He hoped she would be able to smooth things over with her father and step-mother. He knew that was worrying her.

The early morning fog had cleared to leave a bright sunny day. He decided to call in and see Henri. He could not face going back to an empty house. Henri and Sophie were in the kitchen. Sophie was cleaning the gas cooker and Henri was lounging in a battered easy chair watching her. He jumped up with a pleased smile when Raoul entered.

'Hello! I was just thinking of having a look round the tip this morning. It's a while since we had a good rummage.'

'Coffee?' Sophie stopped scrubbing at the burnt-on food on the stove and looked round at Raoul.

'No thanks, Soph, I've already had two at the airport.'

'So she's gone, has she?' Sophie's black eyes regarded him beadily.

'Only for a week', said Raoul. 'She's visiting friends and shopping.'

'Humph!' snorted Sophie. 'Our shops not good enough, eh?'

'No John Lewis or Marks and Spencer.' Raoul grinned at her. 'I might sort out my German bunker while Lizzie's away. It will give me something to do.'

'Ha! I won't hold my breath!' Henri laughed. 'Let's get going; it's a grand day.' He held the door open for Raoul and winked at his sister.

Sophie's face showed the tiniest glimmer of a smile. 'You'll come back with him for your dinner, will you?'

'Thanks Sophie, I'd love to.' He gave her a quick squeeze and a peck on the cheek. She glowered at him and Henri laughed again.

'Come on, dinner's at twelve in this house remember.'

* * *

Lizzie spent her first day in Tonbridge settling back into her flat, doing a supermarket shop and going through the enormous pile of junk mail that had accumulated during her absence. That evening she phoned her father to tell him she was in England and would like to visit him. His reaction surprised her.

'That would be wonderful, Lizzie. Come over for tea tomorrow afternoon. Are you all right for transport? I'm not allowed to drive anymore.'

No mention of Cynthia coming to pick her up she noticed. 'It's all right, Dad, I'll get the train to Penshurst station and walk from there. It's not far.'

The next day was warm and sunny with a gentle breeze. Lizzie always enjoyed the cross-country train ride from Tonbridge to Penshurst, passing through the new Hayesden Country Park and the village of Leigh. It was a fifteen minute walk to her old home which was a small cottage on the outskirts of Penshurst village, set well back from the road in an acre of garden. She was suddenly overcome by a wave of nostalgia as she walked down the lane; the clumps of primroses and lesser celandines in the hedgerow reminding her of the countless times she had walked this same route with her mother. As she rounded the bend and the house came into view her eyes filled with tears.

Lizzie was shocked by the sight of her father as he came down the drive to meet her. He was more bent than she remembered and leaned heavily on his stick. His blue eyes twinkled and he smiled, clearly pleased to see her.

'Hello, Lizzie.'

'Hello, Dad.' She gave him a hug and he returned it warmly. 'How are you?'

'Not bad considering I'll be eighty next year. Come on in. We'll have tea in the conservatory; it's still a bit nippy for sitting outside.'

Cynthia was bustling round the kitchen in her usual efficient manner. A spritely sixty five year old with tightly permed grey hair she nodded briefly at Lizzie. 'So, you've remembered we exist then?'

Lizzie ignored the sarcasm and gave her stepmother a peck on the cheek. 'This is the first time I've been over to England since moving to Ormerey.'

Cynthia sniffed. 'Happy over there are you?'

'Yes, thank you, I'm very happy with Raoul but I do get homesick at times.'

Cynthia finished arranging biscuits on a plate and stared hard at Lizzie. 'Your Dad misses you, you know. He's not getting any younger and would like to see you more often. I think it's time to let bygones be bygones, don't you?'

Lizzie was so surprised she was speechless for a moment. She gathered herself together quickly. 'I agree. We should put the past behind us and make a fresh start. I will visit more often if I'm truly welcome.'

'Of course you are.' Cynthia was brisk. 'Now take this tray through to the conservatory for me. You haven't seen it yet, have you?'

'No,' said Lizzie. 'And I see you've had the kitchen done. It's very modern.'

'It makes life a lot easier now we're both getting on. The old one was so inconvenient. We've had the bathroom done too, with a walk-in shower.'

Lizzie wondered what Cynthia's reaction would be to the kitchen at The Sycamores and smiled to herself. She picked up the tray and went to join her father.

The new conservatory was bright and airy with colourful cushions on the cane furniture. It overlooked the back garden which was now a huge expanse of lawn, neatly trimmed without a flower in sight. The fruit trees had gone along with her mother's herb bed and kitchen garden. At the sight of it Lizzie felt her anger rise but she bit back the comment that sprang to her lips and put the tray down on the coffee table. Her father patted the seat beside him.

'Come and sit down, Lizzie. It's so lovely to see you.' He took her hand. 'I'm sorry things have been so bad between us but I'd like to leave all that in the past. Cynthia has promised to make more of an effort to get along with you. Do you think you could meet her half-way? I know how much you miss Mum, and so do I, but Cynthia and I suit each other very well.'

'I know, Dad, and I will make more effort, I promise. And I'll come and visit more often.'

'I know you hate what we've done to the garden but it was getting too much for us. Cynthia's no gardener like your mother was. We have a chap comes now and he can mow the whole lot in just under an hour on the ride-on mower. We have to adapt to our old age; it comes to us all unfortunately.'

Lizzie felt tears pricking behind her eyelids. She squeezed her father's hand. 'It's all right, Dad, let's make this a new start for us all. I'm so glad we've cleared the air.'

'You are happy with your new man, aren't you?'

'Yes I am, but I miss England dreadfully. Ormerey's a beautiful island but so foreign in many ways. You wouldn't believe how primitive some things are.'

Her father laughed. At that moment Cynthia arrived bearing a homemade ginger cake. 'Everything all right in here?'

Her husband beamed at her. 'Yes, come and sit down, dear. We're gasping for a cuppa, aren't we Lizzie?'

'We are,' said Lizzie, 'and that cake looks delicious.' She smiled at her step-mother. 'Dad and I have had a chat; everything's sorted now.'

The afternoon passed pleasantly. Lizzie admired the new bathroom, feeling a slight stab of envy. She doubted whether Raoul would ever consider updating the ancient bathroom at The Sycamores.

When it was time for her to leave Lizzie hugged her father and much to her surprise Cynthia opened her arms for a hug too. 'Come and see us again soon, dear.'

'I will,' Lizzie promised. She was so glad she had come.

* * *

Francesca was surprised to receive a written invitation to the April meeting of the Ormerey Ladies' Guild. She showed it to Raoul.

'They've obviously missed you.'

'Missed my cakes more like!' snorted Francesca. 'Look what Jean's written across the bottom.'

Raoul took the card from her and read out loud. 'Please bring your friend Elizabeth Bayley but not your dog. Jean Yorke.'

They both laughed. 'You should go; it's an olive branch,' said Raoul. 'Pity Lizzie's away.'

'I'll give it a try and if it's OK Lizzie can come with me in May – if she wants to.'

Jean, Josie and Emily had sent out several invitations and waited in anticipation to see who turned up to the meeting. They were pleasantly surprised.

'It's a good turnout,' said Jean. 'Quite a few new faces, including Natasha. She's never graced us with her presence before.'

'Well, she's usually working,' said Emily. 'Here's Francesca. I'm so pleased.' Her face fell. 'There's no sign of Lizzie.'

Francesca bustled in bearing a large chocolate cake.

'Thank you, dear.' Jean took the cake and placed it on the trestle table. She was determined to be friendly towards Francesca who had always been a popular member of the group. She had not forgotten her humiliation in court but agreed with her friends that it was best to let bygones be bygones. 'No Elizabeth?' she asked.

'She's in England,' said Francesca.

'Best place for her if you ask me!' Alison Soames glided up and fixed Francesca with a stare. 'Good riddance!'

'Nobody did ask you, Alison,' said Jean tartly. 'We don't want any unpleasantness. This is a new beginning for the Ormerey Ladies Guild.'

Francesca smirked at Alison.

'To business now, ladies.' Jean ushered everyone to their seats. 'We'll have our refreshments later.'

Jean's proposals to reorganise the Guild were accepted enthusiastically. Several women felt it was time for the Guild to have a proper structure rather than just being an excuse for a coffee morning. A committee of six was elected and most agreed that, since Jean had set up the group originally, she should be the chairwoman. She was delighted.

'That's a relief!' Josie whispered to Emily. 'She'd have been impossible to live with otherwise.'

Josie was elected secretary and Emily agreed, rather shyly, to be the group's treasurer.

Francesca nudged her neighbour. 'The three stalwarts!'

It was decided that each member should pay an annual subscription of twenty pounds, and fund raising events would be held every so often to raise money for trips or speakers, any surplus to be given to local charities.

'All in all, a very successful meeting,' Jean remarked in conclusion.

The ladies tucked into Francesca's chocolate cake and other home-made offerings while they discussed holding a jumble sale in aid of the RNLI.

'I'm so glad you've decided to come back to us, Francesca.' Josie caught Francesca's arm as she was about to leave. 'Do try to persuade Elizabeth to come with you next time, won't you?'

'I'll do my best, Josie.'

'Well, if that woman joins I definitely won't be coming anymore.' Alison Soames, deliberately hovering within earshot, glared at them both.

'What on earth have you got against Lizzie?' said Francesca, annoyed. 'What has she ever done to upset you?'

'She doesn't belong here. She's too stuck up; she doesn't fit in. Raoul would do so much better married to a local woman instead of shacking up with an outsider. The locals should stick to their own.'

'You should keep your bigoted opinions to yourself,' snapped Francesca, her temper flaring up.

Josie stepped in quickly. 'Francesca's right, Alison. Your bigotry and spite do not belong at the Ladies' Guild. It would be best for everyone if you did not come any more.'

Alison stared at her, open-mouthed, eyes bulging, completely lost for words. *She looks like a goldfish*, Francesca thought and struggled not to giggle, her anger dissipated by her amusement.

'I'll make sure Lizzie comes next time,' she said to Josie.

Scowling furiously, Alison pushed past them and headed for the door.

'She'll be no loss, you know', Josie said thoughtfully. 'She's the main conduit for information getting to the Clerk. She listens to the gossip and passes it on. Good riddance to her.'

Chapter 20

Raoul stood in the kitchen, staring moodily out of the window, while he waited for the kettle to boil for his first cup of coffee of the day. There was a sudden knocking on the front door. Swearing under his breath, he turned the gas off and padded through the hall in his bare feet. He opened the door and came face to face with his cousin Felicity.

'Good heavens, Raoul! Aren't you up yet?' She breezed past him into the hall and made straight for the kitchen, leaving a strong waft of lily-in-the-valley in her wake. 'I could murder a coffee!'

Raoul followed her and re-lit the gas under the kettle. 'Sorry about the mess,' he said tersely.

Felicity sat down at the kitchen table and looked disapprovingly at the piles of unwashed crockery in the sink and on the draining board. 'Where's Lizzie? Still in bed?'

'She's gone to England for a visit.'

'Oh! When's she due back?'

'She was coming back today but she phoned last night to say that she's changed her flight and staying over there for another week, maybe two.' Raoul made the coffee and sat down, pushing one of the mugs towards his cousin.

A look of concern appeared on Felicity's immaculately made-up face. 'She is coming back, is she Raoul? You don't think she'll decide to stay in England?'

'Of course not!' snapped Raoul. 'Anyway, what are you doing turning up unannounced at this ungodly hour? Have you left Julian?'

'Touché!' She smiled suddenly. 'Julian's playing in a bowls match against the Ormerey team. He's gone straight there; it starts at nine. We had to get the early flight. I thought I could spend the day with you and Lizzie. I'm sorry I've missed her.'

'You should have rung. Aren't you seeing Joe and Kate?'

'They've all gone to Guernsey for a week to stay with William and Rosemary. We've seen quite a lot of them while they've been over.'

'That's nice. I wish you'd let me know you were coming, Felicity. You've really caught me on the hop; this kitchen's a tip.'

She looked at him. He had kept the house immaculate when his father was alive. 'I expect you've got used to Lizzie looking after you.'

Raoul sighed. 'I hate it when she's not here; I can't seem to make the effort.'

'Never mind. You go and get yourself organised while I clear up a bit in here.' She found Lizzie's rubber gloves and put them on. 'And have a shave,' she called after him as he left the room, 'then I'll treat you to a slap-up breakfast in the Rock.'

He turned and grinned at her sheepishly. 'I'm so glad you've come.'

Raoul rummaged through his wardrobe looking for something smart to wear. He could not possibly go out with Felicity in his scruffy working clothes. She, as usual, looked immaculate in crisp beige slacks and a pale turquoise cashmere twinset. He found a new pair of jeans which he'd never worn, a checked flannel shirt and his moleskin waistcoat.

Felicity beamed her approval when he reappeared in the kitchen. 'You do look nice.'

'Well, it's not every day my cousin honours me with a visit. You've done an amazing job in here.' He surveyed the tidy room; the crockery washed, dried and piled neatly on the table ready to put away.

'I've left everything out; I don't know where it lives.' She peeled off the rubber gloves. 'I've given the sink a good clean as well.'

'Thanks, you are a brick.'

'I'll just pop up to the bathroom for a minute.' Felicity climbed the stairs, admiring the familiar landscapes on the wall and savouring the smell of the old Axminster carpet which evoked so many childhood memories.

Ten minutes later she re-joined Raoul. He helped her into her jacket. 'You've been ages,' he grumbled. 'I'm starving!'

'I was just exploring the house. I love that little office in the back bedroom.'

'That's Lizzie's domain. She deals with all my paperwork.'

'She keeps a lovely clean home,' said Felicity approvingly. 'I love this house.' She tucked her arm through his as they walked down Main Street. 'I had such happy holidays staying here with Granny and Grandpa. Do you remember?'

Raoul did remember; bossy Felicity always ordering him and Francesca about. She had been insufferable. 'I remember you pushing me off that raft we made,' he said. 'I could have drowned in that pool, it was quite deep.'

'Nonsense! Frankie fished you out! I remember her slapping me. She always did have a temper.'

'It served you right!'

'How is Frankie these days?'

'She's fine. She still has her fiery moments!'

Felicity snorted. She had never cared for Francesca who had always sided with Raoul, leaving her the odd one out. They were still bickering amiably when they reached the Rock Café. Heads turned as they entered. Raoul ordered coffee and full English breakfasts.

'I could eat a horse,' said Felicity. 'What is it about the Ormerey air that makes one so hungry?'

'Do you want to sit outside?'

'It's a bit chilly. I'd rather stay in.' They sat down and the breakfasts arrived almost immediately.

'Will you look at that?' Emily Platt was having coffee with Josie at a corner table at the back of the room. 'No sooner is Lizzie's back turned than Raoul is entertaining another woman; and a very glamorous one at that!'

She frowned disapprovingly and Josie laughed. 'That's Felicity Rockdale, Joe the plumber's mother. She and Raoul are first cousins.'

'Are you sure?'

'Of course I'm sure! I remember her from James St Arnaud's funeral. Can't you see the family likeness?'

Emily stared at Felicity. Several other diners were doing the same.

'We're the subjects of island gossip!' said Felicity. 'Everyone's looking at us.'

'Ignore them, they've nothing better to do.'

Josie stopped by their table as she and Emily left the café. 'Good morning to you both.' She smiled and turned to Raoul. 'When can we expect to see Elizabeth back among us?'

'Very soon,' said Raoul.

'How are you, Mrs Rockdale?'

'I'm very well, thank you.' Felicity waited until Josie had gone before whispering in Raoul's ear. 'Who on earth was that?'

'Josie Cleghorn. You met her at Father's funeral. She was one of Lizzie's *bête noires* but they seem to be building bridges.'

'Are there many *bête noires*?'

'A few!' Raoul laughed. 'She's learning to take them in her stride but I don't think she'll ever be on friendly terms with Prunella.'

'That ghastly woman in the Ormerey Supermart? Is she still there? It can't be easy for Lizzie trying to fit in here. I'm glad she makes you so happy, Raoul. Let's go for a walk along the common. It's turning into a glorious day.'

'Have you arranged to meet Julian for lunch?'

'No, he'll be at the bowls club all day. I'm meeting him back at the airport for the flight home. We're booked on the last one. I'm free all day.'

'I'll treat you to lunch at the Imperial,' said Raoul. 'That will give Daphne Warrington something to think about!'

'She won't be fazed; she knows who I am!'

Felicity paid for the meal and they headed out into the sunshine. They walked across Main Square and turned into Valmont Road. The air was full of birdsong. They passed the small granite cottages with their front gardens full of flowers and walked down the steep hill. As they approached the harbour the roadside verges were white with the dainty bells of three-cornered garlic. Felicity picked a flower and sniffed the strong onion smell. A couple of red-faced cyclists puffed past them on their way up the hill.

'The tourist season's started,' said Felicity, 'funny how the English visitors are instantly recognisable. They don't stand out so much in Guernsey.'

It was breezy on the common. The wind ruffled Felicity's blonde curls and she took deep breaths of the salt-laden air. The sea, aquamarine against the paler blue of the sky, was flecked with white horses.

'It's so quiet here after the hustle and bustle of Guernsey,' said Felicity, 'so peaceful.'

'You and Julian should come for a holiday. It would be nice for the four of us to get together more often.' Raoul was surprised to discover that he meant it.

* * *

Lizzie arrived back on Ormerey on a bright blustery afternoon at the end of April. She had been away for three weeks. The bracing island air hit her like the fizz of champagne as soon as the aircraft door was opened.

'Welcome back, Lizzie,' said the tall fair young man who helped her off the plane. 'Good trip?'

'Yes. Thank you, Paul.' She smiled at him, warmed by his friendly greeting. Perhaps the locals are getting used to me, she thought.

Raoul was waiting for her in the arrivals hall, looking smart in a crisp shirt and his new jeans. He enfolded Lizzie in his arms and kissed her. 'I've missed you, Lizzie. I'm so glad you've come back.'

She looked up at him. 'Of course I've come back. Did you think I wouldn't?'

'Well, I was beginning to wonder. You've been away so long.' He held her tightly. 'I was afraid you might decide to stay in England.'

'Oh Raoul! I do need to go to England from time to time. It doesn't mean I don't love you. I've missed you too.'

He smiled down at her. 'Come on, let's go home. I'll take you the long way so you can see the island.'

They turned left along the airport road towards the west of the island. Raoul stopped the pick-up on the hill overlooking Fort Jackson and Rocky Bay. The tide was right out and the sea seemed a long way away across the vast expanse of rocks and seaweed. Gulls wheeled and soared against the blue sky, the sun glinting on their wings. The smell of the sea filled Lizzie's nostrils and she took a deep breath. 'It's nice to be back, the countryside is lovely but I've missed the sea.'

Raoul squeezed her hand. 'One day Ormerey, not England, will seem like home. Now you've made things up with your father and Cynthia I'm sure you'll find it easier to settle.'

'Yes, I'm sure I shall, but I have promised to visit more often.'

They drove slowly down the long hill to where the road levelled out near the beach. Gulls and oystercatchers were picking about amongst the rocks and seaweed. Raoul found the binoculars and looked through them. 'There are turnstones out there, so well camouflaged it's hard to spot them. See that movement over there? That's where they are, look.'

He handed the binoculars to Lizzie and she watched the turnstones for a few moments. The road continued at sea level around Saline Bay where the coarse sand was piled up high against the dunes. The tank traps were almost buried; only the rusty tips of the metal arms were visible.

'Why don't the States get rid of those horrible things, and all the German barbed wire that's lying about?' asked Lizzie.

'It's forty five years since the war ended. Parts of the island are such a mess.'

'There was so much cleaning up to be done when we came back after the evacuation. All the mines had to be cleared. Now all the bits that are left are tourist attractions. You'd be surprised how many people come over here to see them and explore the bunkers and fortifications.'

They drove on past Fort Juno, another of the Napoleonic forts built by the British to protect Ormerey from a French invasion. This fort was a ruin, battered by the winter storms and gales blowing in from the north. To the east of it lay Breezy Bay which lived up to its name, and farther along Beaumont Bay with its broad stretch of sandy beach popular with surfers and holiday makers. It was bordered at its eastern end by a chain of rocks and the lighthouse.

The road swept on round the eastern end of the island and, instead of taking the quickest route back into town, Raoul drove to the harbour with its myriad of colourful boats bobbing up and down in the sheltered haven. As they passed the Imperial Hotel they saw Natasha and Geoff Prosser leaving through the main entrance.

'Natasha and Geoff are going out together. Did you know?' Raoul turned to Lizzie and raised his eyebrows.

'No! I thought he and Janine Briggs were an item.'

'They may have been for a while but Janine has set her sights on handsome Hugo and now she's going out with him. You shouldn't stay away so long, Lizzie, you miss all the gossip.'

'So it would appear.' Lizzie was delighted for Natasha; she couldn't wait to meet up with her and hear the whole story.

'What else have I missed?'

'According to Frankie, Jean Yorke has re-vamped the Ormerey Ladies Guild. You've been invited to their next meeting.'

'Good heavens!'

'I thought you'd be surprised.' Raoul drove slowly up Valmont Road towards town.

'Did you manage to get your bunker sorted out?' Lizzie asked.

'No.' Raoul looked sheepish. 'I expect it's still wet in there. I'll do it in the summer.' He omitted to tell Lizzie that he had not even been to look at it.

Lizzie was still smiling to herself as they drove up Main Street. They had no sooner got home when Francesca appeared. Zapp hurled himself at Lizzie, nearly knocking her over with his ecstatic welcome.

'Hello, Zapp! Are you pleased to see me?'

Francesca gave her a hug. 'Welcome home!' She nodded towards Raoul. 'He's been like a bear with a sore head while you've been away.'

'I have not!' said Raoul indignantly.

'He's practically lived round at my place,' Francesca went on, 'which hasn't helped my love life one bit!'

'How are things with you and Theo? Get down, Zapp, that's enough now.'

'Really good.' Francesca beamed at Lizzie. 'I've brought you a beef casserole to save you cooking tonight.'

'Thank you Frankie, you are thoughtful. Will you stay and share it with us?'

'No love, I won't play gooseberry! I'll leave you two to have an early night!' She winked at Lizzie. 'See you both tomorrow.'

* * *

Prunella had spent the whole morning hovering by the entrance of the Ormerey Supermart hoping to catch Lizzie as she emerged from the front door of The Sycamores. She had a long and frustrating wait. Lizzie spent her first morning back on the island going through the huge pile of post which had accumulated during her absence. It was nearly mid-day when she was finally ready to go shopping.

Prunella darted across the road as soon as she saw Lizzie and grabbed her by the arm. 'There's something you need to know,' she said smugly, a glint of triumph in her pale protruding eyes.

'Let go of me!' Lizzie shook herself free angrily. 'I'm not interested in anything you may have to say, Prunella.'

'Oh, you'll be interested in this all right so you can just listen to me, you snotty cow! While you've been away Raoul's been seeing another woman.'

Lizzie burst out laughing. Prunella was disconcerted, but only for a moment. She quickly launched herself into another attack.

'You can laugh! He was seen canoodling in the Rock Café with a very sophisticated looking blonde woman, and he was seen having lunch with her at the Imperial. He then took her back into his house with him. I saw that with my own eyes; it was ages before they came back out. What do you make of that, Lizzie Bayley?'

'Not a lot,' said Lizzie calmly.

Prunella stared at her. 'I am surprised. Why don't you ask your saintly Raoul who he's been playing away with behind your back, or don't you want to know?'

Lizzie stared back coldly. 'I can only assume you are talking about Raoul's cousin Felicity. She was over from Guernsey. I'm surprised you didn't know that, Prunella. After all, you are local; I thought you knew everything. Now please excuse me, I've some shopping to do.' She left Prunella open-mouthed on the pavement and headed up the street to Hugo's Emporium.

The whole exchange had been witnessed by the Supermart staff huddled in the shop doorway. 'That's one up to Lizzie,' said Julie.

'Huh!' sniffed Pauline, 'that means Pru will be in a foul mood for the rest of the day.'

* * *

Lizzie met up with Natasha at the Rock Café the following Tuesday morning. It was a beautiful day and they sat outside on the terrace, surrounded by tubs of red and yellow tulips under planted with forget-me-nots.

Josie and Emily passed their table on their way into the café for their usual morning gossip. 'It's very nice to see you back with us, Elizabeth.' Josie beamed at the two younger women. 'Did you enjoy your holiday?'

'Very much, thank you. It's nice to be back.'

'Splendid! I do hope you will join the Ormerey Ladies' Guild. You too Natasha; it was nice to see you at our last meeting.'

'We'll be there,' they replied in unison and exchanged smiles as Josie left them to join Emily inside.

'It looks as though I've finally arrived!' said Lizzie. 'The Ormerey Ladies' Guild no less!' She giggled.

'It's good to have you back, Lizzie. You have been missed, you know, and not just by Raoul.'

Lizzie felt tears pricking at the back of her eyelids. 'I'm surprised at how welcoming people have been. I'm beginning to feel more at home here at last.'

'That's good to hear.' Natasha smiled. 'I'll go and chivvy them up about the coffee; I think they've forgotten us out here.'

'Tell me all your news,' Lizzie said on her return. 'You're looking very pleased with yourself so I'm assuming it's true about you and Geoff?'

'Oh Lizzie, I can't believe it!' Her face glowed and Lizzie thought how lovely she looked, her dark curls tumbling around her shoulders and her green eyes shining.

'I thought he was dating Janine.'

'So did I.' The coffee arrived and Natasha continued. 'I was so jealous and miserable. Geoff's very friendly towards everyone but I've never known him to date anyone before so I thought it must be serious.'

'It obviously wasn't; it didn't last very long.'

Natasha laughed. 'As soon as Janine clapped eyes on my brother she made a beeline for him. Geoff was dumped without a backward glance.'

'And then you stepped in to pick up the pieces?'

Natasha blushed and fiddled with her teaspoon. 'Well yes, sort of. He came into the hotel bar looking very down in the dumps so I asked him if he'd like to have a drink with me to cheer him up.'

'And?'

'He had several drinks and got more and more miserable. Then he said "You're a beautiful woman, Natasha, I've fancied you for years. It's such a pity you're out of my league". I was so surprised. I told him he was an idiot and I'd absolutely love to go out with him. So now we're dating and it's wonderful.'

'I'm so pleased for you both.'

'Geoff really liked Janine but as soon as she found out Hugo was single she was off. She obviously wasn't committed to the relationship.' Natasha rolled her eyes. 'Hugo's very smitten. I hope it doesn't all end in tears.'

'What do your parents think about you going out with Geoff?'

'I don't think they've twigged yet; they haven't said anything. Hugo's always been the blue-eyed boy and now he's back on the island he's the focus of their attention, and they're very taken up with Father's role as President. Mother's even more impossible than usual.'

'What do they think of Janine?'

'They thoroughly approve of her. She's attractive, clever and from the right social background; posh enough to be a Warrington.'

They both laughed again. Raoul stepped up on to the terrace. 'May I join you?'

They both nodded, still giggling.

'What's the joke?'

'Hugo's going out with Janine Briggs,' said Lizzie, pulling up a chair for him.

'And that's funny? I'll never understand the female sense of humour!' Raoul ordered a coffee and sat down. He turned to Natasha. 'I trust things are going well with you and Geoff?'

'Yes thank you, I haven't been this happy for a long time.'

'I'm so glad,' said Raoul, 'I'm really pleased for you both.'

Chapter 21

It was a glorious May morning. Lizzie woke to a chorus of birdsong and lay listening for a few moments until the sound of a lorry rumbling over the cobbles broke the spell. Raoul was still asleep. She climbed out of bed, slipped into her dressing-gown and went downstairs. She made a mug of coffee and took it outside into the back garden.

The grass was heavy with dew, and the clean fresh smell of early morning, flavoured with a tang of the sea, filled her nostrils. She took a deep breath. A wood pigeon cooed somewhere in the depths of the apple tree and after a few moments she spotted him; the soft colours of his plumage blending perfectly with the grey bark and pink blossom. Far away she could hear the clear notes of a cuckoo. She stood on the patio and finished her coffee, feeling happy and relaxed in the beauty of the early morning.

As she made her way back to the kitchen, a young man with dark hair and wearing blue overalls and heavy working boots came into the yard. Lizzie recognised him as one of Joshua Ford's men; she had seen him on the site at Yaffingales.

'Mrs Bayley, I'm sorry to bother you.' He was flustered, the words tumbling over themselves. 'I found Mrs Brockenshaw up on the cliffs. Someone's killed her dogs. She's dreadfully upset. She asked me to bring her here; I do hope that's all right.'

Lizzie stared at him in horror. 'Killed the dogs?'

'Yes, shot them both! She wanted to come here to you; her husband's in Guernsey.'

'Of course, where is she now?'

'In my van. It's parked out front.'

'I'll go and open the front door. Bring her in that way, it'll be quicker.'

He disappeared into the street and Lizzie rushed to unlock the front door, calling up the stairs to Raoul as she did so.

Ruth Brockenshaw, white faced and trembling, her Barbour jacket drenched in blood, stumbled over the threshold helped by the young builder who threw Lizzie a relieved look. 'I'll go straight away and tell the boss what's happened.'

Lizzie gently eased Ruth out of her coat, led her into the sitting room and sat her down on the settee. 'What a dreadful thing to happen. We must phone the police. Let me make you a cup of tea for the shock.' Lizzie found herself babbling, not knowing what to say to the distraught woman who was staring into space with a dazed expression on her face.

Raoul appeared in the doorway wearing his pyjamas.

'What on earth's going on?' He took one look at Ruth and went to the sideboard. 'I think a brandy's called for.'

'Someone's shot both Ruth's dogs. Can you phone the police?'

'Good God!' He handed the brandy to Lizzie. 'I'll do it right away.'

Lizzie sat down next to Ruth and put her arm round her. 'Drink this, Ruth.'

Ruth drank the brandy, spluttered and began to cry, huge sobs shaking her body. Lizzie continued to hold her.

Raoul poked his head round the door. 'I've phoned the police. There's no one at the Police Station, I guess it's still too early. I've left a message for them to come straight round here. I'm going up to get dressed. Are you OK for a minute?'

Lizzie nodded dumbly. Raoul went upstairs and threw some clothes on, not bothering to shave. A few moments later he was back in the sitting room. He knelt on the floor in front of Ruth and took both her hands in his. Lizzie still had her arm round Ruth and he noticed that she was weeping too. 'Try to tell us what happened, Ruth,' he said gently.

Ruth took a deep shuddering breath and looked at Raoul. 'I was walking along the cliff path towards Yaffingales. The dogs were running ahead of me. I heard this terrific bang and Storm just dropped down. He'd been shot through the head. I knew he was dead.' She took another deep breath and reached for a fresh tissue. 'I thought it must have been an accident; someone shooting rabbits. Then there was another shot and Blizzard was hit. It was awful; he was lying on his side whimpering and trying to get up. I held him in my arms. I just couldn't think what to do. I held him while he died.' She broke into fresh sobbing.

'Is that when Barry found you?' said Lizzie.

'Yes, he'd heard the shots from the Portacabin. He came to investigate and he brought me straight here.'

'Where's Simon?' Raoul got to his feet.

'In Guernsey. He's due back on the lunch time flight.'

'Do you think we can get hold of him before then? He ought to be told about this right away.'

'He's staying at Moore's,' said Ruth. 'You could leave a message there; he won't have gone out yet.'

'OK. I'll ask him to ring me as soon as he can. In the meantime I'll make us all a coffee.' He went through to the kitchen and put the kettle on.

Ruth was weeping quietly on Lizzie's shoulder. They both jumped as a loud knocking on the front door reverberated through the house. 'That'll be the police,' said Lizzie, 'they were quick getting here.'

It was not the police. Lizzie opened the door to Joshua Ford, who was white faced with anger. 'Barry and I have put the dogs in the Portacabin. The police will need to examine them.' He followed Lizzie into the sitting room, sat down next to Ruth and took her hand. 'I can't believe this has happened. Did you see anyone?'

'No one at all. They must have been in the bushes.'

Raoul came back into the room with three mugs of coffee and a sugar basin. He set the tray down on the low coffee table and greeted Joshua. 'Bad business this.'

'Yes,' agreed Joshua. 'You've informed the police I take it?'

'A few minutes ago.' He looked at his watch. 'It's only 8.15.' He turned to Lizzie. 'You'd better get dressed, love.'

Lizzie had forgotten she was still in her dressing gown. She ran upstairs quickly. Raoul handed coffee to Ruth and Joshua and took the remaining mug himself. Before he had time to swallow a mouthful the phone rang. It was Simon. Raoul explained what had happened. There was silence on the end of the line, then Simon spoke.

'Both dogs were shot? There's not been a mistake?'

'I'm afraid not. I'm so sorry, Simon, it's a hellish thing to happen. Try not to worry about Ruth; we'll look after her till you get back.'

'Poor Ruth, those dogs were like children to her. How could anyone do such a horrible thing to innocent animals? It's barbaric.'

'You're telling me! I'll meet you at the airport at one. OK?'

'Thanks, Raoul. See you then.'

Raoul replaced the receiver and at that same moment there was a loud knocking on the front door. He opened it to find Constable Derek Peasgood looking flushed and agitated.

'I came as soon as I got your message,' the Constable said.

'Where's Sergeant Green?' Raoul held the door open.

'It's his day off. There's just me, I'm afraid.'

'Bloody typical!' Raoul muttered under his breath. 'You'd better come on through, we're all in the living room. Mrs Brockenshaw's very upset.'

Derek Peasgood followed Raoul into the living room and perched himself on the edge of an easy chair. He looked uncomfortable at the sight of the two weeping women and took out his notebook.

'Could you please tell me exactly what happened, Mrs Brockenshaw? I shall need as much detail as you can give me.'

Ruth sat up straight, blew her nose hard and related her story once again.

'And you're sure there were no witnesses to the incident?' Peasgood was writing in his notebook.

'I didn't see anyone at all.'

'Right. I've got everything down and will write up a full report when I get back to the station. In the meantime I shall go and examine the dogs. They will need to be taken to the vet's to have the bullets extracted. We need to know what type of gun was used.'

'The bangs were very loud,' said Ruth. 'It wasn't an air rifle.'

'Thank you, Mrs Brockenshaw. Rest assured I shall do everything I can.' He turned to Joshua. 'Could you accompany me to the site now to see the dogs? We need to get them to the vet's surgery. Perhaps someone could ring the vet and warn him?'

'I'll do that,' said Raoul. He was impressed by the young Constable's efficiency. 'I do hope your Sergeant will take this incident seriously and not brush it under the carpet as he does with so many things.'

Peasgood flushed crimson. 'I shall endeavour to do my best, Sir,' he said as Raoul showed him and Joshua to the door.

* * *

'Oh dear,' sighed Lizzie munching on a piece of toast and marmalade. 'I'm not sure I want to go to the Ormerey Ladies' Guild after all. I wish now I'd never said I'd go.'

'Of course you must go,' said Raoul. 'You promised Frankie. What are you worried about?'

'It's not really my thing, and so many of those women disapprove of me. I can see it in their faces. Look what happened at the Fords' Christmas party. A lot of those same people go to the Ormerey Ladies' Guild.'

'Lizzie!' Raoul leaned forward across the table and put a hand on her arm. 'If you want to be truly accepted here you must make an effort to join in.'

She looked at him mutinously.

'Just face these people up,' Raoul continued. 'Show them you don't care what they think. You'll have Frankie there for moral support. You might even find you enjoy it.' He grinned mischievously. 'After all, you didn't like Josie Cleghorn to begin with and now you're the best of friends.'

'Hardly!' retorted Lizzie. 'She's all right but she's very opinionated. I don't consider her to be a best friend! Besides, she's got her own little clique, Jean Yorke and Emily Platt. Natasha calls them the three witches.'

'She thinks very well of you. When you were away she told me what a nice woman you are and how lucky I am to have you.'

'Really?' Lizzie gaped at him.

'Yes, really! So off you go and have a nice time. I'll clear up in here.'

'Oh, all right, thanks.' Lizzie gave him a peck on the cheek and headed for the door.

'Lizzie!' he called after her.

She turned round.

'You look very nice, love. That blue really suits you.'

Lizzie looked down at her new royal blue polo-neck sweater which she was wearing with white slacks. 'Thank you Raoul, you are sweet.' She came back into the room and put her arms round him. She kissed him full on the mouth; he tasted of marmalade. 'Do you think I look posh enough for the Ormerey Ladies' Guild?'

'Definitely,' he said. 'You'll knock 'em dead!'

Francesca was waiting in the square for Lizzie. 'The whole island's buzzing with the news about the Brockenshaws' dogs. Isn't it appalling? Do you know how Ruth is?'

'We haven't seen them since the day it happened. I told Ruth to ring or come round anytime they wanted but we haven't heard from them, and we don't like to intrude.'

'No one's seen them apparently; it looks as though they're keeping a low profile and who can blame them? I gather the police have got absolutely nowhere with finding out who's responsible.'

'Raoul says they'll probably never find out. Lots of people have guns and not all of them have gun licences. Someone must know something but there will be the usual island cover-up – that's what he thinks anyway.'

'He's probably right,' said Francesca. 'Come on, we'd better be going inside.' She tucked her arm through Lizzie's and they made their way into the Island Hall.

Lizzie was relieved to see that Francesca had not dressed up. She was wearing her usual outfit of skirt, floral blouse and navy cardigan with casual shoes. Lizzie noticed her smart navy handbag. 'That's nice! Is it new?'

Francesca opened the bag to show Lizzie the bright red interior fitted with numerous pockets. 'Theo and I went to Guernsey for the day. He wanted a new camera from Grut's. We had a slap-up lunch at Creaseys' and I bought this in their sale. My old one's falling to pieces. We had a wonderful day.' She sighed. 'It sounds awful to say it when the Brockenshaws are so devastated but I can't remember when I was so happy.'

'It's not awful, you have every right to be happy, Frankie. You deserve it.'

The Pierre Rachelle room was crowded and noisy with people milling around chatting. Natasha caught sight of Lizzie and hurried over to her. 'I'm so glad you've come. May I sit with you two?' They found themselves three chairs on the back row and sat down together. Jean Yorke clapped her hands loudly and called the meeting to order. The ladies scrambled for chairs.

'Good morning.' Jean took up her customary position seated behind the trestle table at the end of the room, flanked by Josie and Emily. 'I'm delighted to see so many new faces. I do hope you will consider formally joining the Ormerey Ladies Guild. Josie has the membership forms.'

Josie waved a sheaf of papers in the air.

'It's all got very official,' Francesca whispered to Lizzie. 'Shall we join?'

'I'm going to wait until the end before I decide,' said Lizzie.

The forthcoming jumble sale in aid of the RNLI was discussed. Jean asked for cakes and raffle prizes. Francesca nudged Lizzie. 'Go on, make a cake.'

'What!' Lizzie looked horrified. 'My baking isn't up to your standard.'

'It doesn't have to be,' said Natasha, 'no one's up to Francesca's standard.'

Lizzie reluctantly put her hand up and was rewarded with a beaming smile from Jean. Francesca giggled. 'There's no escape now!'

Over coffee and refreshments the sole topic of conversation was the shooting of the Brockenshaws' Dalmatians. Even those who opposed the building of the new hotel were horrified by what had happened and expressed sympathy for Ruth and Simon. The lack of police progress was discussed indignantly and at length.

Lizzie found herself the centre of attention as it had become common knowledge that it was Raoul and herself who had cared for Ruth on that dreadful morning. She was inundated with questions to which she gave brief non-committal answers, not wanting to gossip about the

Brockenshaws' misfortune. In the general hubbub she and Francesca forgot to collect membership forms from Josie who rushed after them as they eventually managed to extricate themselves from the melee.

'Don't forget these,' Josie panted, out of breath. 'You can fill them in at home and let me have them later.'

'Thank you,' said Francesca. 'At least you've met some new people,' she said to Lizzie as they left the Island Hall with Natasha who had also been press-ganged into accepting a membership form.

Geoff was waiting for Natasha on the terrace outside the Rock Café. She ran up to him and they embraced.

'That looks to be going well,' said Francesca.

'It is,' said Lizzie. 'You can tell it's spring; there's so much romance in the air.'

Francesca gave her a very smug smile.

* * *

'We've been invited to the Brockenshaws for coffee.' Raoul poked his head round the door of Lizzie's office.

'Today?'

'Yes, this morning; Simon's just phoned. He sounded fraught. I think we ought to go.'

'OK. Give me five minutes to finish up here.'

A soft drizzle was falling as they drove down Valmont Road and turned into the lane leading to Seagulls Rest. Simon was waiting for them at the front door. He gave them a tight little smile.

'Thank you so much for coming. There's something we need to tell you.'

Raoul and Lizzie exchanged glances as Simon ushered them into the hall. Ruth appeared in the kitchen doorway and Lizzie was shocked to see how pale and drawn she looked.

'I do hope you don't mind having coffee in the kitchen. I can't bear going into the sitting room or the conservatory; it's the sight of those empty sofas.' She was fighting back tears.

'Of course we don't mind,' said Lizzie giving her a peck on the cheek. 'We've been worried about you, Ruth. No one's seen you since it happened.'

'I haven't been out. I can't face seeing people.' She led them into the kitchen where the smell of fresh coffee went a small way to cheering the atmosphere. She poured the coffee and they all sat down at the pine table in the centre of the large kitchen with its gleaming appliances and the bright red Aga. A wide picture window looked out over the garden to the sea beyond, the view obscured today by the quietly falling drizzle. A hopeful looking herring gull sat on the window sill and tapped its beak on the glass. Normally a source of entertainment, it was ignored by everyone in the room and shook its feathers huffily before flying off.

'You tell them, Simon.' Ruth sat with hunched shoulders, her hands wrapped around her coffee mug.

'What?' asked Lizzie. 'Have the police found out who did it?'

'Not that we've heard. To be perfectly honest we don't really care who did it. It's the fact that it's been done that makes us both so sick at heart. We've had enough of this bloody island. We're selling up and leaving.'

'Oh no!' Lizzie's gasp was involuntary. She put her hand to her mouth.

'Yes,' said Ruth. 'Surely you understand?' She looked pleadingly at Raoul and Lizzie.

'Of course we understand.' Raoul sighed heavily. 'I don't blame you but I'm really sorry to hear it. There are times when I despair of this island and this is one of them. I feel ashamed.'

'Please don't,' said Ruth. 'You two have been good friends to us.' She paused. 'There are cruel and spiteful people everywhere. We just didn't expect it here. Visitors think Ormerey is such a warm friendly place, they love it.'

'They don't see what goes on underneath,' said Raoul. 'When will you go?'

'As soon as we can get organised.' Simon stood up and moved over to look out of the window. 'We're putting this place on the market, the Yaffingales site too. Ford's as sick as a parrot and I feel bad about that but we've had enough. I'll see he's not out of pocket. My advocates are sorting it all out.' He came back to the table and sat down again. 'I've arranged with a removals firm in Guernsey to ship all our stuff back to the UK and we'll stay in our Eastbourne hotel for the time being.'

'We're hoping to go in the next few days,' said Ruth. 'We can't get off the island soon enough.'

Chapter 22

The brutal slaughter of the Brockenshaws' beloved pets, coming so soon after her return from England, had thoroughly unsettled Lizzie. Her warm welcome back had gone some way towards alleviating the misgivings about her future that had beset her while she had been away. Now all her doubts resurfaced with a vengeance.

She had spent the last few nights tossing and turning, unable to sleep. While the soft salt-laden breeze ruffled the curtains and Raoul snored gently beside her, Lizzie turned her face into her pillow and wept. She wept for Ruth and Simon, for Blizzard and Storm and for herself, wracked by doubts and torn between her love for Raoul and the safe familiar things of home.

Now, back in her office at The Sycamores, looking out over the back garden where the fallen apple blossom carpeted the lawn like snow, she could see a thrush banging a snail on a rockery stone. It smashed the shell and gulped down the soft body. Lizzie had a sudden mental picture of Blizzard whimpering and bleeding in Ruth's arms. Her eyes filled with tears.

The office door was opened and Lizzie jumped. 'Sorry,' said Raoul, 'did I startle you? I wondered what you were doing. It's lunch time.'

'Is it?' Lizzie hastily pulled herself together. She had not discussed her recent misgivings with Raoul or anyone else on Ormerey; she did not want Raoul to worry. 'I haven't even thought about lunch yet. I was thinking about Ruth and Simon.'

'They're safely in Guernsey. Simon's just phoned. I'll just pop over the road and get something for lunch. What do you fancy?'

'Oh, anything; whatever you'd like. I'm not very hungry.'

Raoul looked at her. Normally she ate like a horse, and she would have expressed disgust about him patronising the Ormerey Supermart. He frowned. 'Are you all right?'

She smiled at him. 'I'm fine, just a bit tired that's all.'

In the shop Prunella was holding forth as usual. 'All their stuff has already gone,' she was saying to a rapt audience of holidaymakers and a few local women. 'Two containers left on this morning's boat. It won't be long before they've left Ormerey, and good riddance.'

Raoul rummaged in the freezer cabinet and extracted a cauliflower cheese dinner for two. He brushed a thick layer of ice crystals off it and checked the date before queuing up at the till.

'Well, Raoul! Fancy you gracing us with your presence,' Prunella said archly, batting her sandy eyelashes at him.

He ignored the comment. 'If you're talking about the Brockenshaws then they've already gone,' he said shortly and banged the cauliflower cheese down on the counter.

'Oh no, Raoul, you're quite wrong there. My Georgie would know if they'd left and he says…'

'Your Georgie's antennae are obviously malfunctioning,' said Raoul. There were titters from the onlookers. It was common knowledge amongst the islanders that George and Bertie Soames had a mole at the airport and another at the harbour who kept them informed about arrivals and departures.

Prunella glared, her pale eyes protruding even more than usual.

'They were picked up by boat before dawn and taken off the island. You should check your facts before you start spreading gossip. And while we're on the subject of gossip Prunella, I'd be obliged if you'd refrain from slandering my cousin. The Rockdales have some standing in Guernsey and they don't appreciate being the subject of malicious tittle-tattle.'

Conscious of the people listening, Prunella went red and spluttered. 'You've no right to come in here and speak to me like this when I'm working.' She eyed the cauliflower cheese. 'Is this all you want?'

'Yes,' said Raoul. 'You should watch that spiteful tongue of yours or one of these days you'll find yourself in court for slander.'

Lizzie was laying the table when he got home. He told her about his conversation with Prunella and was relieved to see her smile. 'It's worth going in there just to wind her up,' he chuckled.

* * *

Francesca's birthday was on the 9th May which was Liberation Day; bank holidays in both Guernsey and Jersey to celebrate the anniversary of the end of the war when the German occupying forces had surrendered to the British. It was a day of rejoicing in both islands where lavish celebrations were enjoyed by residents and visitors.

Liberation had come later to Ormerey on the 16th May when the British troops found an island devastated by war and devoid of its population; all but a few of its inhabitants had been evacuated in 1940.

To the on-going annoyance of Francesca and Raoul no celebrations were held on Ormerey. 'There was no one here to liberate,' was the view expressed by the majority of islanders and this was endorsed by the States.

'Of course the island was liberated,' Francesca said crossly to anyone who would listen. 'Otherwise we'd still be living under German rule. We should have our own Liberation celebrations.'

Six years previously, on the fortieth anniversary, Francesca had persuaded the head teacher of St Mark's School to give all the pupils a day's holiday on the 9th May so they could learn and appreciate what Liberation meant to the islands. Some parents took the opportunity of taking their children to Guernsey to experience the euphoric atmosphere and enjoy the fun fair.

This year Francesca had a day off on her birthday. She had parked Zapp with Raoul and Lizzie and been treated to a sumptuous lunch at the Imperial Hotel by Theo. Afterwards he had driven her up to the cliffs to enjoy a leisurely stroll among the spring flowers.

May was the month when Ormerey's floral display was at its finest, enticing naturalists from England to examine species that could not be found on the mainland. It was also the best month for birdwatchers; spring migrants flew in for a brief stop-over and summer visitors settled on the island to nest and raise their young.

Francesca and Theo sat on a lichen covered granite boulder and watched a buzzard flying lazily into the valley below them where it perched on a fence post. A stiff breeze was blowing, ruffling Francesca's curls, and even Theo's immaculate slicked-down hairstyle showed signs of disturbance. They sat in companionable silence admiring the scenery. The sea shone aquamarine in the sunshine, darkening to Prussian blue in the shadow of the rocks where the deep water churned in endless agitation. Wrens sang in chorus and meadow pipits flew up from the ground close by and glided downwards with trilling cascades of high pitched notes.

'If the weather stays as clear as this we'll be able to see the Liberation fireworks from up here,' said Francesca gazing out to sea where the islands of Guernsey, Sark, Herm and Jethou lay brooding on the horizon.

'Really?' Theo looked surprised.

'Yes, Raoul and I always come up here on Liberation Day if the weather's clear. It's a family tradition.'

'We could come up here together this evening if you like.' He paused. 'Frankie…'

'Yes.' She looked at him His dark eyes were serious and held hers for a long moment. He took her hand in his and the words came out in a rush. 'I'd like to marry you, Frankie, but I don't think I could live with the dog.'

It was the last thing Francesca was expecting; she recovered herself quickly. 'You wouldn't have to. I'll give him to Raoul and Lizzie. I'm sure they'd have him.'

'Does that mean you'll marry me?'

'Of course it does, better late than never, eh!'

Theo put both his arms round her and kissed her.

'There is just one thing,' she said after a few minutes.

'What is it?' He pulled away from her, suddenly anxious.

She hesitated. 'Oh dear! I don't know how to say it.'

'What? You can say anything to me, Frankie.'

'I really don't like Rachelle House. I don't think I could be happy living there, even as your wife. I'm so sorry, Theo.'

Relief spread over Theo's face. He burst out laughing and hugged her tightly. 'Is that all? I don't like it either. I hate the place; it's so full of unhappy memories. I'll sell it and we'll start afresh somewhere else. How about that?'

'That would be ideal, a new start for us both.' Francesca took his hand and wondered how Raoul would react to the prospect of having Zapp on a permanent basis.

* * *

Later that evening while Francesca, Theo, Raoul and Lizzie were up on the cliffs watching the pinpricks of light soaring into the sky over Guernsey and drinking champagne, Geoff and Natasha were spending a cosy evening in Geoff's one-bedroom flat over the bank in Main Street.

'I really ought to be going.' Natasha slipped out of bed and started to pick her clothes up off the floor.

'Do you have to? I wish you could stay all night.'

'I know, darling, but Belle won't go to sleep until I'm home. She needs to know I'm there.'

'I could look for a bigger place then you and Belle could move in with me.' Geoff sighed as he got dressed. 'We can't go on like this. When are you going to tell your parents about us?'

'As soon as I can get their attention for five minutes. They're so busy these days. I will tell them, I promise.' She kissed him. 'I'd love to move in with you, Geoff. Are you sure about Belle?'

He put his arms round her. 'Of course I am, darling. She's a sweet kid; we get on fine. I think we'd make a lovely little family and I think she likes me.'

'She does, she thinks you're wonderful.'

'I'll go to the estate agent's first thing in the morning.'

The foyer was deserted as Natasha entered the hotel. She peered into the bar where one or two people were chatting quietly. There was no sign of her parents. She went upstairs and tiptoed into Belle's room.

'Mummy?'

'Good night, sweetheart.' Natasha kissed her and went to her own room. She got ready for bed, her head whirling at the thought of moving in with Geoff. Once in bed she found she could not sleep. She tossed and turned and eventually decided that a hot milky drink might help.

She donned her old pink candlewick dressing-gown and fluffy slippers and crept downstairs. As she walked through the hall on her way to the passage that led to the kitchens she noticed a light under the door of her father's study. She stopped in surprise, thinking he must have forgotten to turn the light off. She was about to enter the room when Ian's voice, raised in anger, assailed her ears.

'I'm not discussing this now. Have you any idea what time it is? Yes, I know we've achieved our objective but you've gone too far. Killing both the woman's dogs. Was that really necessary?'

Natasha froze, her hand on the door handle, waiting for her father to speak again.

'Yes, I did give you a free hand, and of course you'll get your money. But you're on your own if the police catch up with you. The whole island's up in arms about this, you bloody fool.'

Natasha flung open the study door. Ian jumped. He swung round crashing the telephone receiver back into place. 'What are you doing up at his hour? What do you want?'

'I heard every word, Father. You had the Brockenshaws' dogs killed.' She rushed at him and pummelled his chest with her fists, tears pouring down her face.

He took hold of her arms. 'Calm down, for God's sake. You'll wake the whole building.'

'I don't care!' Natasha jerked both her arms upwards and broke free. 'What sort of person are you?' she raged. 'Killing defenceless animals to get rid of someone you don't want here.'

'Listen to me, Natasha. I didn't tell the bloody man to shoot the dogs; I told him to do whatever it took to get Brockenshaw to abandon his hotel before it ruins our business. It was his decision and it will probably backfire. The whole place is up in arms over two wretched animals.'

'Serves you right,' Natasha screamed. She was becoming hysterical.

'What's happening here?' Daphne, wearing a black negligee and a hair net, stood in the open doorway. She walked up to her daughter and slapped her hard on the cheek. Natasha collapsed into a chair, still sobbing.

'Well?' Daphne turned to her husband.

He looked uncomfortable. 'Nat's got herself into a state over nothing. You know what a drama queen she is.'

'He's had the Brockenshaws' dogs shot to make them leave the island,' Natasha wailed.

'Ian, is this true?'

'Of course not! The girl's hysterical.'

Natasha, calmer now, turned to her mother. 'I heard him on the phone. I heard him admit it. I shall go to the police and tell them.'

Ian laughed. 'Go ahead. Who do you think they'll believe, the island's president or his hysterical daughter?'

'Go to bed, Natasha.' Daphne hauled her daughter out of the chair, pushed her out of the room and shut the door behind her.

'Now tell me, Ian, is what Natasha says true?'

'No.' Ian looked his wife straight in the eye. 'She's misunderstood what she heard. I was discussing the incident on the phone and she got the wrong end of the stick.'

'Who were you talking to in the middle of the night?'

Ian never took his eyes from his wife's face. 'Bertie Soames, more States business, the wretched man never sleeps.' He took her arm. 'Come on, I could use a drink.'

Natasha fled to her room. She grabbed her handbag and flew down the stairs and out of the hotel. A few men lounging outside watched with mild curiosity as she jumped into her car and roared up the hill towards town.

Geoff Prosser was woken by the continuous ringing of his front door bell. He leaned out of the window and looked down into the street. 'Nat!'

He ran downstairs and unlocked the door. Natasha flung herself into his arms. She was shaking. His fingers closed on the softness of her dressing-gown and he held her tightly.

'What's happened? Is it Belle?'

'No, it's Father. I hate him. How I hate him.'

Geoff went cold. 'Has he hurt you?'

'No.' She was crying. He led her upstairs, sat her on the sofa and poured her a brandy. 'Here, drink this. Tell me what's happened, Nat.'

She poured out the whole story and Geoff listened in horrified silence until she'd finished speaking.

'Will you go to the police?'

'Yes,' said Natasha. 'I will. First thing in the morning.'

Chapter 23

Josie and Emily stood in Main Square and watched Mark, the estate agent, erecting a For Sale sign in the front garden of Rachelle House supervised by Theo. News of Theo's and Francesca's engagement had already done the rounds and superseded the gossip about the Brockenshaws' departure.

'So many changes on the island,' murmured Emily. 'I wonder where Theo and Francesca will live when they are married.'

'Let's ask him,' said Josie briskly marching up to Theo's front gate. 'Good morning, Mr Rachelle, may we congratulate you on your forthcoming marriage.'

Theo beamed. 'Thank you, Ladies, how very kind of you.'

'I see you are selling your family home,' Josie continued. 'We were wondering where you and the future Mrs Rachelle will be living.'

'We'll live in Francesca's cottage to begin with,' said Theo, 'while we look around for a suitable house with a nice garden. New beginnings, you know.'

'Quite,' said Josie. 'Well, we wish you both the very best of everything in your new life together.'

'Thank you,' said Theo again, warmed by the kindness he and Francesca had been shown by so many people. He went indoors to join Mark who was now measuring up rooms and taking down particulars for the sale brochure.

Josie and Emily wandered over to the Rock Café where they were greeted animatedly by Jean Yorke who was having coffee with her husband. 'You've heard the latest, I suppose?' she said.

'What?' asked Josie. 'If you mean Rachelle House going on the market we already know about that.'

'Is it?' Harold Yorke emerged from behind his Daily Telegraph and squinted at Josie through his reading glasses.

'Yes,' said Emily. 'We've just seen the sign going up.'

'Really, how much are they asking for it?'

'I've no idea,' said Josie. 'We didn't ask; we aren't nosy like some people.'

Harold snorted and disappeared behind his newspaper.

'Sit here with us.' Jean moved her handbag off an adjacent chair. 'You obviously haven't heard the latest scandal.'

Josie and Emily sat down and ordered coffee. Jean could hardly contain herself. 'Natasha has walked out of the hotel. She and her little girl have moved in with Geoff Prosser.'

'Are you sure?' Josie eyed Jean suspiciously; her sources were not always reliable.

'Quite sure. Natasha was seen outside the bank at seven o'clock this morning. She and Geoff were unloading her car; several cases and bags and a cardboard box full of toys. The woman who saw her said Natasha looked dreadful; she'd obviously been crying and Belle looked bewildered, poor little mite. What do you suppose has happened?'

'Perhaps she's fallen out with her parents,' said Josie. 'I can't imagine they would approve of her relationship with Geoff Prosser. He's hardly her type.'

'Don't be such a snob, Josie,' said Emily reprovingly. 'He's a very nice man.'

They were interrupted by Susan Cottingham who rushed over to them, pulled up a chair and sat down. Harold glared at her before burying himself behind his paper again. Susan appeared not to notice, she was out of breath. 'I've just seen Ian and Daphne Warrington coming out of the police station. They looked absolutely furious and completely ignored me when I said "good morning" to them. I wonder what's going on.'

* * *

Ian Warrington was satisfied that he had successfully fobbed off Sergeant Malcolm Green during his interview at the police station. It had been a degrading experience answering a lot of questions as a result of his daughter's accusations and he hoped that was the end of the matter.

'I can't face going back to the hotel yet,' Daphne said as they got into the car. 'I need some time to calm down.'

'You and me both,' said Ian shortly. He slammed the car into gear and roared down Valmont Road. There was a small crowd of people outside the hotel. He drove straight past without slowing down and followed the coast road round to the lighthouse. He parked the car on the small grassy promontory, which was deserted, and switched off the engine.

An oystercatcher perched on a rock nearby uttered shrill piping cries, a warning to his mate who scuttled away from the shallow dip in the ground that was her nest. Four perfectly camouflaged eggs were left unattended. The little drama went unnoticed by the couple in the car and the oystercatcher quickly returned to her parental duties.

'What are we going to do, Ian?'

'Nothing. It will blow over. The police can't take any action without evidence. Someone's shot some animals; no one's committed murder.'

'Not just animals; two pedigree Dalmatians. It's a dreadful business.'

'I've no doubt they were insured.'

'That's not the point,' said Daphne. 'Anyway, what I meant was what are we going to do about Natasha?'

Ian snorted. 'I wash my hands of the girl; she's gone too far this time, reporting her own father to the police. She's been nothing but trouble since she was a teenager. I disown her. She's on her own from now on.'

Daphne looked at him. She had never seen him so angry and wondered for a moment if her daughter was right and he had orchestrated the Brockenshaws' departure. She dismissed the thought as quickly as it had come. She could not believe it of him and he was right about Natasha. She had always been a difficult girl.

'But she's not on her own, is she? She's with that oaf Geoff Prosser. If only she'd married Raoul St Arnaud.' Daphne sighed wearily. 'He would have been ideal; that bit older than her and of some standing in the community. He'd have settled her down.'

'For God's sake!' Ian turned on her furiously. 'Can't you let that go? It's ancient history. She's made her bed and has to lie on it. It's time she moved out. You're always complaining the child's under your feet. Let Prosser take responsibility for them.'

'You're forgetting she works for us. We need her, Ian. Whatever you think, she's an asset to the hotel.'

'We can get someone to replace her. I don't want her back under any circumstances. I meant what I said; I disown her and that's the end of the matter.'

Daphne was silent. She felt a stab of guilt remembering how Belle had looked at her as the child had climbed into Natasha's car, clutching her favourite toy rabbit. "I shall like living at Geoff's, Granny. He never tells me I'm in the way."' Daphne bit her lip. The hotel had always been her top priority; she had not been a good mother or grandmother. Despite her iron control tears slid down her cheeks.

'Stop snivelling,' said Ian, 'and pull yourself together. We need to put a brave face on this and act as though nothing untoward has happened.'

* * *

Natasha packed Belle off to school as usual, thinking it was best to keep the child in her normal routine as much as possible so she would not be too disturbed by her sudden change in circumstances. Natasha need not have worried. At break time Belle skipped up to Francesca and tapped her arm.

'Miss Saviano, Mummy and I are going to live with Geoff in his flat. Isn't it exciting?'

Francesca was surprised. She smiled down at Belle. 'Very exciting! Will there be room for you all?'

'I'm going to sleep in the living room till Geoff finds somewhere bigger for us all to live. He's going to find a bed for me today.' She raced back to her friends, leaving Francesca marvelling at the resilience of children.

Geoff and Natasha meanwhile had re-arranged the living room furniture, unpacked Natasha's and Belle's belongings and headed up the street to Hugo's Emporium to stock up with groceries.

Hugo was on edge having just listened to his mother on the telephone for the past twenty minutes, filling him in on the happenings of the previous night and Natasha's subsequent departure. He was about to go out and look for her when he spotted her and Geoff loading up a trolley with provisions. He walked over and grabbed his sister by the arm.

'I want a word with you, Nat. Excuse us for a moment,' he said curtly to Geoff, and pulled Natasha unceremoniously into his office. 'What's this I hear about you reporting Father to the police? Did Prosser put you up to it?'

'It's nothing to do with Geoff.' Natasha was defensive. She was fond of her brother and did not want to argue with him. She sat down on an office chair and told him calmly about the telephone call she'd overheard in the middle of the night between her father and an unknown person.

Hugo rounded on her; she was startled by the anger on his face. 'You do realise the amount of damage this will do to both Father and Mother. Where's your family loyalty?'

Natasha ignored the last part of the question. 'What about the damage he's done to the Brockenshaws? I can't just ignore this. Whoever shot those dogs should be brought to justice and if Father's implicated in the crime he'll have to face the consequences. It was a dreadful thing to do.'

'But not a crime. There are no laws here protecting animals. If a person had been shot it would be a very different matter.'

'Surely bribery is a crime? Father paid whoever it was to get the Brockenshaws off the island. I heard him say so.'

'Are you sure you heard him correctly? Mother says you misunderstood what you heard and have got the wrong end of the stick. She's furious by the way.'

'Well of course she'll stick up for Father. I know what I heard, Hugo; he was shouting. He's not going to admit it to anyone, is he? He's the President; he's got a position to uphold.'

'Precisely, which is why you shouldn't have gone running to the police. God, what a mess.'

'I'm sure he'll lie his way out of it,' Natasha said bitterly. 'No one will believe me.'

'No they won't.'

'What about you? Do you believe me, Hugo?'

Hugo looked at her. His face softened and he spoke more gently. 'I don't think you're making this up, Nat. I think you genuinely believe what you think you heard, but you misunderstood what Father was saying.'

'I did not, Hugo. I'm not backing down. I have to do what I feel is right.' She spoke coldly. 'Belle and I have moved out of the hotel. We're living with Geoff now.'

Natasha marched out of the office and joined Geoff who was talking to Raoul and Lizzie.

'I've got a camp bed somewhere at home,' Raoul was saying to Geoff. 'You're very welcome to borrow it.'

'That would be great.' Geoff turned to Natasha, 'OK?'

'Not really. Hugo thinks I misunderstood what I heard. He's livid with me.' She smiled ruefully at Lizzie. 'Has Geoff told you what's happened?'

'Yes,' said Lizzie. 'It's awful, Natasha, I'm so sorry. What will happen now?'

'It will all be brushed under the carpet,' said Raoul. 'Ian will hide behind his presidential position, the police will do nothing and the culprit will never be found. Another typical Ormerey cover up.'

They queued up at the till and paid for their shopping before walking out into the bright sunshine. The street was crowded; the tourist season was now well under way and no one took any notice of the four as they wandered down to The Sycamores.

Geoff took Natasha's arm. 'I think we should call in at the police station and see what, if anything, is being done.'

'I wouldn't hold your breath,' said Raoul. 'Come in for coffee while I hunt around for that camp bed.'

* * *

It was nearly mid-day when Geoff and Natasha arrived at the police station for the second time that morning. Sergeant Malcolm Green was on the point of closing for lunch. He frowned with annoyance as Geoff and Natasha strode purposefully up to the counter.

'We've come to see how your enquiries into the dog shooting incident are coming along,' said Geoff.

The Sergeant tightened his lips. Geoff Prosser had been a thorn in his side for years; for ever poking his nose into police business. 'The matter's been dropped,' he said shortly. 'No law has been broken.'

'What?' Natasha flared up immediately. 'So it's all right to go around destroying domestic pets, is it?'

'It's a waste of police time and resources. We've more important matters to attend to.' He looked pointedly at his watch as Derek Peasgood poked his head round the door.

'Are you coming to lunch, Sarge?'

'A very important matter,' sneered Geoff. 'I assume that you are not taking Mrs Roche's statement seriously then?'

'Mrs Roche?' Malcolm Green raised his bushy grey eyebrows. 'Oh, you mean Natasha.'

'It's Mrs Roche to you,' said Natasha coldly. 'Well?'

'I have spoken to the President – the Sergeant emphasised the word *president* – and he says that you misunderstood what you heard from behind a closed door. He's very angry about you coming here to make a false statement; malicious he called it.'

'He's obviously not going to admit to anything,' said Geoff. 'Did you find out who he was speaking to on the phone?'

The Sergeant blustered. 'That's confidential police business.'

'It's one person's word against another,' said Derek Peasgood. 'It's only fair that we consider both statements. Perhaps Natasha, er… Mrs Roche, is right about her father. Shouldn't we make some enquiries?'

Malcolm Green threw him a furious look which the Constable ignored. He had admired Natasha for years and still harboured secret fantasies about her. He was not going to let the opportunity of doing her a favour slip past him. 'I'll ask around among the locals and check up on all the gun licences. Whoever did it might have been careless covering his tracks. He may have boasted about it after he'd had a skinful in the pub. Somebody must know something.'

Natasha turned her green eyes, brimming with tears, full on him. He blushed.

'You'll do no such thing,' the Sergeant thundered. 'The President is a fine gentleman; his word is his bond. I, for one, believe he's telling the truth. The whole matter is dropped; there will be no further enquiries.'

Geoff snorted derisively. He took Natasha's arm and propelled her out of the police station. 'What's the betting your father has bunged a large sum in his direction to keep him sweet?'

'I wouldn't be at all surprised,' said Natasha. 'Raoul's right; it will be another Ormerey cover-up and I shall be made to look a complete fool.'

Chapter 24

To his surprise, Theo had an offer for Rachelle House within a week of it going on the market. An English couple on the point of retirement who were visiting the island for a short break decided, on the spur of the moment, that Ormerey was the place where they wanted to spend the rest of their lives.

Lizzie was incredulous. 'How could they make up their minds so quickly? They know nothing about the island or how things work here. Frankie says it's their first visit.'

Raoul laughed. 'It often happens; people come here, fall in love with the place and decide they want to live here.'

'Does it work out?'

'Sometimes it does. Some people settle here and never regret it, for others it's a huge mistake. The house buying process is much quicker and more straightforward than it is in England. That attracts people; they don't need a solicitor and most of them never bother with a survey. It all goes through very quickly.'

Lizzie tutted. 'No one in their right mind buys a house without having a survey done, especially an old one, and what about land searches?'

'Things often come to light after the purchase has gone through. There have been some real disasters; boundary disputes, rights of way, that sort of thing. It keeps the court busy.'

'Who tells these people they don't need a solicitor or a surveyor, the vendors?'

'Possibly, but it's usually the estate agents who are after a quick sale. One of the problems is that there is no qualified surveyor on the island which means flying one over from Guernsey or the UK so people don't usually bother. It holds things up, and you need a Guernsey advocate who understands the laws here.'

'What about the couple buying Rachelle House? A property of that age is bound to have some structural defects.'

'Oh Lizzie, I can tell you used to work for an estate agent.' He gave her a warning look. 'We can't interfere. Theo is desperate for this sale to go through so he can buy somewhere else. That reminds me, I've promised to go and help him sort out his loft this afternoon. He's drowning in clutter; a lot of it belonged to his parents and grandparents. Frankie's suggested he starts at the top and works downwards.'

'Sounds logical,' said Lizzie. 'No wonder Frankie feels the ghost of Claudine Rachelle haunting the place if all her clothes are still in the cupboards.'

'What nonsense!' Raoul laughed. 'What will you do this afternoon?'

'Frankie and I thought we'd walk over to Yaffingales and see what's what.'

'I can't think why,' said Raoul. 'There are few things more depressing than an abandoned building site. It will never be cleared up and will become yet another eyesore; right in the middle of the green belt too. It will ruin the coastal walk.' He sighed heavily, his brow furrowed. 'This whole dreadful business will damage our tourist industry. The Brockenshaws are bound to relate their story back in England; word will soon get around especially on the south coast which is where many of our tourists come from. The trouble is, Lizzie, I've seen this kind of thing happen before. There have been other incidents over the years when good people who would have been an asset to the island have been driven away.'

'Things happen on the mainland,' said Lizzie. 'There's crime and violence, people get murdered, but you'd think that on a tiny island like this people would try to get on with each other and do what's best for the community. There are so few of you and outsiders could contribute so much if only the island would let them.'

'The locals stick up for their own and people do pull together if there's a real crisis. There's a lot of good will. But bad news always overshadows the good news, doesn't it? Everyone here is on top of each other; when people fall out there's nowhere to go to cool off. Bad feelings build up, there's no way of diffusing them; they fester for years.'

'It doesn't bode well for the future of the island, does it, if incomers who want to settle are driven away?'

'It depends on who they are.' Raoul gave a derisive snort. 'If they have pots of money, or some claim to fame like that disgraced English politician who lives up near Frankie, they'll be welcomed with open arms and invited to all the posh parties.'

'The Brockenshaws had pots of money.'

'They had the temerity to want to make changes and the locals hate that, as you know.'

'People don't like me,' said Lizzie, 'they made that obvious from day one, when they knew nothing about me.'

'Oh sweetheart, I've told you before it's nothing personal; it's because you're with me. In the eyes of the locals I should have married a local girl to keep the St Arnaud money on the island.' He put his arms round her. 'You've been here nearly a year now and have made some good friends so ignore the nasty ones. You are happy here aren't you, Lizzie?'

'Of course I am.' She smiled up at him and he kissed her. 'I'm off now. See you later. Enjoy your walk with Frankie. It won't be long before we have that diabolical dog of hers here for keeps.'

* * *

It was a warm sunny afternoon. The light breeze wafted the sharp pungent scent of hawthorn blossom over the two walkers and the dog as they wandered over the fields towards Yaffingales. Skylarks soared overhead and dunnocks and wrens were singing in the hedgerows.

Zapp made a sudden dart into a clump of long grass, startling a hen pheasant which flew up under his nose and clattered away uttering harsh staccato cries.

'She was probably on a nest,' said Francesca. 'Come here, Zapp.' She shortened his lead and he glared at her, the short fur along his spine standing up in a stiff crest revealing his African ancestry.

'Poor Zapp,' said Lizzie, 'he's desperate to run loose.'

'He can when we get to the Yaffingales garden; he can't escape from there. Has Raoul come round to the idea of having Zapp to live with you permanently?'

'Yes, he loves him really. He enjoyed having him before despite his mischief. He's a constant source of entertainment.'

'He's that all right. Oh look!' Francesca peered over the gate at the Yaffingales field.

All traces of the building work had disappeared. The foundations had been filled in and the ground levelled over the top. Seedlings of sea radish, common mallow and other weeds were already germinating in the bare earth, and round the edges of the field wild carrot, clover and various types of vetch flowered in profusion.

'It doesn't take long for nature to reassert itself,' said Lizzie. 'Raoul will be surprised; he thought this place would remain an eyesore for years.'

'Simon must have arranged with Joshua to have the field reinstated to how it was,' said Francesca. 'How nice of him after all that's happened.'

'They were nice people. I'm sorry they've gone.'

'I wonder who will buy Yaffingales now.' Francesca was thoughtful for a moment. 'This land is no longer part of the green belt so anyone could come along and build on it – and knock the cottage down. We're back to square one.'

Lizzie thought that no one in their right mind would try building anything on Ormerey but she kept her thoughts to herself. They walked through the tunnel of trees to the cottage, then pushed their way through the undergrowth to the terrace overlooking the back garden and sat down on the steps. Francesca let Zapp off the lead and he charged joyfully across the lawn, startling a blackbird in the process of pulling up a worm.

'We shouldn't be here really,' said Francesca.

'It's all right. Simon said Raoul and I could bring Zapp here whenever we wanted and it's still his land.'

'I love it here,' said Francesca turning her face up to the sun. 'It's always had such a peaceful feel to it. I can still picture my mother hanging up the washing across the lawn, and my father digging his vegetable plot down the bottom there, beyond the apple trees. He used to give me rides in his wheelbarrow.'

'Doesn't it make you sad?'

'A little, but in a nice way. I have such happy memories of living here and now I have a whole happy future ahead of me with Theo. I still can't believe it's true; I have to pinch myself every morning when I wake up. You never know what's waiting round the corner, do you?'

'No. I never ever thought I'd fall in love again and come to live on an island. I'd got so used to being on my own after my divorce and had settled into a quiet little rut. Then I met Raoul trying to get off a train at Waterloo and here I am. There are thousands of people rushing through that station every day and I met Raoul. How amazing is that?'

'Fate,' said Francesca. 'It was obviously meant to be, and if you hadn't come to live with Raoul, Theo would never have walked into the Rock Café that day and joined us for coffee. He said that seeing the three of us together, and you and Raoul so happy, made him realise how alone he was. He acted on the spur of the moment and look how it's turned out.'

They sat listening to the hum of insects, the tinkling of the little stream as it trickled through the valley, and the surf shushing on the beach far below them. The overgrown garden was a riot of colour with marigolds, lupins and foxgloves struggling through the long grass in the neglected borders. Zapp had tired of chasing birds and jumping at butterflies. He joined them on the terrace and lay down on the warm stones.

'I hope no one buys Yaffingales,' said Francesca, 'then we can come here whenever we want. Wouldn't that be nice?'

* * *

Jean, Josie and Emily were having morning coffee at the Imperial Hotel. It was pouring with rain outside. The sea was grey and turbulent with white horses dancing towards the shore. A few gulls hovered disconsolately just above the surface, and yet more were huddled together on the beach with a flock of oystercatchers.

The hotel dining room was crowded with holidaymakers and smelt of wet hair and rainwear, masking the usually delicious aroma of coffee. There were no fresh flowers on the tables as there usually were. Daphne's mood matched the weather. She was curt to the point of rudeness when she brought the coffee.

'You look tired, dear.' Emily looked at her sympathetically.

'We're short staffed,' said Daphne abruptly.

'She must be missing Natasha,' said Jean in a low voice when Daphne had moved out of earshot. 'She's working at The Lord Nelson up in town now. There's been the most dreadful row.'

'We know all about that,' said Josie. 'I hear Bill and Val are delighted to have her. They always need extra staff in the summer.'

'What about little Belle?' asked Emily.

'Natasha's only working four evenings a week,' said Josie. 'Geoff gives Belle her supper and puts her to bed and Natasha pops in to kiss her goodnight. It's only a few yards up the street.'

'It's amazing how Geoff Prosser has taken to surrogate fatherhood.' Jean took a bite of gâche while eyeing the chocolate biscuits longingly. Her dentures still made eating biscuits difficult. 'It will be interesting to see how long their little arrangement lasts. Geoff may get fed up; he's so used to being on his own and it's all happened in such a rush.'

'It's a big change for all of them,' said Emily. 'It's strange not seeing Natasha in here; she's such a pleasant friendly girl, a real asset to the place. I do wonder if it's true what she said about her father.'

'Oh, I'm sure it isn't.' Jean poured them all a second cup of coffee and watched disapprovingly as a sodden couple in oilskins sat down, shedding their outer garments to reveal scruffy shorts and tea shirts. 'I can't believe Ian Warrington could be behind anything so cruel and underhand. He and Harold have played golf together for years and Harold is a very good judge of character. He says Ian is always the perfect gentleman. Natasha must be mistaken.'

'Well, whatever the truth of the matter, it's played straight into the Warringtons' hands,' said Josie. 'They did not want that new hotel. Everyone knows that.' She had never liked Ian Warrington. She had known him for years and considered him quite capable of getting rid of the Brockenshaws and sacrificing his own daughter to protect his position and his good name. She did not, however, voice these opinions to the others and kept her thoughts to herself.

Chapter 25

For the past three days Ormerey had been shrouded in mist and drizzle, drenching the island in a fine grey haze which kept many of the holiday makers mooching round the town or in the pub. For the islanders, life carried on as usual and the disruption to flying was stoically endured by those who had wished to travel.

Theo stood on his landing gloomily surveying the heap of suitcases, boxes and piles of assorted objects which he and Raoul had brought down from the loft a few days earlier. He really ought to sort through it; maybe a caffeine fix would pull him out of his inertia.

He turned to go downstairs to the kitchen when his eye was caught by a small brown leather writing case which had slipped off the pile and was lying on the floor. It bore the initials P.J.R. Theo stared at it; those initials belonged to his grandfather Pierre Jean Rachelle. His interest was suddenly sparked. He picked up the case, carried it downstairs and placed it on the kitchen table which was still littered with his breakfast things.

The lock was rusty, the case grey with mildew on its underside. Theo made himself a mug of instant coffee, then found a kitchen knife and prised the lid open to reveal a jumbled pile of documents and photographs. He gazed fascinated as he sifted through old bills and receipts, some dating back to the beginning of the century. His coffee was forgotten as he read postcards sent from France in 1917 from someone called Jean-Claude. Who was he? Theo wondered. The messages, written in English, were brief and optimistic with no mention of the horror of the trenches. *I am well and hope this finds you the same. My good wishes to all on Ormerey. Jean-Claude.*

There were dozens of letters, most of them still in the original envelopes. Theo took a slurp of the now tepid coffee and decided to go through them at his leisure that evening. It was obviously going to be a long job; he ought to be sorting out the heap of junk on the landing. Raoul had promised to take any rubbish to the tip in his pick-up. He gathered up the papers off the table and replaced them in the writing case. As he did so his attention was caught by an Australian stamp. His heart gave a sudden lurch. He held the envelope in his hands, his thoughts racing. His uncle, Jean Rachelle, had gone to Australia when Theo was a small child, never to return. Could this letter be from him? He remembered the desolation he had felt after his uncle had left and he was told he would never see him again.

The letter was postmarked Sydney, Australia, 7th April 1938. His fingers trembled slightly as he withdrew the flimsy paper from its envelope. The ink had faded but the bold writing was still legible. As he read it his face paled; he felt sick. After a few minutes he picked up the phone.

* * *

Raoul and Lizzie were just about to go shopping when the phone rang. 'Damn!' said Raoul. 'I'd better answer it. I'll catch you up.' He picked up the receiver, 'Raoul St Arnaud.'

'Raoul, thank God you're home. Something quite dreadful has happened. Can you come round?'

'What, straight away?'

'Yes, if you wouldn't mind. Come to the back door. I'm in the kitchen.'

'OK. I'll see you in a few minutes.' Raoul replaced the receiver and peered out of the front door. He could just see Lizzie through the drizzle talking to Natasha. He hurried up to her. 'That was Theo on the phone. He wants me to go round there straight away; some sort of crisis I gather.'

'Oh dear,' said Lizzie. 'I hope he's all right.'

'He doesn't sound it,' said Raoul. 'I'll see you later.' He nodded briefly to Natasha and hurried down the street.

'I wonder what all that's about,' said Lizzie. 'Nothing to do with Frankie I hope.'

Raoul walked round to the rear of Rachelle House, surprised to see how neat the kitchen garden was looking with its rows of lettuces, peas and French beans. The kitchen door was open. He tapped on it before entering the room. Theo was sitting at the table, his head in his hands. He looked up and Raoul was horrified to see the ravaged look on his face.

'What's happened? Is it Frankie?'

'Sort of,' said Theo. 'Take a look at this.' He pushed a piece of paper across the table. Raoul sat down opposite Theo and reached across to pick it up.

'What is it?'

'It's a letter from my Uncle Jean in Australia, written to my grandfather.'

'I never knew you had an uncle.'

'He was my father's younger brother. I was very fond of him. He went to Australia in 1935 when I was five years old and whenever I asked about him I was fobbed off. When I was older I was told that his name was never to be mentioned. Now I know why. Read it for yourself.'

Raoul scrutinised the faded handwriting. The letter was dated 5th April 1938.

My dear Papa,

I have been here for three years now and have never received a word from you or Mama in all that time. Surely the scandal has died down and it is safe for me to return home now. The Police have surely given up the search for Saviano's killer. You know it was an accident. I explained to you that I never meant to kill him, only to warn him to keep out of my way. Am I to be punished for ever? Please forgive me, Papa. I miss you all and my life on Ormerey. I am so very homesick. Little Theo must have grown into a big boy now. Please, please, let me come home and I will never cause any trouble again.

Your ever loving son

Jean.

Raoul read the letter through again. He sat back in his chair and looked across at Theo. 'Good God! This is a turn up for the book; I can hardly believe my own eyes.' He exhaled a long drawn out breath. 'And he never came back?'

'No.'

'Have you found anything else; any more letters?'

'No, I've only had a quick look through but there's nothing else with an Australian stamp. I'll have to go through everything properly. What on earth am I going to do, Raoul?'

'The first thing is to have a stiff drink; we've both had a shock.'

'Help yourself. There's whiskey or brandy in the dining room.'

Raoul poured brandy into two glasses. He put one in front of Theo and sat down again. 'No wonder your grandfather refused to have Antonio's shooting investigated. He knew all along it was his own son who'd done it and had him shipped off to Australia. Murder was a hanging offence in those days. Do you think your parents knew?'

'They must have done. Why else would they refuse to have his name mentioned? I asked and asked what had happened to him and why he never came back to see us. I was told never to speak of him.'

There was anguish in Theo's dark eyes. 'What am I going to do about Frankie?'

'What do you mean?'

'She'll have to know the truth; she won't want to marry me now.'

Raoul looked at his friend in exasperation. 'Don't be ridiculous, Theo. Frankie won't hold you responsible for the killing of her father. She loves you. It will be a terrible shock for her but you don't know her very well if you seriously think this is going to make any difference to how she feels about you.'

'She'll have to be told.'

'Of course she will but I'll tell her. May I borrow the letter?'

Theo looked relieved. 'I'd be so grateful, Raoul.'

* * *

Raoul walked round to Puffin Cottage with the letter. Francesca was out. He looked at his watch; she should be back from school by now. He let Zapp out of the cottage and sat down to wait on the stone bench outside the front door. The drizzle had stopped and the sun was making valiant efforts to shine through the mist, a pale disc in the grey sky. Zapp climbed up on to seat and sat upright beside him, his eyes fixed on the gate.

Bright petunias in shades of pink and mauve drooped in their pots; flowers and foliage glistening with rain. The lawn was lush and green and speckled with dandelions. It was in need of a cut but Raoul was oblivious to his surroundings. His brain was in a whirl. What an extraordinary find, he thought, a family secret buried for over fifty years. He tried to recall what he had been told by his father. His Aunt Rosamund and little Francesca had come to live with them after Old Pierre had thrown them out of Yaffingales. No one had ever found out who had killed Antonio. His father and grandfather had always suspected there had been a cover up and they had been right.

Zapp leapt off the bench as Francesca came bustling through the gate laden with shopping and poked his nose into one of the bags.

'Get out of there, Zapp. Hello, Raoul.' She beamed with pleasure. 'This is a nice surprise.' She took in his serious face. 'Has something happened?'

'Yes, an interesting discovery. Come inside and I'll make a cup of tea. I've something to show you.'

They went inside to the bright colourful kitchen. Francesca placed the shopping in the middle of the table out of Zapp's reach and sat down while Raoul busied himself making two mugs of tea. He found a packet of digestive biscuits and put some on a plate. Francesca broke one up and fed it to Zapp, wondering what could have provoked this unexpected visit from her cousin on his own without Lizzie. He was wearing the little frown that always furrowed his brow when he was troubled or perplexed. A small frisson of foreboding passed through her making her shiver. Raoul finally sat down opposite her. He looked at her intently and hesitated, as if trying to decide what to say.

'What is it? You've got me worried now.'

Raoul pulled the letter from his pocket. 'Theo found this amongst all the old papers in his loft. It's a letter written to his grandfather, Old Pierre; it explains what happened to your father all those years ago.'

Francesca's brown eyes widened with shock. Her face paled. 'Let me see.'

Raoul pushed the letter across the table and Francesca read it, her hands trembling so much that the paper shook. Raoul placed his hands over hers to steady them. She was silent for several minutes.

'I don't understand. Who was this Jean?'

'Old Pierre's younger son, Theo's uncle. He shot your father, Frankie. No wonder there was a cover up. He was packed off to Australia to get him out of the way but he wanted to come home.'

'I never knew there was a younger son. I always thought Young Pierre was an only child, like Theo.'

'So did I.' Raoul frowned. 'I've never heard any mention of him before.'

'He never did come back or we'd have remembered him. The letter says it was an accident.'

'It wasn't Frankie. Dad was always adamant about that; he'd read the reports by the police and the coroner. Antonio was killed by person or persons unknown. Dad always maintained that he either turned his back on someone during an argument or he was running away from an assailant. Old Pierre obviously never believed it was an accident, that's why he packed Jean off the island. It was for his son's own protection. Murder was a capital offence.'

'But why? Why did Jean kill him? There must have been a reason.' Tears ran down Francesca's cheeks.

'A quarrel gone wrong, perhaps? We'll never know. Theo says he's going to sort through everything to see what he can find out. He's in a dreadful panic over this.'

'Is he?'

'He thinks you won't want to marry him now.'

Francesca sniffed and wiped her face with a tissue. She took a deep breath. 'He can be such an idiot.'

'That's what I told him. He's insecure, Frankie, and desperately lonely. He's always been on his own, no one to bounce his ideas off or discuss problems with. You know how hard it is being an only child but you and I have always had each other.' He took her hand. 'Are you all right?'

'I'll be OK in a minute.' She took a gulp of the now lukewarm tea. 'Yuk! You've put sugar in it.'

'It's for the shock. Drink up.'

She finished the tea obediently. Zapp, hoping for another biscuit while attention was diverted elsewhere, jumped up on to Raoul's lap and grabbed one off the plate.

'Get down, you little devil. You won't be allowed to do that when you're living with Lizzie and me.'

Francesca got up from her chair. 'You couldn't take him out for me, could you? I must go and see Theo.'

'Of course, love.'

She found Zapp's lead and clipped it on to his collar. Biscuits demolished, he jumped down enthusiastically and headed for the door. The two cousins walked into town together and parted outside The Sycamores.

'You're sure you're all right, Frankie?'

She smiled tremulously. 'I'm fine, don't worry.'

'Take care, then.' He gave her a peck on the cheek. 'We'll hang on to Zapp till you're ready to collect him. Good luck.'

* * *

Theo had searched through all the documents and letters in his grandfather's writing case but had found no further reference to his Uncle Jean and, to his disappointment, no photographs of him either. It was as if Old Pierre had wiped out all evidence of his younger son's existence – except for that one letter. Why had he kept that? It was clear evidence of Jean Rachelle's guilt. Theo wondered if his uncle was still alive; he would be in his eighties now. Suppose Raoul wanted to find him and bring him to trial? Theo suddenly doubted his wisdom in showing the letter to Raoul. Perhaps it would have been sensible to destroy it without saying anything to anyone. On the other hand could he, in all conscience, have kept the knowledge from Francesca? It would always have been there, a barrier between them even though she would have been unaware of it. She deserved to know what had happened to her father.

He was so deep in thought that the tap on the kitchen door startled him. He looked up to see Francesca and quickly got to his feet scattering papers as he did so.

'Frankie!'

'Oh darling, darling Theo. Don't worry, everything's going to be all right.' She ran across the room into his arms.

Chapter 26

Constable Derek Peasgood was sitting with his feet up on the desk, drinking a cup of tea and reading the Daily Mail. He always enjoyed Sergeant Green's day off and hoped he would not be presented with anything too onerous to deal with – hopefully there would be nothing at all.

It was a warm afternoon and he was on the point of nodding off when a middle-aged couple walked into the police station.

'Damn!' Derek muttered under his breath and quickly changed it to 'ahem' as the strangers approached the desk. 'What can I do for you?'

'Good afternoon,' said the man. He was small and skinny with spindly legs showing beneath his knee-length shorts. His wife, by contrast, was a large woman wearing a puce vest-top which clashed with her complexion, and whose shorts looked uncomfortably tight. She lowered her backpack and smiled at the Constable.

'We've just found this,' she said and laid a man's gold watch on the counter. Derek picked it up and looked at it closely. It was made by Longines.

'It's real gold,' the man said. 'It's hallmarked. Do you think there will be a reward?'

Derek ran the gold linked strap through his fingers thoughtfully. 'I know who has a watch just like this one,' he said, 'but he hasn't reported it missing. No one has reported losing a watch. Where did you find it?'

'We were walking along the south cliffs and my wife – er – my wife went into some bushes to answer a call of nature.'

'And there it was,' the woman said, 'I saw something glinting in the grass. I nearly peed on it.'

Derek noticed that the catch was slightly distorted and came undone easily. He frowned. 'It's strange no one has reported it missing. Would you mind showing me exactly where you found it?'

The couple looked at each other. 'We were about to have a cup of tea somewhere,' the woman said. 'It's a long walk back up there.'

'We can go in the Land Rover,' said Derek. 'Please, it could be very important.'

'Oh all right.' The woman sighed heavily. 'As long as we can have a ride there and back; my feet are killing me.'

Derek locked the watch in the drawer of the desk and wrote down the couple's particulars. They were Eric and Diana Good from Nottingham, staying at the Imperial Hotel. He grabbed the keys to the Land Rover and escorted the couple out of the police station to the waiting vehicle. His mind was racing. He was almost sure he knew who the watch belonged to and if he was correct he could deal with the situation before the Sergeant was back on duty the following day. That would serve him right. Derek smirked to himself as he drove over the bumpy track towards the south cliffs.

'I hope we can find the right clump of gorse bushes,' Diana said as they turned on to the coastal path. 'They all look the same but I know it was further along than this.'

'It was just in front of a German bunker.' Eric turned to his wife. 'I had a quick look inside while you were in the bushes.'

'I hope you can remember which bunker; there are quite a few along here.' Derek slowed down to almost a walking pace. 'Was it this one?'

'No, there were a lot more bushes and you couldn't see it from the path.'

'I know the one.' Derek drove on and drew to a halt at the side of the track. 'Here we are. There isn't another bunker till we get to Yaffingales.'

They all alighted from the vehicle. 'This is the place,' Diana said confidently. 'There's that little path through the gorse. My legs got scratched to pieces.'

A narrow rabbit path, barely discernible, ran through the gorse bushes. Derek fetched a stick from the Land Rover and held the gorse branches aside before following the couple as they made their way gingerly through the prickles. A small grass clearing opened out in front of a flight of overgrown steps leading down into a half-buried German bunker. The clearing, peppered with rabbit droppings, was completely surrounded by gorse.

Diana looked round. 'This is definitely the place.' She indicated a spot at the edge of the clearing where the bushes were particularly dense and the grass was longer. 'It's private here; you can't be seen from the path when you squat down. There appear to be no public conveniences anywhere on this island.' She looked at Derek accusingly.

The policeman blushed. 'There's one in town,' he muttered. 'Are you quite sure this is the place?' He looked round. The woman was right; anyone bending down would not be visible from the coastal path.

'Positive. Eric went down into that bunker, didn't you, dear?'

'With difficulty, it's very overgrown. It would make a wonderful bird hide; the view across to France is spectacular. I don't know why the island government doesn't make more of its assets to encourage tourism. So much of the place is unkempt and strewn with rubbish.'

Under normal circumstances Derek, who was island born, would have bristled indignantly at these comments by visitors but his mind was occupied elsewhere. This is where those dogs were shot he thought. Someone crouching in this clearing would not have been seen by Ruth Brockenshaw. 'Thank you both very much,' he said. 'This has been very helpful.' He held the gorse aside once more so the couple could squeeze through the narrow gap back on to the track.

Diana looked at Derek's grim face. 'Helpful in what way? Solving a crime you mean? What happened?'

'Two dogs were shot and killed on this path just about here. The watch you found may belong to the culprit.'

'How dreadful!' Diana was horrified. 'Was it deliberate?'

'Oh yes. I mean to get to the bottom of it, and hopefully before the day is out I shall have done.' For the second time that afternoon he was thankful that it was the Sergeant's day off.

'We thought Ormerey was such a peaceful crime-free place where everyone could leave their doors unlocked.' Diana squeezed her ample behind into the front of the Land Rover. 'Do move up a bit, Eric.'

'Only a fool leaves his house or car unlocked.' Derek manoeuvred the vehicle back on to the track and set off back to town. 'There's crime everywhere these days; Ormerey's no different. Every time an article about the island appears in a newspaper or magazine some idiot writes that no one ever locks their doors. The crime-free myth is perpetuated and we get a spate of burglaries.' He pulled up outside the Rock Café. 'Here we are. Enjoy your tea, and thanks again for your help.'

Eric and Diana clambered down and made their way into the café. Derek parked the Land Rover and headed straight for the pub.

* * *

The back garden at The Sycamores was a haven of tranquillity on a hot sunny afternoon. Lizzie had carried a tea tray outside and she and Raoul were relaxing in deck-chairs in the shade of one of the huge trees for which the house was named.

Bees buzzed round the lavender hedge and the buddleia, trailing its deep mauve flowers almost to the ground, was alive with butterflies; peacocks, red admirals, small tortoiseshells and painted ladies shimmered like dancing fairy lights as they fluttered in and out of the foliage. Lizzie watched the humming-bird hawk moths hovering almost motionless around the honeysuckle flowers.

'They are just like miniature humming birds,' she said.

Raoul was not listening. The heavy scent of roses, mixed with that of the lavender and honeysuckle, the buzzing of insects and the continuous chatter and laughter drifting over from Main Street had made him drowsy. He was on the point of falling asleep when a question from Lizzie jerked him instantly into wakefulness.

'Are you going to try and find Jean Rachelle?'

'What?'

'He could still be alive, Raoul, and if so don't you think he should be brought to justice? After all, he is a murderer.'

Raoul, wide awake now, looked at her. 'I doubt whether he could be found even if he is still alive. He's probably changed his name. He could be anywhere; he may not have stayed in Australia. I don't really think there's much point in trying to find him now.'

'Justice, Raoul, that's the point. No one should get away with killing someone. He should be brought to trial.'

'He's served a life sentence, Lizzie, banished from his home; leaving everyone he loved and never able to return. Maybe he left a sweetheart. We'll never know. He's had to live with his conscience for all these years. Don't you think that's punishment enough?'

Lizzie was thoughtful. 'Maybe? What does Frankie think about it? I presume you've discussed it with her.'

'Yes, we've discussed it at length. Frankie thinks it's best left in the past and she and Theo should concentrate on their future together with no shadows lurking between them. I agree with her; there's no point in raking it all up. Besides, no one will be interested in a case that's over fifty years old, especially here.'

'People are still hunting for Nazi war criminals.'

'It's hardly the same thing. Just drop it, Lizzie. Let Frankie and Theo deal with it their way.' He lay back in the deckchair and closed his eyes.

Lizzie sighed. There were some things about which she and Raoul would never agree but at the end of the day this was none of her business.

* * *

The Lord Nelson was crowded. Derek scanned the throng and saw the man he was looking for. He made his way to the bar where Natasha smiled and greeted him warmly. 'Hello, Derek. What can I get you?'

'A pint of my usual, please.' He leaned across the bar and lowered his voice. 'I may have some news for you later.' He gave her a solemn wink, leaving her frowning in perplexity, and pushed his way sideways until he was standing next to his quarry.

'Hello, George, you don't happen to have the time on you, do you?' He nodded politely to Prunella who was standing on the other side of her husband with a glass of white wine in front of her. She gave him a sharp look.

'No. There's a perfectly good clock over there if you bother to look.' George grunted into his beer.

'Not wearing your gold watch tonight? That's not like you.' Derek remembered back to when George had first flashed his gold watch around the pub. It had been last Christmas and caused a sensation at the time. How could someone like George Soames buy a watch like that on his wages? It was a present, George had explained, from a relative. Few of the regulars had believed him; it was common knowledge that George, along with his brother, was part of the Ormerey mafia.

'He's lost it, haven't you Georgie?' Prunella's high pitched voice could be heard above the general hubbub. Several people looked over in their direction.

'Really? I'm surprised you haven't reported it missing; it's a valuable piece of kit.' Derek's excitement grew. He knew he was on the right track. 'You were quick enough to flash it around when you got it; telling everyone how valuable it is.'

'It's at home somewhere,' George was sullen. He drained his glass and banged it down on the bar.

'I don't think it is, Georgie. We've looked everywhere in the house and the garden. The catch was loose; you could have dropped it anywhere. You ought to report it to the police, someone might find it and hand it in.'

'Be quiet, Prunella, and drink up. We're going home.' George's ferret-like face, so like his brother's, had turned an angry red.

'Hang on a minute, George. A watch just like yours was handed in this afternoon. If you come back with me now we can verify whether it's yours or not.'

'Oh, that's brilliant.' Prunella beamed at the Constable, her pale eyes shining. 'Who found it?'

'You go on home, Prunella, while I go to the police station. It's time you were getting the tea on anyway.' George pushed his way towards the door, closely followed by Derek. Annoyed, Prunella finished her drink and ordered another. Georgie could make do with frozen beef burgers and oven chips tonight.

It took only a few minutes to walk down Main Street to the police station. Derek unlocked the desk drawer and laid the watch on the counter.

George's eyes gleamed. 'That's my watch all right.'

'You're quite sure?'

'Absolutely.' George picked the watch up and examined the catch. 'See, the catch is a bit bent; it sometimes comes loose. It happened when I caught my wrist on something and pulled the watch right off. I'd been meaning to get it fixed next time I went to Guernsey. Who found it?'

'It was found by a couple of visitors who are staying at the Imperial; Eric and Diana Good. Honest of them to hand it in. It's where they found it that's interesting.'

'Oh?'

'Yes. They found it lying on the ground behind some gorse bushes up on the south cliffs, right close to where the Brockenshaws' Dalmatians were shot. How did it get there, George?'

He noticed the flash of panic that crossed George's face and felt a surge of triumph. He knew he was right.

'It must have fallen off when I went for a walk.'

'It wasn't found on the path; it was behind the gorse. Besides, you're no walker. Everyone knows that. You never go a hundred yards without your car.' He stared hard into the other man's face. George shuffled uncomfortably.

Derek continued, his voice cold and formal. 'You have two guns haven't you, Mr Soames, an air rifle and a revolver? Why do you own a revolver?'

'It was my father's, left over from the war. I've got licences for both guns.'

'I know that. What I want to know is did you use your revolver to shoot those dogs?'

George's state of panic was obvious now. He was sweating profusely. 'Of course not. Why are you accusing me?'

'Because your watch was found at the scene and you'd never reported it missing. I reckon you realised when you got home that morning that you'd dropped it somewhere. Maybe you've been back to look for it. Also, you have a revolver. Bullets, not air rifle pellets or shotgun cartridges killed those animals.'

'You can't prove it was me.'

'Unfortunately not.'

'Anyway, even if you could you can't arrest me; it's not a criminal offence.'

'Is that an admission, Mr Soames?'

'No, it bloody well isn't. Just you wait till your Sergeant hears about this.'

'Oh, he'll hear about it all right. I'm writing a full report and I've a good mind to send a copy of it to Mr and Mrs Brockenshaw.'

'You can't do that.' George sat down suddenly on a nearby chair. He was shaking. 'Not without proof.'

'I don't need proof; it's written all over you. You're right, I can't arrest you but it is possible that the Brockenshaws will bring a private prosecution against you.'

'From over on the mainland? I don't think so.' George curled his lip up in a sneer. 'You've made a very bad mistake, young man, one you'll live to regret.'

Derek refused to be ruffled. He continued calmly. 'Were you acting under somebody's instructions? The President's perhaps?'

'What?'

'Ian Warrington. Did he ask you to assist him in driving the Brockenshaws away from the island?'

George spluttered. 'Why would he do that?'

'Please answer the question, Mr Soames. Were you, or were you not, acting under instructions from Ian Warrington?'

'I was not.' George pulled a handkerchief out of his pocket and wiped his brow.

Derek was barely able to keep a note of triumph out of his voice. 'Are you sure that's the answer you want to give me,

Mr Soames. What if I were to tell you that Sergeant Green has already interviewed the President on this very subject.'

George threw a venomous look at the Constable. 'Go to hell,' he spat. He grabbed his watch and made for the door. Derek let him go. He had heard and seen enough.

Chapter 27

June's heat wave continued into July. Main Street was crowded with holidaymakers and locals as Lizzie passed the long queue outside the bread shop on her way to the Rock Café. The narrow pavement was cluttered with baby buggies, bicycles and gossiping bystanders so she gave up trying to negotiate her way along it and walked down the cobbled street, nimbly jumping out of the way when a vehicle approached. She was worried. Natasha had sounded tearful on the phone a few moments ago.

Lizzie was hot by the time she reached the café. She saw Natasha sitting alone at a table on the terrace and waved to her. She was answered with a tremulous smile.

Josie, Emily and Jean were having coffee at a nearby table and greeted Lizzie as she squeezed by.

'Natasha's looking rather pale, don't you think?' Josie asked. 'Is she all right?'

'Yes, as far as I know.' Lizzie smiled at the three women who were all wearing garish sunhats of indeterminate age. 'She has a very fair skin.'

'She's looked peaky for a while,' Jean muttered under her breath. 'Trouble in paradise I wouldn't wonder.'

'Let's go inside,' Natasha said as Lizzie pulled out a chair to sit down. 'It'll be cooler, and those old biddies have got their antennae on red alert.'

'They think you look pale.'

Natasha snorted. 'Nosy old bats.'

Lizzie frowned. 'That's not like you. What's the matter, Nat, you sounded upset on the phone? You've not fallen out with Geoff, have you?'

'No, not yet anyway.' Natasha waited until the waitress had served their cappuccinos. She lowered her voice to a whisper. 'I'm pregnant!'

Lizzie was not sure how to respond to this sudden announcement. She studied Natasha's distraught face. 'You're not happy about it?'

'No. It wasn't planned, I'm on the pill. I'm still in shock.' Natasha was on the verge of tears.

Lizzie frowned in concern. 'It's not a problem is it, Nat? Don't you want another child?'

'It's not that. I just don't know what on earth Geoff is going to say.' Natasha fished in her shoulder bag for a tissue and blew her nose. 'You're the first person I've told. You will keep it to yourself, won't you?'

'Of course.' Lizzie reached out her hand and laid it on Natasha's arm. 'Surely Geoff will be pleased.'

'Will he? Not everyone wants kids, Lizzie.'

'I know that,' Lizzie said sadly thinking of her own failed marriage.

'I'm sorry, I wasn't thinking. Trust me to put my big foot in it.'

'It's OK.' Lizzie pulled herself together. 'It's just something I have to accept.' She gave Natasha's arm a reassuring squeeze. 'Try not to worry. Geoff adores Belle; he'll probably be over the moon at the prospect of being a proper father.'

'I do hope so. He might just want out.'

'Not Geoff surely?' said Lizzie.

'He might panic at the thought of all the responsibility involved. He's always been so self-sufficient; a bit of a loner really. Suppose he goes back to Janine? She's on the loose again and I know he liked her.'

'He loves you,' Lizzie said. 'Anyone can see that. Tell him, Nat, and put yourself out of this misery. Have another coffee,' she added, 'it will make you feel better.'

'Yes please. I need it, I hardly slept last night.'

Lizzie ordered two more cappuccinos and they sat in silence until the waitress had served them.

'What do you mean about Janine being on the loose again?' Lizzie sprinkled sugar on her cappuccino and spooned off the froth. 'Have she and Hugo split up?'

'Yes, haven't you heard? There's been a terrific row. The Guernsey Evening Press asked Janine to interview my father in the wake of the George Soames scandal. Hugo asked her not to do it but she said it was part of her job as a journalist and she had to remain impartial. He said she was being disloyal to his family and had to make up her mind whose side she was on.'

'Did she do the interview?'

'Yes, it will be in Saturday's Press. Father is denying all knowledge of the incident, of course, but Hugo has dumped Janine.'

'I'm surprised your father agreed to be interviewed,' said Lizzie.

'He's the President. If he'd refused it would have looked suspicious. George Soames is public enemy number one. Prunella's getting a lot of nastiness in the shop apparently. I don't think she knew anything about it. I feel quite sorry for her.'

'I don't; she's a nasty, spiteful woman. What goes around comes around.' Lizzie returned to the subject of Natasha's pregnancy. 'Do you think you might be reconciled with your parents when they know about the baby? It is their grandchild, after all.'

'I doubt it.' Natasha pulled a face. 'They show precious little interest in Belle and I was respectably married when she was born. Besides, Father's made it very plain he's in no mood to forgive me and Mother always sides with him. It's Geoff I'm worried about.'

'Don't be,' Lizzie said gently. 'He adores you. It will all work out, you'll see.'

* * *

Prunella was struggling. She dreaded going to work now that the news of George's perfidy had circulated round the island. She found herself the target for malicious comments from nearly everyone who entered the shop. Only Pauline remained loyal.

Things came to a head one hot July afternoon. The island was busy. Private schools had already broken up for the summer holidays and yachties and holiday home owners had descended on masse, swelling the population to almost double its normal size. Prunella found herself on the receiving end of a complaint by a regular visitor who was bemoaning the fact that she could not find any pink toilet paper.

'We've only got white or blue, I'm afraid,' explained Prunella.

'Neither of which will go in my bathroom,' snapped the woman. 'I must have pink. I can't believe you haven't got any.'

Pauline chimed in. 'We've sold out of pink and we have to wait until the next boat arrives with fresh supplies.' The woman snorted. 'This is an island, you know,' Pauline continued, 'and it's our busiest time of year. You should be thankful we've got any toilet paper left at all.'

'Well really! It's not good enough. If we can get a man to the moon, surely you can get toilet paper to Ormerey.' She picked up a pack of white toilet paper and banged her basket down on the counter before flouncing out of the shop.

'Stuck up cow!' said Prunella and burst into tears.

Josie Cleghorn was passing the door as the woman came out. 'I don't know what this place is coming to,' she said pushing past Josie. Josie saw Prunella crying and went into the shop.

'It's not my fault there's no pink loo paper,' Prunella wailed.

'Never mind, dear. Don't take it to heart. Some people are never satisfied.'

Prunella broke into fresh sobbing and Josie motioned to Pauline to take over the till. She led Prunella into the small room at the back of the shop, filled the kettle and put it on the gas. 'Now Prunella, whatever's the matter? This isn't like you at all.'

'Oh Mrs Cleghorn, everyone's being so nasty to me and all because Georgie shot those poor dogs. I didn't know anything about it, I swear I didn't. I don't know why everyone is having a go at me.' Prunella sniffled noisily into a tissue. 'And another thing,' she continued amidst hiccups, 'I've been ticked off by head office in Guernsey because the shop is doing so badly. They're threatening to close us down.'

'Oh dear,' said Josie looking round the dingy little room.

She was not surprised the business was failing; the whole premises needed a good overhaul.

'It's all that Hugo Warrington's fault, opening that posh supermarket.' There was no mistaking the bitterness in Prunella's voice. 'I hate him. I hate everybody.'

Josie made a pot of tea and poured it into two chipped mugs. She sat down opposite Prunella and regarded her seriously. She spoke briskly.

'Now drink this, Prunella, and listen to me. That is at the root of all your problems, you know.'

Prunella stared in surprise. 'What is?'

'Hating everybody. If you don't like people they won't like you. You've a reputation for being spiteful, Prunella. People are using this dog incident as an opportunity to get back at you for unkind things you've said to them in the past.'

'So you're saying I deserve it?'

'Yes,' said Josie. 'What you send out comes back to you. That's a universal truth.'

Prunella stood up, pale eyes gleaming, her tears forgotten. 'How dare you,' she hissed. 'How dare you speak to me like this. Go away. Get out of here.'

Josie was unruffled. 'It's for your own good. Think about what I've said.' Her voice softened. 'Why don't you and George go away for a while? Have a holiday. All this fuss will die down and when you get back you could try being a bit nicer to people.' She paused. 'I suppose it is true that George shot those animals?'

Prunella's tears broke out afresh. She nodded miserably. 'He confessed after Derek Peasgood found his watch up on the cliffs.'

'Did he say why he did it?'

'He said he hates newcomers who come to the island and throw their weight about and try to change things.'

'How very sad,' said Josie. 'Now dry your eyes Prunella and get back in the shop, there's a good girl. Stiff upper lip and all that.' She smiled and patted Prunella's arm. 'Think about that holiday.'

* * *

Jean Yorke and the Ormerey Ladies' Guild had volunteered to help with the church fête which was always held on the second Saturday in August. Preparations were well under way but a few volunteers to run stalls were still needed.

Jean was in her element presiding over an extra meeting of the Guild in the Island Hall. It was hot. A fly buzzed over the cakes and Josie swatted it away. Jean looked around the room.

'Where's Francesca?' she asked, patting her newly permed curls self-consciously. 'Not here? Where is she I wonder?'

'She's in Guernsey,' said Lizzie. 'She and Theo will be away for a few days.'

'That's too bad of her. She knew we were having this special meeting today.' Jean tutted with annoyance. 'I was relying on her to run the cake stall. I don't suppose she's said anything to you about that, Elizabeth?'

'No, she hasn't mentioned it,' said Lizzie. 'I'm sure she would have done if she was intending to do it; she'd have roped me in to help with the baking.'

Jean tutted again. 'Well, I wish she had told me if she wasn't prepared to do it. It's most annoying of her.'

'She and Theo are awfully busy at the moment,' Lizzie said, 'with the wedding to organise and everything.'

'The wedding obviously isn't happening before the fête,' Emily chipped in, 'that's in two weeks and the vicar hasn't read any banns in church yet.'

'True,' said Jean. 'I shall ask her as soon as she gets back. When is she due to return, Elizabeth?'

Lizzie shrugged. 'I think you need to arrange for someone else to run the cake stall, Jean, just in case Frankie's not available.'

'I'll do it,' said Josie, 'if Emily will help me.'

Emily looked resigned and Jean looked relieved.

'We'll need someone to help us fetch and carry things,' Emily said. 'We're not as fit as we once were. Perhaps Harold could help us?'

'I expect he could,' Jean said rather doubtfully, 'I'll ask him anyway. We'll break for coffee now which will give you all time to think about what you'd like to volunteer for.'

'Be press-ganged into more likely,' Natasha whispered to Lizzie. As soon as they had sat down with their coffee Jean made a beeline for them.

'I hear congratulations are in order, Natasha,' she gushed. 'When are you getting married?'

'At the end of August,' said Natasha.

'My goodness, that's quick!' Jean raised her eyebrows. 'You and Geoff haven't been courting long.'

Natasha smiled at the use of the old fashioned word. 'We're neither of us getting any younger, why wait?'

'What a summer this is for weddings,' Jean continued. 'It will be you and Raoul next I expect, Elizabeth.'

Lizzie ignored the remark. 'Natasha and I would like to man the book stall at the fête, Jean, if no one else has already offered.'

Flustered, Jean rummaged in her bag for her note pad. 'That would be splendid. Thank you both very much. I'll be in touch with the details later.' She turned to go and then hesitated. 'I see the sale of Rachelle House has completed. Do you know who has bought it?'

'A retired English couple according to Frankie,' said Lizzie.

'How nice,' said Jean. 'I do hope they play golf.'

Chapter 28

'Well, Mrs Rachelle, are you ready to fly home this morning?'

'Not really,' said Francesca. 'It's so nice here. It's been a wonderful few days.'

'It has, hasn't it?' Theo squeezed his wife's hand. They were having breakfast in the bright, airy conservatory at Moore's Hotel.

'I don't want it to end. It's so nice being away from everyone and the endless gossip. Won't people be surprised when we get back and they find out we're married.' She giggled. 'I hope Zapp's behaving himself.'

'I expect Lizzie's spoiling him rotten,' said Theo. He hoped fervently that Zap had settled down at The Sycamores and was not pining for his former mistress. 'I've got a surprise waiting for you on Ormerey,' he announced.

'What kind of surprise?'

'Wait and see.'

'You can be so annoying sometimes,' said Francesca.

'It's all part of my charm.' He grinned at her.

Francesca looked at her husband and marvelled at the change in him. He'd sloughed off the burden of presidential responsibilities like a butterfly emerging from its chrysalis. She smiled at the thought of Theo as a butterfly; what species would he be she wondered, a purple emperor or a peacock? She giggled suddenly.

'What's so funny?'

'Nothing,' she said quickly. 'I'm just happy, that's all.'

Ormerey was looking its best, surrounded by the sparkling blue sea as the Trislander swooped low over the Gannet Rocks and came to land with a bump on the short runway. Several rabbits scuttled across the grass as the plane taxied to a halt in front of the airport building.

'Ready for the surprise?' Theo helped Francesca down the steps on to the tarmac.

'What?' Francesca looked around. Everything looked the same as usual. She had half expected a welcoming committee.

They walked to the car. Theo stowed their luggage in the boot and slammed it shut. He held the passenger door open for Francesca. 'Hop in.'

Theo drove along the airport road towards the town then turned off on to the wide grassy track that led to the south cliffs.

'Aren't we going home?'

Theo smiled. 'Yes,' he said.

Francesca gave up. They bumped slowly over the rough track until they reached the Yaffingales field where Joshua Ford was climbing down from his Land Rover. He waved to them.

'Hi there, you two,' he said with a wide grin as Theo wound the car window down. 'Congratulations, and welcome home.'

'I haven't told her yet,' said Theo.

'Told me what?'

'Patience, my dear.' Theo took her hand and led her through the tunnel of hawthorn trees to the cottage. 'There,' he said. 'Our new home; I've bought Yaffingales.'

Francesca stared at him. 'You've bought it?'

'Yes, for us to live in. If you'd like to, Frankie?'

'Like to? I'd love to. Oh Theo, what a wonderful, wonderful surprise.' She flung herself into her husband's arms. 'Oh, thank you, thank you.' She found she was crying.

Theo held her close for a long time. 'You are a dark horse,' she said when he released her. She looked through one of the broken windows. 'There's a lot of work to be done.'

'That's why Joshua's here; I've hired him to do the restoration work. He's removed a lot of the rubbish already. It needs gutting completely. We'll be starting from scratch so you can have anything you want.' He squeezed her hand and smiled.

'We'll need to work out a budget,' said Francesca. 'Should I sell Puffin Cottage to help pay for all this?'

'Good Lord, no. There's more than enough money from the sale of my house, and the Brockenshaws have let me have this at a very good price. They are just glad to be rid of it.'

'Is the field ours as well?'

'Yes, so it won't be built on.'

'Oh Theo, what an amazing man you are. I love you so much.'

'And I you.' He kissed her passionately.

* * *

'Well, really!' Jean Yorke exclaimed crossly as she poured milk into her coffee. 'Fancy sneaking off to Guernsey like that. I would have thought our ex-president would have had a church wedding here on Ormerey. After all, it is the first marriage for both of them, there's no reason why they couldn't have a church wedding.'

'They obviously didn't want one,' said Josie. She, Jean and Emily were sitting on the terrace at the Imperial Hotel. It was a glorious day. The beach below them was crowded with holidaymakers; shouts and laughter drifted upwards, mingling with the cries of the gulls and the soft chugging of a boat's engine far out to sea.

'It was a private ceremony,' said Emily, 'even Raoul and Lizzie didn't go.'

Jean snorted impatiently. 'They obviously knew about it. They've got themselves saddled with that dreadful dog. Theo's had a lucky escape there. It is very disappointing though; Harold and I were so looking forward to a nice wedding. How often do we get a really good "do" here on Ormerey?'

'I doubt whether you'd have been invited.' Josie helped herself to another piece of gâche and spread it liberally with butter. 'You and Harold took Francesca to court over that dreadful dog remember.'

'Oh, we would have been. Think of all the times we've invited Theo to have Christmas lunch with us.'

Josie and Emily exchanged smiles.

'You know they have bought Yaffingales,' Jean continued. 'Why they want to live right out there I can't imagine. The house is a complete wreck.'

'Francesca was born in that house.' Josie poured them all a second cup of coffee. 'She lived there with her parents when she was a small child.'

'I think it's wonderful,' said Emily, 'we won't have to worry about the land being developed now.'

Jean ignored her. 'I thought Francesca lived with the St Arnauds and that she and Raoul grew up together.'

'That was later.' Josie dismissed the subject; she did not want to go into the details of Francesca's family history with Jean.

'I wonder if Natasha and Geoff will have a big wedding,' said Emily, 'they could have the reception here at the hotel.'

'That won't happen,' said Jean. 'There's still a huge rift in that family; poor Daphne's dreadfully upset.' She leaned forward and lowered her voice. 'I hear there's another grandchild on the way, that's why Natasha's in such a rush to get married.'

'How lovely, another sibling for Belle.' Emily smiled. 'Perhaps it will be a sister this time; she's got two little brothers. That might bring the family back together.'

'I wouldn't bank on it,' said Jean tartly. 'Natasha's still in disgrace; she refuses to retract her accusation against her father.'

'That shooting business,' said Emily sadly. 'I don't suppose we'll ever know the truth of it.'

* * *

Geoff took advantage of the post lunchtime lull at The Lord Nelson to sit quietly and think over the momentous changes that had occurred over the past ten days.

Bill, the landlord, approached with Geoff's pint of bitter. 'Congratulations, old man.'

'Thanks,' said Geoff and took a noisy slurp.

'You're full of surprises, aren't you?' Bill continued. 'We all had you down as a confirmed bachelor.'

'No one's more surprised than me. I'm on cloud nine.'

'I must say Natasha's looking very bonny. When's the wedding?'

'The end of August hopefully. We need to find somewhere to live. My flat's far too small for me, Nat, Belle and the new baby. Let me know if you hear of anything suitable for us to rent, won't you.'

'I'll keep my ear close to the ground.' Bill collected up the empty glasses and headed back to the bar.

Geoff sat back in the battered easy chair and relaxed. The street outside was quiet; it was another hot sunny day and most people were on the beaches. Geoff could not remember a more glorious summer on Ormerey.

He saw Janine enter the pub and cross to the bar. He called to her. 'Hi Janine, come and join me. It's ages since we had a catch up.'

Janine hesitated. She still felt awkward with Geoff having dropped him so suddenly for Hugo.

'Have a drink with me,' said Geoff, 'no hard feelings, eh?'

Janine flashed him a smile. 'Thanks.' She settled herself opposite him. 'How are you these days, Geoff?'

'Grand. You know Natasha and I are getting married.'

'Really?' Janine's eyes widened. 'I hadn't heard. I knew you were going out together of course. Congratulations.' She felt a pang of regret. Geoff was worth ten of Hugo. She'd been in such a hurry to dump him and run after Hugo, and look where that had ended up. 'When's the wedding?'

'At the end of August, just a quiet do at the Greffe. How's life treating you?'

'I've been offered a full-time job with the Evening Press in Guernsey so I'm thinking of moving over there. Hugo and I have split.' She pulled a face. 'I think I need a new start.'

'For what it's worth,' said Geoff, 'I think you're right. It was very courageous of you to interview Warrington over that dog shooting business. It can't have been easy. You're very good at your job, Janine, very professional.'

Janine blushed to the roots of her hair and beamed at him. 'So you think I should go then?'

'Definitely. When would you start?'

'September. One of their regular reporters is retiring. That will give me time to find somewhere to live which I gather is quite difficult in Guernsey.'

'Same as here,' said Geoff. 'We're looking for somewhere bigger. Well, all the best, Janine, it's a real feather in your cap.'

Chapter 29

Belle was excited. 'What time are we going to Miss Saviano's, Mummy?' She was wearing her new pink and white sundress and could not wait to show it off.

'Any minute now,' said Natasha, 'and you must remember to call her Mrs Rachelle now she's married. Are you ready?'

'Yes, I'm ready. Mummy, when you and Geoff are married will you be Mrs Prosser?'

Natasha smiled. 'Yes, darling. Come along now.' She took her daughter's hand and locked the door of the flat behind them.

Belle clattered down the stairs and into the street. 'Where's Geoff?'

'We're meeting him at Puffin Cottage.'

'Mummy, when you're Mrs Prosser will I be Belle Prosser?'

Natasha stopped and looked down into her daughter's earnest face. 'No darling, you'll still be Belle Roche. Daddy will always be your daddy. Geoff will be your step-father.'

'Oh.' Belle digested this piece of information. Her brow creased.

'That's OK isn't it?' said Natasha.

Belle thought for a moment. 'Yes, I'll have two dads, won't I? Jamie at school has two dads. His proper dad's in England. He doesn't like his new one much.'

'You like Geoff, don't you?'

'Oh yes, I love Geoff. I love Daddy too,' she added hastily.

'That's good. Look, there's Geoff now at the top of the street. If we hurry we can catch up with him.'

Belle raced up the road calling as she ran. Geoff turned and swung her up into his arms. 'Hello, sweetheart, don't you look pretty?' He waited for Natasha. 'Do you know what this is all about?'

'No. Francesca just invited us all to tea. I expect she and Theo are widening their social circle now they're married, and she's always been fond of Belle.'

'It's odd though,' said Geoff. 'I don't know either of them particularly well and Theo and I have had a few spats over political issues.'

'I don't expect he cares about that now he's no longer the President. Besides, we seem to be accepted as a couple now so they've invited all three of us.'

Francesca welcomed them warmly. 'Come round to the back garden; we're having tea outside, it's such a lovely afternoon.'

Natasha had never seen the back garden at Puffin Cottage and gazed round in delight. The immaculate lawn was bordered by flower beds where scarlet runner beans entwined themselves among herbaceous perennials in a riot of colour. A winding gravel path led down a gentle slope to the bottom of the garden where an ornamental pond, surrounded by water plants and sedges, nestled in one corner. Belle squealed with delight.

'Look, Mummy, water boatmen!' She lay on her stomach and peered into the water. 'And goldfish,' she shouted excitedly.

Theo, seated at the rustic table on the patio, got to his feet and held out his hand formally to Natasha and then to Geoff. 'How nice to see you and the child too.' He beamed and Natasha thought how different he looked, less care worn and ten years younger.

'What a lovely garden you've got,' said Geoff. 'It must take a lot of hard work to keep it looking so good.'

'I love gardening and I've plenty of time for it now I've retired.'

'Belle,' called Francesca, 'come and wash your hands ready for tea.'

Francesca had baked scones, fairy cakes and a chocolate sponge. Soon they were all tucking in.

'Well,' said Francesca as she poured out the tea, 'I expect you are wondering why we have invited you here today. We have a proposition for you.'

Geoff and Natasha exchanged glances. Belle, who had stuffed a whole fairy cake into her mouth, stopped munching and looked round at the adults.

'You know Theo and I will be moving into Yaffingales as soon as the renovations are finished,' Francesca continued. 'We're hoping to be there for Christmas. We were wondering if you would like to come and live here. We heard you are looking for a house to rent and this would be ideal for a growing family.'

Geoff and Natasha were speechless. They stared at Francesca. There was a pause, broken by Belle who squeaked excitedly through a mouthful of crumbs.

'Could we, Mummy, could we?'

'We do realise it may not be quite what you're looking for,' said Francesca, 'but we thought we'd give you first refusal. You'd be ideal tenants. Of course you'll need to look over the house properly and have a good think about it.'

Natasha found her voice at last. 'We'd absolutely love to live here, wouldn't we Geoff?'

'Yes we would. We don't need to go away and think about it; it's ideal for us, just what we're looking for and the garden is a huge bonus. It's incredibly kind of you.'

'You haven't even seen over the house yet,' laughed Theo.

'There are three bedrooms,' said Francesca, 'so it will be plenty big enough. We'll look round as soon as we've finished tea.'

Belle bounced up and down on her chair. 'Oh please hurry up and finish, everybody. I can't wait.'

'Try and be patient,' said Francesca. 'Wouldn't you like a piece of chocolate cake?'

'Yes please,' said Belle.

After they had all finished eating and Belle had demolished two slices of chocolate cake, Geoff took Natasha's hand and they followed Francesca through the back door into the bright airy kitchen. Theo followed behind and Belle squeezed past everyone, opening cupboard doors with exclamations of delight.

'Come out of the cupboards, Belle,' said Natasha. 'It's rude to poke about in someone else's house.'

'She's all right,' said Francesca. 'What do you think?'

'It's lovely,' said Natasha admiring the brightly coloured curtains and the potted geraniums on the window sill. The pine table in the middle of the room matched the modern units round the walls and there was a gleaming gas cooker and a stainless steel sink.

'I'll leave the cooker, fridge and washing machine if you'd like them, and any of the furniture too if you can find a use for it. You'd be doing me a favour; we're having everything new at Yaffingales.'

'I think I've married a shopaholic,' said Theo with a smile.

'That would be brilliant,' said Geoff, 'wouldn't it Nat? Most of my stuff is so tatty.'

Natasha nodded. She was close to tears. Geoff squeezed her hand as Francesca led them through the rest of the cottage. Belle thought about jumping on the beds but caught Theo's eye and thought better of it. She sidled up to Francesca and slipped her hand into hers.

'Do you miss Zapp?' she whispered.

'Sometimes,' Francesca whispered back,' but he's very happy living with Raoul and Lizzie and I see him quite often.'

'Maybe when we move here we can have a dog,' said Belle. 'I do hope so.'

Francesca marvelled at the change in the child; transformed from a quiet lonely little girl into a bundle of energy and happiness. Whoever would have believed it she thought? Geoff Prosser had taken to fatherhood like a duck to water.

* * *

The hot weather continued into August. Jean Yorke was in her element organising the church fête which this year, with the good weather guaranteed, was being held in the gardens of the Island Hall.

Lizzie and Natasha arrived early to set up their book stall. Cardboard cartons full of paperbacks needed to be sorted.

'Should we arrange them in categories?' said Lizzie, 'or alphabetically?'

'Neither,' said Natasha. 'There isn't time. Just arrange them neatly and make sure they are the right way round. There's nothing more irritating than trying to read upside down. There are a few hardbacks in this box; we'll put them at one end.'

'You've done this before,' said Lizzie.

Natasha grinned. 'I've been helping Francesca at fêtes and things since I was knee high.'

'When do you think you'll move into Puffin Cottage? Frankie says the work at Yaffingales is coming on really well. I bet you can't wait.'

'At the end of November hopefully. I can hardly believe it's really happening. Belle's decided she wants a dog.'

'Will you get one?'

'Yes, we'll get a puppy in the spring, after the baby's arrived.'

'You'll have your hands full. What does Geoff think?'

Natasha turned to Lizzie with a dazzling smile. 'He's over the moon. He says he's always wanted a proper family but he never thought he'd be lucky enough to get one.'

'That's wonderful. I'm so happy for you, Nat.' Lizzie could not help a small stab of envy. She wondered if Raoul would ever ask her to marry him, and dismissed the thought quickly knowing it was never likely to happen. She placed the remaining few books on the stall.

Jean approached them. 'How are you getting on, ladies?' She cast a critical eye over their display and straightened a couple of books. 'It's a great pity Francesca isn't helping us this year,' she said. 'We really miss her. I see Raoul's other cousin is over here, Elizabeth.'

'Yes, Felicity and Julian are here for a week,' said Lizzie. 'They're staying with their son and his family.'

'How nice,' Jean murmured as she drifted off to the next stall.

Lizzie was relieved that neither Raoul nor Felicity had suggested that the Rockdales stay at The Sycamores for their week's holiday. She had dreaded the thought of preparing meals for guests in that awkward kitchen. 'Where's Belle this afternoon?' she asked.

'Geoff's taken her to the beach; they'll be here later if he can tear her away from the water.'

Ian Warrington was scheduled to open the fête at two o'clock.

'The Vicar should have asked Theo,' Natasha said crossly. She was still convinced her father was instrumental in driving the Brockenshaws away from the island. She narrowed her eyes as she watched her parents saunter into the gardens, her father in a smart suit and her mother in yet another outfit Natasha had not seen before.

'You know Derek did really well getting George Soames to confess to shooting those dogs,' Natasha continued, 'but he couldn't get him to come clean about Father's involvement. Geoff and I think Sergeant Green insisted that the matter was dropped. Father must have bunged George a huge sum to keep him quiet and take all the blame. No wonder he can afford to whizz Prunella over to California for a month.'

'She'll get a shock when she comes back,' said Lizzie, 'now the Ormerey Supermart is closed and all boarded up. She's out of a job.'

'That won't worry her. George and Bertie Soames must have amassed thousands in bribes over the years.'

'Are you sure about that?' Lizzie looked sceptical.

'Well, it can't be proved of course but it's funny how certain people always get exactly what they want and the rest of us don't. Geoff says he only has to look at the list of planning applications and he can tell whose plans will be passed and whose will be turned down. Ninety five per cent of the time he's right.'

'Raoul applied to have UPVC windows put in at The Sycamores but his application was turned down.'

'What reason was given?'

'It's a historic building, part of the island's heritage. Yet three other buildings of the same age in Main Street have been allowed to install them.'

'There you are then,' said Natasha. If Raoul wants UPVC windows he'll have to bung a fat brown envelope at someone.'

'He'll never do that.' Lizzie was emphatic. 'We'll just have to put up with the draughts.'

'Ladies and Gentlemen!' Ian Warrington, flanked by the Vicar and the Church Wardens, boomed through a loud hailer. 'I declare the 1991 Ormerey church fête well and truly open.' A resounding cheer arose from the waiting crowd. Natasha scowled. There was no opportunity for further conversation as people surged through the gate and made a rush for the stalls.

* * *

The August heatwave continued and Geoff and Natasha's wedding day was blessed with glorious sunshine, tempered by a gentle breeze which rustled through the sycamore trees in the Island Hall gardens.

'What a lovely party,' sighed Emily. 'It was so kind of Natasha and Geoff to invite us to their reception. What a nice speech Geoff made. Natasha is positively glowing. That pale green frock looks wonderful on her and little Belle is such a pretty flower girl.'

'Yes, it's a jolly gathering,' said Josie. The two friends were sitting together in a shady corner watching the chattering throng. 'I see Natasha did not invite her parents, or if she did they haven't come.'

'No, but Hugo's here. I can see him over there talking to Raoul and Lizzie. They were the witnesses you know.'

'Jean and Harold weren't invited,' Josie continued. 'Jean is very miffed. It's hardly surprising though. Harold is so pally with Ian Warrington, they play golf together, and he and Jean are convinced that Ian had nothing to do with the dog shooting incident.'

'Well, I think he could be innocent,' said Emily. 'Don't you? I think Natasha may be mistaken. It's a real shame the family is split in this unfortunate way, and with a new baby on the way too.'

'I wouldn't put anything past that man,' said Josie tartly. 'I've never cared for him. He can be quite ruthless when it comes to business. I don't think Natasha would be so adamant if she had any doubts about the matter. We'll probably never know the truth, I'm afraid.'

She changed the subject. 'Let's get another cup of tea, the wedding cake's being cut, they'll be bringing it round soon.'

* * *

There was a hint of seasonal change in the air as Lizzie sat outside the airport terminal building waiting to board the 8.30am plane to Southampton. A few dead sycamore leaves blew around her feet, taking her back to the previous August when autumn had crept in almost unnoticed while holidaymakers were still enjoying the beaches. She wondered if it was the same every year on the island; long winters, late springs, short summers and early autumns. She still missed the gentler change of seasons that graced the English countryside.

Raoul appeared with two cups of coffee and sat down opposite her at the small rickety table. 'Gosh, I need this. I'm usually in bed at this hour.'

Lizzie smiled at him. 'Never mind, you can have a long lie-in every morning while I'm away.'

'Don't stay away so long this time, will you?'

'No more than a fortnight, I promise, and I'll ring every day. You could clear out that awful German bunker while I'm away.'

He laughed. 'Don't hold your breath.'

They watched the luggage being loaded on to the Trislander.

'Drink your coffee; they'll call you in a minute.'

Lizzie downed the last of her coffee and picked up her bag. They walked together into the terminal building and Raoul gave her a hug.

'Come back soon.'

'I will.'

He watched her walk through departures and returned outside to lean over the fence with a small group of people seeing off friends and relatives. Lizzie turned and waved as she climbed into the plane. Raoul waved back and blew her a kiss.

'You all right, mate?'

He turned to see Henri standing behind him.

'What are you doing here?'

'Collecting a parcel for Sophie. Your Lizzie going away then?'

'Just a quick visit to see her father. She'll be back soon. I ought to tackle that bunker while she's away. It should have dried out after all this fine weather.'

'I'll come and help you. How about we start this morning?'

'What?'

Henri grinned. 'Too late to back out now.'

As the plane took off Raoul could see Lizzie waving to him through the small window. He waved back and watched the plane until it disappeared from sight. His heart was lighter than it had been the last time he had watched her go. He knew now for certain that she would be back.

As the plane soared over the gannet rocks Lizzie took a last look at the island and settled back in her seat with a contented sigh. She was excited about her stay in England and seeing her father and all her friends again but she knew she would miss Raoul. At long last Ormerey was beginning to feel like home and she looked forward to her return.